THE BALLOCHBRAE BOOK CLUB

M C MACKAY

Copyright © M C Mackay 2025

The moral right of M C Mackay to be identified as author of this work has been asserted in accordance with the Copyright, Designs and Patents Act, 1988.

All rights reserved. No part of this publication may be reproduced or transmitted in any form or by any means, electronic or mechanical, including photocopy, recording, or any information storage and retrieval system, without prior written permission of the copyright holder.

Scripture taken from the New King James Version®. Copyright © 1982 by Thomas Nelson. Used by permission. All rights reserved.

EBook ISBN: 978 1 0684475 0 1
Paperback ISBN: 978 1 0684475 1 8

This book is a work of fiction. Names, characters, businesses, organisations, places and events are either the product of the author's imagination or are used fictitiously. Any resemblance to actual persons, living or dead, events or locales is entirely coincidental.

Cover design: davethompsonillustration.com

Published by: Ballochbrae Press

For Alistair

Prologue

MacDuff picked his way along the riverside until he neared the bridge.

Gaining its stone supporting wall, he stopped. Between that and deep water was nothing but a narrow ledge, what little footing it afforded slimy with lichen.

He was debating his next move when his eye was caught by a flash of white. Back pressed to the wall, he inched into the gloom, arms outstretched. Against his spread palms, the granite slabs were ice-cold, damp and smelling of decay.

MacDuff had almost reached the far side when he saw it: an amorphous mass corralled by giant boulders.

Heart pounding under his heavy uniform, he strained forward.

Fought to focus in the fading light.

Beneath him bobbed a bloated human body, the face identifiable only by an obscenely engorged tongue.

One

Flora MacPhee studied her reflection in the mirror of the oak hallstand. High cheekbones jutted from a heart-shaped face, to which a distinctive nose – not quite patrician – lent character. Fine lines sun-rayed from the outer corners of green eyes. Her cropped bob, once a fiery red, had faded to strawberry blonde.

She ran a mental checklist of the contents of her shoulder bag: phone, shopping list, debit card, small change, tissue, keys. Pulling the front door to, she proceeded down the sloping driveway and walked briskly towards the village.

It was a clear day, the sky near cloudless over Lochnagar, the hills darkly forested with Sitka spruce and Scots pine. Alongside the stony footpath, bracken fronds trembled amidst a carpet of heather. As she approached, a bird flew, squawking, from its nest. From a hillside chimney, pungent wood smoke drifted into the air.

"All seemed to breathe freedom and peace, and to make one forget the world and its sad turmoils", wrote Queen Victoria, who did much to romanticise the Highlands, a century after Jacobite attempts to oust her ancestors from the British throne. As the village came into view, those words echoed in Flora's head.

In the heart of Royal Deeside – so named for its popularity with Queen Victoria and her descendants – Ballochbrae lies on a fertile alluvial plain bounded by low hills to the north and the river to the south. Like many a Highland village, it is defined by the loose string of cottages fringing the main road. With traditional quartered sash windows and slate roofs pierced by pitched dormers, they could be lifted straight out of a tourist brochure. Beyond the cottages stands the village's one hotel, the imposing three-storey Ballochbrae Arms. But the focal point of the village is the kirk. Set back from the road and fronted by a paved square edged with flowerbeds, it is constructed of the same silver granite as the cottages, with shallow steps leading up to an arched double oak doorway and a tower topped by a Gothic steeple.

Picture perfect! The sight never failed to gladden Flora's heart. She'd left Ballochbrae a rebellious teenager to live in Aberdeen, where nursing studies allowed scarce more than a flying visit. Then – after she met and married doctor Allan Rentoul – there was always an excuse: pressure of work, activities with their children, Scott and Isla.

Flora's footsteps faltered as she recalled the chain of events that had prompted her return.

Like dominos falling.

Only ten times the speed, and far less orderly.

And now, here she was.

Age fifty-six.

Right back where she started.

Two

Chatty MacIntyre turned her face up to the trickle of tepid water. Like everything in Castle View, her bathroom had seen better days. Originally named Dalnacreich and her husband's ancestral home, the substantial granite property stands on the crest of a grassy incline set back from the A93. With stepped gables and a vestibule crowned with a pepperpot turret, it is a vision in Scottish Baronial architecture. But there the vision ends. Dark and ponderous in the Gothic Revival style, Chatty hated the place on first sight.

Stepping out of the cramped corner shower cabinet onto a faded candlewick mat, she reached for the bath sheet draped over a bulbous towel rail. Towelling herself vigorously, she let her mind wander. Whilst her in-laws were alive, visits had been infrequent, governed as they were by Roderick's naval postings and her own recalcitrance. After his parents died and her husband inherited the property, Chatty realised absence hadn't diminished her distaste.

Unexpectedly finding herself a widow, she wasted no time. Following a perfunctory cremation and the pantomime of scattering her husband's ashes at sea, she booked a one-way flight to that north-east outpost of the British Isles, Aberdeen. She'd planned to sell Dalnacreich. Start afresh.

But the Aberdeenshire property market had taken a nosedive alongside the price of oil. With no fallback position – the couple had spoken of investing in a retirement home, but never had the cash – Chatty had taken the only obvious path open to her: to convert the mouldering property into a paying business. Capitalising on its position within a quarter mile of Balmoral Castle, she wasted no time, kitting the place out as a guesthouse and renaming it Castle View. Something of misnomer, since its two acres of grounds are planted with mature trees, as are the policies surrounding the castle.

Padding through to the bedroom, she let the towel drop and struck a pose in front of an antique mahogany cheval mirror. At a curvaceous five foot seven and a half, Chatty cut – still – a striking figure, though her breasts drooped and her bum was heading in the same direction. Eyeing her sagging stomach, she made a mental note to cut down on the pastries. The alcohol, too, though that would be more of a challenge. The life she'd been reduced to was rendered bearable only by dint of a stiff gin on the stroke of six o'clock.

Shaking bleached-blonde hair from the band which held it in a topknot, she let it fall in loose curls to her shoulders, noting with dismay that dark roots were showing. Again. She'd spent sixty pounds at the hairdresser only three weeks before.

'Mrs MacIntyre?'

Chatty started at the rap on the bedroom door.

Making a frantic grab for the towel, 'Who is it?'

'The laundry hasn't come,' bawled the hired help, an elderly charlady by the name of Etta. 'I can't change the sheets in Glen Tanar.'

'Well, do something else,' said Chatty irritably.

'I finish at eleven, mind.'

'Then turn them top to tail. And keep your voice down.'

'Whatever,' muttered Etta, her steps receding along the landing and down the stairs.

Three

Heather Garden was forty-six and looked sixty-four. In her coomb-ceilinged bedroom at Thistle Cottage, she checked the time on the vintage alarm clock that sat on a mahogany pot cupboard by the bed.

'Morning, sweetheart.' Bestowing a fond look on the somnolent figure lying alongside, she threw back a corner of the Paisley-pattern down quilt and swung her feet onto the floor.

The two-bedroom Victorian property had been purchased by Heather's father when he retired from the ministry and moved out of the much larger Ballochbrae manse. Over the years, Kenneth and Isobel Garden made judicious improvements, draught-proofing windows and installing central heating. Otherwise, little had changed since the day Thistle Cottage was built. None of which bothered Heather, who was of the firm opinion the old ways were far superior. Aside from splurging on a few feminine touches like floral-pattern Laura Ashley curtains and cushions, she liked things just the way they were.

Now, a diminutive figure clad in chin-to-toe flannelette, she pushed her feet into sheepskin slippers and descended the stairs to the only bathroom. There, she performed her morning ablutions at a wall-hung washbasin supported by ornate cast-iron brackets. An amber oval of Pears soap sat on a perforated china soap dish. Heather lathered and rinsed. Then, patting herself dry, applied a slick of Nivea cold cream to plump cheeks and an indulgent spritz of Yardley English Lavender behind both ears.

Back in the bedroom, she tugged the nightgown over her head, shucked off her slippers and reached for the underclothes which lay neatly folded on a rush-seated chair. Crossing to the dormer window, she drew back sill-length curtains and took a peek outside. The hills soared skywards, their slopes carpeted with spruce, pine and larch. By the roadside, silver birches trembled in the breeze. Happily, the day was – as forecast – dry.

With a small tut of satisfaction, Heather wriggled into a pair of thick, ribbed tights, slipped on a long-sleeved blouse and zipped a pleated tweed skirt at her waist.

With another glance at the clock, 'Sweetheart?'

No response.

'Breakfast time.'

From the single iron bedstead, a Norwegian Forest cat regarded her with baleful gold eyes.

She crossed the room, bent to ruffle his head.

The tabby's tail shot up, fur bristling.

Yawning, he displayed a mouthful of pointed teeth.

Stretched languidly.

Shook himself.

Jumped off the bed.

Heather smiled in satisfaction.

She'd laid the breakfast table the night before.

Put a bowl of prunes to soak.

Set aside a fresh brown egg.

Once Darcy feasted on the Gourmet Gold salmon in his special bowl, they'd be all set.

Four

Fergus McCracken stabbed a fork into his plate. 'Where's the meat?'

'There's no meat,' daughter Morag replied from across the kitchen table. 'It's macaroni cheese.'

'What are you thinking, woman?'

With a shrug. 'I was pushed for time.'

'A man needs his meat,' Fergus grumbled. 'Put marrow in his bones.'

'There's ham hock in it. Says so on the sleeve.'

His fork raked the glutinous tubes of pasta. 'Could have fooled me.'

Spearing a few, Morag held them aloft. 'See!'

Fergus peered through his cataracts. 'Give me mince an' tatties any day.'

'We've had mince and potatoes every Monday since I don't know when.'

'An' a fine plate o' stew on Tuesday, lamb shank on Wednesday. A man needs his dinner if he's to work the land.'

Morag kept her counsel. Her dad contributed less and less to the running of Cairnshiel, their hundred-and-fifty-acre hill-farm.

'Since your mother went, this place has gone to pot.'

'That's down to me, is it? Nothing to do with you?'

He set down his fork. 'What about me?'

'Your imaginary arthritis, for a start. Stops you doing all sorts. And if you're to be believed, it's not that, it's your angina.'

'I'm coming on eighty. No wonder my old body's complaining.'

'Except on mart days. You never miss a chance to meet up with your pals at Thainstone.'

'That's work,' Fergus protested. 'You can't buy or sell beasts on that ... What do you call it?'

'Internet. Fair enough, but it's me gets landed with the heavy lifting.'

'You're a big lass. An' I'm getting on.'

'So am I,' said Morag, pushing her plate aside.

'Time you found yourself a man.'

'I've got a man.'

'That so?' Looking her up and down, Fergus sneered. 'Who would have you?'

'You'd be surprised.'

'You can say that again. You're past the age where you'll give a man a son.'

Morag flinched. At forty-nine, her menopause had come and gone.

'An ugly one at that.'

'Try telling that to Duncan Kelman.'

'Call thon a man? Dunc Kelman couldn't service a ...'

His words were drowned by the scrape of Morag's chair. Crossing to the sink, she opened the unit door and scraped the congealing macaroni into a discoloured plastic bin.

Turning. 'You done?'

Fergus bent his head, shovelled the remains on his plate into a slack, wet mouth. Wiping his lips with the back of his hand, he threw her an ingratiating look. 'Any chance o' a pudding?' he said.

Five

In the front parlour of Thistle Cottage, Heather Garden dispensed tea from a Royal Albert teapot florid with crimson and yellow cabbage roses into matching gilt-edged cups. Passing cups and saucers around, she offered plates, paper serviettes and a selection of fancies from a wheeled hostess trolley. Then, when she was assured the ladies were settled comfortably, waved aloft a paperback book. 'This week's book club read is *Sorrow and Bliss* by New Zealand author Meg Mason. I've taken the liberty of listing a few questions to guide our discussion, but before we get started, hands up: who's read the book?'

Seated on a cut-moquette settee in front of the tiled fireplace, where a cheerful fire flickered in the grate, Flora said, 'Not me. Sorry.'

'Wasn't it your suggestion?'

'It was. Couldn't get hold of a copy.'

'Me neither,' added Chatty, seated alongside.

'Well.' Heather huffed. 'That's not a good start.'

'Before we go any further, can I check …' She cast a wary glance at the door. 'Where the cat …?'

'There is no possibility whatever of Darcy joining us,' Heather cut in. She'd fed him an extra helping of chicken and liver and tucked him up on her bed.

'That's okay then,' said Chatty, who claimed to be allergic to cat hair. In truth, she didn't trust Darcy, ever since she'd caught him trying to service a wildly expensive faux-leopard-skin handbag. 'To answer your question, I only managed a quick run through.'

Heather eyeballed the last member of the club.

Big-boned limbs folded into the other armchair of the fawn three-piece suite, Morag McCracken said, 'Don't look at me. We'll be into lambing in no time. It's a wonder I'm here at all.'

'How can we call ourselves a book club if nobody reads the books? One book a week is hardly a big ask. I can get through one of an evening.'

Chatty said, 'It's not as if you're doing much else.'

'It would be a whole lot easier,' Flora intervened, 'if the council reinstated the mobile library.'

'Never going to happen,' mumbled Morag through a mouthful of petticoat tail shortbread. 'Not with the economy in tatters.'

Heather said, 'There's a delivery service.'

'That you have to be at death's door to take advantage of.'

'Plus,' Flora added, 'Ballater Library's never open.'

'Now, dear, you know that's not the case.'

'It may be open seven days, but it's hardly ever manned.'

Chatty broke off from nibbling an iced ginger slice. 'I agree. Ten till three on Tuesdays and Wednesdays and noon till five on Thursdays is no use to me. Ever since the library moved across the road from the Victoria and Albert Halls to the Old Station, things have gone down the drain.'

'Any time I've visited,' countered Heather, 'I've found the librarians knowledgeable as ever. And when the library isn't manned, the tourist office staff are most helpful when it comes to using the self-service machine.'

'You don't even have to go near,' said Morag, stretching for a second cinnamon swirl. 'You can use the phone app, as I do.'

'Only not,' Flora observed, 'if you haven't read the book.'

Morag's already ruddy face heightened in colour. 'There's no need to be sarcastic.'

'Now, now,' said Heather. 'Let's not get overheated.'

'You wouldn't know overheated if it was staring you in the face.'

It was Heather's turn to flush, colour rising at the neck of her pearl-buttoned blouse and creeping up to the hairline of her soft perm.

'It was a joke.'

'In poor taste, if I may say, but who am I to judge? Moving on, three months in, how many books have we actually read? Barely a handful.'

Chatty said, 'And whose fault is that? If you didn't keep ramming highfalutin literary titles down our throats …'

Morag nodded. 'She's right. I didn't get past the first chapter of *Crime and Punishment*. Couldn't get my head around the names. *1984* was an uphill struggle. As for *Ulysses*: nightmare! And not a full stop in sight.'

'Maybe if we chose something a bit lighter.'

'With a shudder, Heather said, 'If you're talking chick lit—'

'We all have different levels of ...' 'Ability', was on the tip of Flora's tongue. 'Expectation,' she said pragmatically. 'That's why I suggested *Sorrow and Bliss* for this week. Might speak to us all.'

'If anyone had bothered to read it. But if you're not prepared to devote the time—'

'It's all right for you,' Chatty interrupted. 'Done and dusted by four o'clock and weekends free. Some of us have to work all hours.'

'I'll have you know there's a lot more to teaching than standing in a classroom.'

Morag said, 'Come off it. If you had a farm to run—'

'Or,' Chatty came back, 'a residential establishment like mine.'

'A B&B,' Flora qualified, for devilment. 'Thought you chucked your guests out straight after breakfast and were free the rest of the day.'

Chatty snapped, 'It's not that simple. And not the occupation of my choosing. Had the Commodore still been alive ...' Delicately dabbing fingertips at the inner corners of her eyes, she confided, 'I could have been a model, I'll have you know.'

'Plus size,' Flora joked, earning a poisonous look.

Heather reached for the teapot. 'More tea, anyone?'

'Please,' said Morag.

'Chatty?'
'Not for me.'
'Flora?'
'Just a drop.'

When she'd done the rounds, Heather said, 'The Ballochbrae Book Club, it has a ring to it don't you think? Perhaps we need to give it more time.'

'Why don't we drop the whole idea,' Morag argued. 'Meet up on a purely social basis.'

'We could keep the name,' Chatty suggested. 'Broaden the concept: talk about art, for instance. Or music. Think about it: a little salon. We might even indulge in a wee refreshment.'

'Alcohol?' spluttered Heather, dribbling tea down her front. 'I think not.' She snatched up her serviette and dabbed furiously at her blouse.

'Great idea,' enthused Morag. 'Lord knows I could do with a snifter after a day standing up to my ankles in dung. Plus, begs the question: what do we really want from this? Can't speak for the rest of you, but all I want is to get out of the house and have a good gossip.'

Chatty said, 'I wholeheartedly agree. I thought this would be fun, but when it comes down to it, I'm not really a book club sort of person.'

Heather set her jaw. 'That's as may be, but not everyone cares to imbibe. And there's the cost to consider.' Turning to Flora. 'What do you think, dear?'

'We've been here since seven and achieved sod all. Why don't we give the rest of the time over to current affairs?'

Affecting a yawn, Chatty said, 'Boring.'

'Anyone watch the evening news?' Flora persisted.

'Too much going on.'

'Me and all,' said Morag.

'How about you, Heather?'

'Caught the tail end of it: nothing but the National Health Service and cost of living.'

'Anything of local interest?'

'Dolly Peterkin's gone into hospital: diabetes. Weight's ballooned since her mother died, God love her.'

'It's not love she needs,' Flora shot back, 'so much as a week or two on a liquid diet.' Deftly changing the subject, 'Any other news?'

Morag said, 'Neighbour had his quad bike stolen. Not that it's news, exactly. Happens too often.'

'Anything else worth mentioning?'

Heather ventured, 'One of my students claims to have seen a wildcat down the Beltie Burn. Might not be kosher. They have such fertile minds at that age.'

'What if it's for real?' asked Chatty, eyes out on stalks.

'It's possible,' Flora conceded. 'The Royal Zoological Society of Scotland released nineteen captive-bred wildcats in the Cairngorms National Park, and those wildcats have since produced two litters of kittens. But I wouldn't put money on Heather's student. Wild cats are more likely seen at night.'

Heather said, 'Let's face it, there hasn't been anything of note happened since our late Queen died.' Wistfully, she added, 'Hard to believe how much time has passed.' Then, brightening, 'The funeral, wasn't that something: the cortege, the crowds, the camera crews. And the weather! Couldn't have been better.' Piously, she clasped her hands. 'The Lord was looking down on our dear Queen that day.'

'Him and a couple of helicopters,' Morag joked. 'One for filming, one for security. Best bit of the TV coverage, in my opinion, was the aerial footage of the cortege leaving Balmoral.'

Chatty said, 'Those tractors lined up at Drumoak to form a roadside guard of honour. Don't know about you, but I was in bits.'

'I'm told that was a spur-of-the-moment thing. The two lads came up with the idea on the Friday night. They were power-washing tractors into the wee small hours. Bet some had never been cleaned since the day they were bought.'

'And the horses, weren't they sweet?'

'You've obviously never been kicked by one. But the King must have appreciated the gesture, for he invited the tractor lads and the woman who organised the horses to the Halls when he came up in October and thanked them personally.'

'I think we're all agreed Deeside's contribution to the late Queen's funeral was an unqualified success,' said Flora decisively. 'Now, if we can get back to—'

'Except for the hearse,' Heather cut in. 'I think it was disgusting to display the funeral company's name on the side like that. Free advertising.' She sniffed. 'Newspapers said Purves had so many enquiries afterwards their website crashed.'

'Regardless, the name had vanished by the time the cortege left the comfort stop at Brechin Castle. And talking of moving on, when I mooted we discuss current affairs, this isn't what I had in mind.'

'Since – demonstrably – there's nothing newsworthy to talk about,' Heather argued, 'I say we give books another shot.'

'Nah!' said Morag. 'Unlike some, I don't have a minute in the day to call my own, never mind a quiet hour to sit and read.'

Chatty said, 'We all have busy lives.'

'Some busier than others.'

'Now, now,' said Flora. 'We're not here to insult folk and argue with one another. Admitted, we have our differences, but we are – let's face it – "women of a certain age". Surely we can reach a consensus.'

'If you say so.'

'It's clear, noble aim notwithstanding, we've neither the time nor capacity to tackle high-end literature.'

'But,' Heather complained, 'the whole point was to stretch our minds.'

'We can still read a book now and again: something pacey that moves along without heavy content. A book club pick, perhaps. A crime novel, even.'

Morag said, 'Now you're talking.'

Heather winced. The book club had been her idea. She had grandiose plans for growing the membership and took ill with the direction of travel. 'I'm of the firm opinion a book club is what we convened, and, given time, a book club can succeed.'

'No way!'

Flora said, 'I propose we each come back next week with a topical theme for discussion. Agreed?'

'Fine by me,' said Chatty. 'So long as I get shot of my paying guests for an hour or two, I don't give a monkey's what we talk about.'

'Morag?'

She made to rise. 'I don't mind, but I've really got to go.'

'Who's in favour of a book club?' Heather persisted. 'Let's have a show of hands.'

Nobody moved.

'Current affairs it is, then,' said Flora, with a thin, but palpably triumphant smile.

Six

Listening to the rain battering his bedroom window, Police Constable Alexander MacDuff wished he could stay in bed a while longer. There was no satisfaction in the job anymore. The reason he joined the force – to keep the Queen's peace, to prevent crime, to pursue and bring to justice those that break the law – had been lost in a sea of woke speak and paperwork, policing strategies and drink-driving targets.

Opening one eye, he took in the unsullied pillow next his own. For a nanosecond, MacDuff wished Moira hadn't left him. How long was it? He couldn't remember. What he did know: there was a while he thought there was a chance. No hope now. With a grunt, he rolled onto his back, gave his balls a good scratch, and slid from under the duvet.

Blearily, he washed and shaved, wishing he hadn't accepted a chaser with that last pint in the pub. But the price of a drink these days, on his pay grade you couldn't look a gift horse in the mouth.

Straining to fasten the waistband of his uniform trousers over his burgeoning belly, MacDuff wished he could lose a couple of stone. Not that he hadn't tried. He'd lost count of the number of times in the past twelve months he'd passed up a fish supper from the Phoenix in Ballater in favour of heading home to eat a sensible meal. But his rural beat being what it was, he too often ended up in a farm kitchen with a mug of tea and a fine piece: a thick, moist slab of Dundee cake, or a fluffy scone still warm from the oven. And you couldn't refuse, not if you wanted to keep in with the community.

Sitting down to a place laid for one at his kitchen table, MacDuff wished he was anywhere but here: a nondescript nineteen-sixties end-of-terrace council house with single-storey police office attached. Office was maybe pushing it, since the one small room was dominated by a sizeable counter. No longer in use. Along with Ballater and Braemar, Ballochbrae had no provision for a public counter, the nearest being at Banchory or Stonehaven. Time was, MacDuff enjoyed the comings and goings. Now, the space functioned as a storeroom and general dumping ground.

Shovelling down the porridge oats he'd made in the microwave, MacDuff wished he had someone to share a meal with, pass the time of day. Not a woman. Women were nothing but trouble. Since Moira, he'd been with a few – bad news every one. A dog, maybe. Alongside all the other things he'd learned to be suspicious of in twenty-plus years policing, MacDuff didn't trust cats. But it wouldn't be fair on the dog, being left on its own. Him neither. He'd have to walk it and feed it. Plus, dogs cost big money these days.

Unhooking his yellow high-vis jacket from the back of the chair, MacDuff wished he'd put in more effort to make sergeant. Time and again, he'd started studying for the exam, but something always got in the way. Too late now. In the fallout from the sale of Police Scotland's Aberdeen Queen Street HQ, cops were lucky to be stationed within spitting distance of their home address. If they had a job at all.

Dumping his porridge bowl and spoon in the sink, he reached for the keys to his police Land Rover. Fingers crossed he'd get the darn thing started. It was forever breaking down.

As MacDuff went out the door, head bowed into the driving rain, he wished he was a bit closer to drawing his pension.

Seven

Standing in half a wooded acre on the outskirts of the village, Albert Villa enjoys an open outlook, facing south across the valley. Two-storey, with generous bay windows flanking the front door, the Edwardian granite property had been built by Flora MacPhee's great-grandfather to house his growing brood. It had passed down the family to Flora's father and had been her childhood home.

If you asked Flora what prompted her return to Ballochbrae, she'd have said duty: her widowed mother was no longer able to live independently. Dial back, she put it down to sex. In the long, lonely hours of the night, she'd revisit – like a dog scratching a sore – the moment she walked into Allan's surgery.

In her job as Team Leader, District Nursing Services, she must have done so a hundred times: given the door a cursory tap, barged in, having first checked with Reception he wasn't with a patient. Most times, she'd find Allan sitting, head bent in concentration over a cluttered desk. He'd be writing up patient notes. Occasionally, on the telephone. But that day her husband of almost thirty years had been standing with his back to her, enthusiastically pleasuring Tracey, Aboyne Health Centre's nubile new Practice Nurse.

Now, her thoughts were shattered by the doorbell. Switching off the vacuum cleaner, she ran through the hall. 'Didn't think you'd make it.'

Morag said, 'Nor me. The old fella has been acting up something awful.'

They'd re-established a connection through the book club. Flora had extended the invitation on the spur of the moment. Was already asking herself if it was a good idea, her trust in relationships at rock bottom. 'Don't know how you cope.' She ushered Morag into a spacious kitchen with doors to the garden. Drawing out a hoop-back chair from the Ercol table, 'Make yourself at home.'

'Some days I just about manage to stay below the parapet. Others, I could put a hatchet in his head.'

'I know the feeling. When Dad retired, I thought they were all set for a comfortable life, but after he died Mum became quite needy.'

'Tell me about it,' Morag sighed. 'Fergus has me on twenty-four-hour call.'

'At the time, I put her memory lapses down to delayed shock. The death was sudden: a thrombosis. In the event, I stepped up my visits home, encouraged Mum to socialise. That helped a bit, but she was constantly on the phone, sometimes in the middle of the night. Things would go wrong. Nothing major: shower controls out of sync; TV remote going missing …'

'Where were you living at the time?'

'Rented accommodation in Aberdeen. I'd put in for a job move when my marriage broke down. You'll have heard the gossip.'

'Greatly exaggerated, I don't doubt. One rumour even had a machete involved.'

'Can't deny it. Tracey's husband was into body-building. Took strong exception.'

'Wow! Must have given Allan a real fright.'

'He'd have lost more than his job if I'd had a machete to hand.'

Morag grinned. 'I can believe you.'

'In the end, he didn't pursue the assault charge. Resigned the practice. His partners left him no choice. He went back to Glasgow. I gave my notice not long after.'

'Poor you. They'll have found your replacement, I suppose.'

'Expect so. Haven't been near the health centre, to tell the truth. The finger-pointing in the village was bad enough. Seemed, every time I ventured out, someone I hadn't seen in years would bump into me.' Flora made quotation marks of her hands. '"Accidentally on purpose." So the thought of facing my former colleagues ...'

'I see where you're coming from.'

'Getting back to Mum, when the drive back and forth got too much, I was forced to weigh my options, reckoned someone had to be there 24/7. She was officially diagnosed with Alzheimer's a year past.'

'Poor Kate! After losing her husband and all.'

'I thought the diagnosis would be welcome. But that day, when Mum did the tests ...' Flora broke off, her voice ragged. 'It completely floored me.'

'I can imagine. Even if you're used to it, must be hard.'

'Believe me, when it's someone that close to you, it's a whole different story.'

'What was the upshot?'

'Bit the bullet, took early retirement and came back to live at home.'

'Couldn't you have got social services in?'

'Doesn't happen overnight.'

'I'd have thought, with your connections, they'd have speeded things up.'

'Even I was prepared to take advantage of my position, Mum would have hated a stranger coming into the house to help her bathe or dress. After everything I'd been through, it was a relief, if I'm honest: running back home, sleeping in my old room, in my old bed.'

Morag winced. 'Unlike me. When my marriage collapsed, I had nowhere else to go.'

'At the beginning, I was happy to settle for a quiet life: pottering in the garden, watching soaps on TV. Things I hadn't done in years. We could still enjoy our own space. Mum would be happy enough knitting or watching TV in the breakfast room. I'd get peace and quiet to sit on my laptop in Dad's old snug. Sharing a kitchen, mind you ...' Flora pulled a comic face. 'Had its moments, I must admit. Speaking of which, what can I get for you?'

'I'd kill for a mug of tea. I've been out on the hill since breakfast.'

'Sit you down.' Crossing to the sink, Flora filled a fat cream Dualit kettle. Switching it on, she fetched mugs and teabags from a cupboard and milk from the fridge.

Morag said, 'How did things pan out? Hope you don't mind me asking. Truth be told, I've been wanting to pick your brains for ages. Reckon I might end up in much the same situation.'

'As Mum's condition deteriorated, I felt the ground shift beneath my feet.' Flora's voice wobbled. 'I thought, after all these years in nursing, I'd be able to cope. Did the best I could: invested in memory aids, digital watch, safety plugs, a simple remote control for the TV. Plastered Post-it notes all over the house. We were both terrified she would end up in a home.'

'Couldn't the doctor have given Kate something? I read in the papers there's drugs slow things down.'

'They can produce some benefit in mental function. Sadly, they don't halt the progression of the disease.'

'Your kids, where are they?'

'Scott's in Australia. Went out to work with my brother after university. Settled there. Isla's been in London for ten years or more. I don't see her coming back.' Arranging biscuits on a plate, 'You'll have heard Mum's gone into care.'

Morag nodded. 'What changed your mind?'

'She took to wandering, to the extent I'd to keep the front and back doors locked and hide the keys. I bought her a tracker lanyard, but she kept taking it off and forgetting where she'd put it. Then, one day I forgot to lock the front door. Mum got out. Wandered down to the main road. Luckily the post-van was passing at the time. It was Rab Kelman brought her back.'

'Nightmare!'

'And how.' Setting two pottery mugs on cork mats, Flora dropped onto a chair and offered biscuits. 'The traffic on that road, she could easily have been knocked down. And her balance hasn't been great. If she'd got as far as the river, she could have fallen in.'

'The amount of rain we've had,' said Morag, through a mouthful of chocolate digestive, 'she'd have drowned, no question.'

'Don't even go there. But the incident forced my hand. I thought if I could find a care home that was right for Mum ... Researched homes within a thirty-mile radius. Drew up a short list. Failed to find a single vacant bed. So when I got a call last week to say a room had become available in Darroch View, I didn't hesitate.'

Eight

'Mrs MacIntyre?'

Chatty looked the length of her nose. 'Yes?'

'Christopher Calthorpe-Drummond-Smythe.'

She took in a well-cut tweed jacket over a Tattersall check shirt, a tie in broad navy and maroon stripes. Below a vintage pair of cuffed cavalry-twill trousers, brown brogues buffed to a high shine spoke to a military background.

'Ooh,' she breathed, not quite managing to conceal her excitement. Time was, Chatty would have been in thrall to a double-barrelled name. Not any more, when every Tom, Dick and Harry was stringing surnames together. Triple-barrelled, that was another thing entirely.

Straightening, she pulled in her tummy and thrust out her boobs. 'I wasn't expecting you until much later.'

'Managed to get on an earlier flight. Hope this doesn't cause inconvenience.'

'Not at all,' she fibbed, mind working overtime. When the booking had come in, she'd Googled the name. Found a possible match: Eton and Guards, office in St James. Made a mental note to run a further search. 'Welcome to Castle View.' Chatty cursed herself for not finding the time to follow through. Then she focused on more mundane matters: had Etta made up the room to a passable standard? If the guest chose to dine in that evening, could she squeeze another portion?

Switching her focus back to the new arrival, she clocked the absence of luggage.

Following her eyes, he said, 'Suitcase is in the car. I'll fetch it later.'

'As you wish,' Chatty acknowledged, voice belying her disappointment. In her reluctant reincarnation as a hotelier, she'd learned you could tell a lot from a guest's luggage. 'If you care to follow me.' Turning, she wiggled down the hall, wishing she was wearing heels, and started up the staircase, praying her bum didn't look as big as it felt.

*

'I've put you in Glen Muick, one of our Executive Rooms,' Chatty announced, throwing open the bedroom door.

Ushering her guest inside, she scoped the room.

The bed was straight, if not exactly tailored.

The carpet bore vacuum cleaner tracks.

The waste bin had been emptied.

She was congratulating herself when she clocked the dirty water glass sitting on the bedside table.

Chatty zipped across the room. Standing by the bed, her back to the offending item, she waved a hand. 'Take a look at the view.'

Obediently, Calthorpe-Drummond-Smythe crossed to the window.

In one silken movement, Chatty whipped the glass off the bedside table and – lifting the hem of her leopard-print shirt – stuffed it down the back of her control knickers.

Face a study in puzzlement, her guest turned. 'Should I be looking for anything in particular?'

'Lochnagar,' Chatty shot back. When she was stuck for an answer, it usually filled the bill, either that or Balmoral. Crossing to his side, 'If you look through that gap in the trees, you'll see the river.'

He brightened. 'Good show. I'll be down there first thing tomorrow morning.'

'Fished the Dee before?'

'Not for some years.'

Up close, Chatty detected a whiff of something subtle: Floris, at a guess. Founded in 1730, the renowned family perfumers would be close to Christopher's place of work. Shortly before Roderick's demise, she'd popped into their Jermyn Street shop for a bottle of her favourite Chypress eau de toilette following afternoon tea at Fortnum and Mason in Piccadilly.

If you'd asked Chatty MacIntyre what brought her back to Ballochbrae, she'd have said heritage. The truth was more prosaic. When Roderick went under the wheels of the number 94 bus, he generated scarce a column inch in the London *Evening Standard*. But if some eager young hack from one of the red-tops were to pick up the story …

Now, Chatty speculated as to Christopher's line of business. Investment banking? Property? The name thrown up by her Google search hadn't given a lot away. He'd be married, she presumed. Eyes dropping to his left hand, she zeroed in on the crested gold signet ring on his little finger. Divorced, with a bit of luck. Since The Incident, she'd sworn off men, but old habits die hard.

'There's nothing like crisp mountain air,' she declared, bending from the knees to throw up the sash window. 'Shake off those city cobwebs.' Filling her lungs, she gave him an eyeful of cleavage.

'No, indeed,' he said, bug-eyed.

'But first, you'll be needing a hot meal. And ...' with a suggestive glance towards the bed, 'a good night's sleep.'

'If you'll forgive me, I'll pass on supper. Had something at the airport.'

Thank God! Chatty relaxed, just a tad.

'Been a long day.' Turning to face her, he thrust out a hand. 'I answer to Chipper.'

Furiously batting her eyelashes, 'Catriona,' she replied. Then, praying her Spanx knickers still had firm hold of the tumbler, she backed cautiously out the room.

Nine

The river Dee is perfect for fly fishing. From its source at the Wells of Dee – perched at four thousand feet on the upper slopes of Braeriach – it tumbles down through the Cairngorms until it reaches the Linn of Dee, a narrow passage with sheer rock on either side and favourite picnic spot of Queen Victoria. After the Linn, the river clatters through a series of beautiful, boulder-strewn pools as it travels past Braemar and Ballater to Aboyne.

On the riverbank, 'Aye, aye?' said ghillie Stuart Thom creeping up behind the hooded figure. 'What are you up to?'

Kenny Tinsley whirled to face him. 'Just taking the air.'

'On a day like this?' Stuart cast a glance over his shoulder. The hills sat under a heavy blanket of mist, trees blurred by a veil of drizzle.

With a nonchalant shrug, 'Yup.'

'On your own?'

Shielding his eyes with one hand, Kenny made a show of scanning the horizon. 'Can't see anyone else. Can you?'

'Strange place to be out walking,' Stuart came back. 'Wouldn't have anything to do with the salmon?'

A fishing ghillie's job encompasses maintenance of the riverbanks and salmon fishing hut, and they were close enough to Crathie, one of the best fishing beats, offering unrivalled individual rod space on both right and left bank over its six-mile length. In most rivers the upper sections are the least prolific, but on the Dee they are some of the most storied, notable amongst them Crathie, Mar Lodge, Invercauld and the royal beats themselves: Birkhall, Abergeldie and Balmoral.

'It's a free country,' said Kenny, unable to keep the smirk off his face. 'Leastways, was last time I looked.'

'What have you got under that coat?'

'A sweater.'

'Don't come the smart aleck with me.'

Laconically, Kenny unzipped his waxed Barbour jacket. 'See.'

Stuart clocked it was a Beaufort.

Zoomed into the double-zipped game pocket at the back.

Registered it was empty.

'Hah,' he said.

Turning away, he scanned the undergrowth for a hiding place. Found none.

Turning back, 'You wouldn't have come from yon farm steading?'

Kenny's eyes slid sideways. 'Why would I?'

'Lost a tankful of oil a couple days back. Thief might have nipped back, see if there was anything else worth stealing.'

'You can't lay that at my door.'

'Mebbe. Mebbe not.'

The Tinsley clan, of which Kenneth was a scion, were travellers with a long history of poaching and agricultural theft. Oil tanks were repeatedly targeted, farm machinery and equipment stolen with such frequency incidents often went unreported.

'But don't think you've free rein. This is my patch.' Jabbing a warning finger, Stuart ordered, 'Stay away.'

Head lowered, Kenny muttered, 'Ye're only an effing ghillie, not the police.'

'Aye, but I've good connections. And I'll be keeping a close eye on you, and anyone like you. Cross the line and you'll suffer the consequences.'

Kenny's chin jutted. 'That a threat?'

'Look on it as good advice. Now, clear off.' Stuart gave him a helpful shove.

'Take your hands of me,' Kenny hissed, spittle flying.

Stuart stood his ground. 'On your way.'

Fists balled, Kenny turned.

Halfway up the riverbank, he threw over his shoulder, 'I've got your number. Better watch your back.'

Ten

At the western edge of the village, Ballochbrae Primary School occupies an extended two-storey Edwardian granite villa, with later outbuildings for lunch-room and toilets. A wraparound tarmac playground backs onto an expanse of native woodland, where the children have the added opportunity to learn and explore.

Heather Garden rapped a wooden ruler on the desk. 'Settle down.'

Students – dressed in the uniform of white polo shirt and forest-green sweatshirt over dark skirt or trousers – joshed and fidgeted and finally sat still.

Methodically, Heather worked her way through the attendance register. Not that she need have bothered. She could spot the absentees at a glance. Notwithstanding a catchment area that embraced outlying hamlets and estates, the school roll had plummeted, a single combined class currently totalling eleven.

Raising her head, she asked, 'Anyone seen Lachlan?'

This was met by a sea of blank faces.

'How about Ruaridh?'

Children nudged one another and whispered behind their hands.

For some weeks, nine-and-a-half-year-old Lachlan Burnett and his sidekick Ruaridh Shirras – eighteen months younger – had truanted persistently, their absences justified by a series of dodgy sick notes, to the extent their parents been called to attend on more than one occasion.

Heather said, 'I'll take that as a "no".' She jotted a note.

She was about to start the lesson, when the classroom door opened a crack.

A small, dark head poked round. 'Sorry, miss,' said Ruaridh Shirras. 'Slept in.'

'Again?'

'Sorry.'

'Well, come away in.'

When Ruaridh had found his seat, 'I don't suppose you've seen your pal.' Where one went, the other was usually not far behind.

His eyes slid away. 'No, miss.'

'He's not unwell, is he?'

'Don't know.'

Heather eyed him with suspicion. Sighing, 'I suppose he'll turn up in his own good time.'

If you asked Heather Garden what brought her back to Ballochbrae, she'd have said God. A late only child, she lived quietly at home until age seventeen, when she enrolled on a teacher training course in Dundee. And found love. But the year after she graduated – and before her love had a chance to fully blossom – Isobel Garden was diagnosed with cancer. When, unexpectedly, a vacancy arose at Ballochbrae

Primary, Heather resigned her post and moved back to care, first for her mother, then father until both passed away.

Now – still years short of retirement – Heather wanted nothing more than to see out her teaching career in Ballochbrae, putting heart and soul into nurturing her school 'family' and living quietly with her beloved Darcy in Thistle Cottage. But the council had a timetable of planned school closures. Who would be next? Every time she lost a pupil, Heather died a small death. Worse, she was powerless to influence the situation. Students moved up to secondary school with dispiriting regularity. More families moved out of the village than in.

As to Lachlan Burnett and Ruaridh Shirras, they were at that stage: pushing the boundaries. Heather had seen it before, and no doubt would again. She allowed herself a small smile. Except Lachlan was a troubled lad. There were problems at home. And if the pair were to get up to serious mischief, be excluded from school—

Beneath her sensible underpinnings, Heather's stomach performed an uncomfortable somersault.

Lips framing a silent prayer it wouldn't come to that, she said, 'Open your workbooks and let's get on.'

Eleven

The blade flashed silver as the axe cleaved the log in two.

Exiting his police Land Rover, 'Nice one!' MacDuff joshed. 'Wouldn't like to get on the wrong side of you.'

Plaid lumberjack shirt unbuttoned over a sweat-stained tee, Hector Pirie straightened, axe dangling loose from one hand. Standing well over six feet, and built like an ox, the forestry worker personified his part-time pursuit of champion caber-tosser. 'Fit like?' He voiced the Doric equivalent of, 'How's things?'

'Doin' awa.'

Setting the cut logs on top of a tidy woodpile, 'What can I do for you?'

'I'm on the scrounge.' Inhaling the sweet smell of resin, 'Any offcuts going spare?'

'Hang on a mo.'

MacDuff recoiled as Hector swung the axe overarm. The blade embedded in a block of wood, haft sticking up at an alarming angle.

With a yank of his head, Hector said, 'Come in the workshop.'

'If I'm not keeping you back.'

'Nae bother. Kids are out. Jean's at work.'

MacDuff followed him around the back of the single-storey cottage, where the doors of a timber outbuilding stood open, revealing a pristine woodworking bench. Approaching, MacDuff bent for a closer look. 'I'd give my eyeteeth for a set-up like this,' he marvelled, taking in the top-of-the-range circular saw, the lathe, the chisels and planes. His own rusting toolbox was a hotchpotch of hand-me-downs and car-boot-sale finds.

'Aye,' said Hector, stroking his ginger beard. 'Well.' He indicated a row of plastic crates on the concrete floor. 'Help yourself.'

'Thanks.' Dropping to a crouch, MacDuff pulled a stout plastic bag from his pocket and proceeded to fill it.

Hector eyed the process with asperity. 'Expecting visitors?'

'As if I'd have time for entertaining,' MacDuff complained, not looking up. 'Police Scotland!' he exclaimed, shoulders stiff with tension. 'The amount of paperwork I have to get through in a week you wouldn't believe. Takes up that much time, I scarce know my arse from my elbow.'

'Thought you might have found yourself a bidey-in,' Hector ribbed, using the local term for a fancy woman.

'Chance would be a fine thing.' He sat back on his heels. 'Women!'

Hector said, 'You wouldn't want to be in my shoes. I've two of them. Give me nothing but grief.'

MacDuff turned, grim faced. 'Tell me about it.'

'And when they're not on at me, they're at each other's throats.' He threw the policeman a cautionary glance. 'Maybe just as well you and Moira didn't have kids.'

'Suppose.'

'Sighing, Hector continued, 'My lad, now, he's the opposite. Can hardly get a word out of him these days, and when you do it's not civil.'

MacDuff struggled to his feet. 'You're more than able for them, I don't doubt.'

'I wish. You can't lift a finger to anyone these days.'

'Don't get me started.'

Flexing bulging biceps, Hector spread meaty hands. 'Time was ...' He threw MacDuff a look heavy with meaning. 'You'd sort your problems your own way.'

Twelve

'Good morning.' Chatty greeted the last of that morning's guests with a forced smile. By nature, she was not an early riser and, taking hard to her daily 6 a.m. start, was ready for a lie-down.

Nothing if not resourceful – years negotiating naval life had stood her in good stead – she'd tackled the challenge of setting up in business head-on. But even the minimum entry requirements for VisitScotland's Quality Assurance Scheme were daunting. Chatty had no idea there were so many regulations: Licensing, Health & Safety, Food Hygiene, Data and Consumer Protection. And it didn't stop there. The list of furnishings and equipment was exhaustive: fire extinguishers and kettles and hairdryers and non-flammable waste bins. Pillows (two per person) and coat hangers (wire hangers not acceptable). Towels and non-slip bathmats and lidded disposal bins.

An online trawl of the local bed and breakfast websites set a benchmark. Mumsnet and Pinterest offered a goldmine of tips. Operating on the slenderest of shoestrings, Chatty set to replacing her in-laws' store of greying linen sheets with hotel-standard white cotton sourced from Primark. Scorched parchment lampshades were swapped for taupe fabric ordered on Amazon, the depleted Spode Italian dinner service augmented with seconds from an outlet store, and worn silver-plated cutlery replaced with stainless steel. What the ensuing promotional blurb described as a 'major refurbishment' was, in reality, a quick coat of emulsion slapped on by a local handyman and the purchase of a selection of stick-on door signs from the closing-down sale at Cassie's hardware store in Ballater.

Now, 'And good morning to you, ma'am,' the tall American replied, baring a perfectly aligned set of Colgate-white teeth.

Chatty reckoned they were false, either that or the product of mouth-wateringly expensive dentistry. Pondering the current price of implants, she asked, 'Where would you like to sit?'

Brett Sanders – impeccably turned out in sharp-creased chinos and polo shirt – turned. 'What do you think, hun?' Indicating a window table, 'How about over there? Make the most of the view.' He ushered his wife – her name was Marvel – across the naked expanse of parquet floor.

Dressed in matching shirt and chinos over pristine white sneakers, Marvel had that stick-thin lollipop-head look Chatty inwardly aspired to, but affected to despise. Craning her neck through the tall windows, she complained, 'I thought you said we'd have a view of the castle.'

Nine miles west of Ballater, Balmoral Castle sits on the River Dee, close to the village of Crathie. One of the residences of the British Royal Family, it is set in woodland

and formal gardens encircled by a protective ring of forest and heather-clad hills, notable of which are Craig Gowan to the south and the Munro of Lochnagar to the south-west.

'It's the time of year,' breezed Chatty. 'Forest canopy at its densest.' Catching Marvel's dubious expression, 'You can see the castle from the roadside.'

What Chatty didn't say: on those stretches of the A93, where from certain angles a fleeting glimpse of the castle might be afforded, police road signs prohibit vehicles from stopping.

'You don't say,' Marvel responded, looking mutinous.

Brett said, 'Balmoral is only minutes away, right?'

Chatty nodded. *On Balmoral's doorstep* was what she'd said in her tourist listing, penned late one night in a gin-soaked haze. The Quality Assurance Scheme stipulated a map and/or directions showing the location. It hadn't said anything about the view.

Once the Americans were seated on Xanthe's barley-twist oak dining chairs, upholstered in faux tapestry, Marvel announced. 'We're gonna do the tour. Whaddya say we bump into the King?'

Chatty couldn't resist. 'Wrong time of year.'

Beneath a razor-cut blonde bob, Marvel's perfectly made-up jaw dropped onto her immaculate powder-blue Ralph Lauren polo shirt. 'When we did Buckingham Palace, they told us King Charles was coming up to Balmoral. Isn't that right, hun?'

'Yup.'

'Doubt it,' said Chatty. 'You can tell by whichever flag is flying: Royal Banner of the Royal Arms of Scotland, otherwise known as the Lion Rampant, or – when the sovereign is in residence – the Royal Standard of the United Kingdom. It's very distinctive: the arms of England quartered with those of Scotland and Ireland.'

Eyes narrowed beneath a rigidly Botoxed forehead, Marvel turned on Brett. 'Looks like you've dragged me up to this godforsaken place for nothing.'

He laid a hand on her arm. 'Now, baby,' he soothed.

'Don't "baby" me,' she replied, false eyelashes batting furiously.

Feeling sorry for the poor schmuck, Chatty said, 'Even if your information is correct, King Charles wouldn't be at the castle. He'd be at Birkhall. That's over seven miles away.'

'Do they do a tour?'

'Sorry. You've more chance of meeting the King on the grouse moor or walking around Loch Muick.' Chatty looked on in satisfaction as Marvel gave her husband the full evils. 'Doing his shopping in Ballater, even. Look out for the sepia direction signs bearing Queen Victoria's head and the royal warrants over the shop doorways.' Tiring of the charade, Chatty added, 'If you do go to Balmoral, there's five miles of walks in the grounds. A tearoom. Gift shop, if you're that way inclined.' She thrust out a menu. 'I expect you'll want the full Scottish, seeing as you'll be out all day.' Hopefully, they'd take the hint. She couldn't be doing with folk who hung around, getting under her feet.

Marvel scanned the printed card with palpable distaste. 'Not for me. Give me an egg-white omelette. Two eggs. And a peppermint tea. Fresh mint, if you have it.'

Fresh mint? Chatty couldn't keep the scowl off her face. As for an egg-white omelette. 'And for you, sir?'

Reading from the menu, Brett enunciated, 'Smoked back bacon, pork sausage, eggs, fried, poached or scrambled. Stornoway black pudding.' Looking up, 'That's sorta blood sausage, right?'

'Correct,' said Chatty. 'And very tasty it is too.'

'It's banned in the US. For sanitary reasons,' he expanded. 'Seeing as it contains sheep's lungs.'

Nose thoroughly out of joint, Chatty fibbed, 'It's a favourite with the royals.'

'Sold,' said Brett. 'I'll go for the full Scottish.'

A movement caught Chatty's eye.

Her head swivelled. Chipper was approaching a nearby table.

As he drew out a chair, he cast an appreciative look over Marvel's groomed figure and flawless maquillage.

Chatty's gaze dropped to the baggy black leggings and scuffed trainers she wore to get through the morning shift.

Dammit! She'd have to up her game.

Thirteen

With a screech of brakes, Lachie Burnett brought his bike to a standstill. Dismounting with one fluid movement, he let it fall onto its side.

'What's up?' queried Ruaridh Shirras, skidding to a halt alongside.

'Fancy a shufti at the suspension bridge?'

Ruaridh clocked the rusty lock on the tall iron gate. 'You're not allowed.'

'Och,' said Lachie. 'Who's to know?'

'Someone might see us.'

Waving an arm in the direction of the thickly forested hills, Lachie asked, 'Like who?'

Ruaridh eyed the gate, uncertain. 'What about them spikes? I'll get murdered if I tear my breeks.'

'We don't have to go over the gate, dummy.' Pointing to the gap between a low wall and the bridge supports, 'We could squeeze through there and climb onto the walkway.'

Ruaridh strained forward. The narrow stone parapet was damp with moss. Far below, the river tumbled and swirled. He shook his head. 'We'll go for the gate.'

'Don't be such a sissy,' scoffed Lachie.

Ruaridh squared up. 'Who are you calling a sissy?'

Starting forward, Lachie said, 'You coming, or not?'

Fourteen

'Fine day.' Flora smiled, as she came through the door.

From the high-backed orthopaedic chair by the window, Kate MacPhee (Flora had reverted to her maiden name) regarded her daughter with open hostility. 'Where's my bag?'

Flora held out a paper bag bearing the logo of Ballater's Byron Bakery. Located in Golf Road, the double-fronted shop is crowned with a royal warrant and home to the famed Balmoral Bread. 'I've brought something for us to have with our cuppa.'

Forehead creased in a frown, Kate's thin fingers scrabbled at the baker's bag, then forcefully batted it away. 'It's my weekend bag I'm talking about. Have you come to take me home?'

Flora crossed the room. Dropped to a crouch at her mother's knee, as she'd done a thousand times. Only not under these circumstances. 'Not today, Mum,' she said softly. 'You'll be a wee while yet.'

Confusion flooded Kate's face. 'A week,' she insisted. 'That's what they said.'

'You're right,' Flora soothed. 'But that was last year, when you came to Darroch View for respite care.'

'That's not what you told me yesterday.' Eyes blazing, she thrust her face up close. 'Am I right?'

Flora drew a calming breath. Her mother's sudden eruptions of rage were all-too-frequent. 'I'll have a word at the desk before I go.'

Kate's face clouded. 'It was yesterday?' she faltered.

Flora was saved by the rattle of an approaching tea trolley.

There was a tap on the door.

A head poked round: pink-cheeked, topped by a high ponytail.

'Cup of tea, ladies?' asked the care assistant.

'Please,' said Flora, turning. 'Drop of milk. No sugar.'

'Biscuit?'

'No, thanks.'

She turned back. 'Mum?'

In the chair by the window, Kate MacPhee's head lolled in slumber.

'I'll take that as a "no".'

Flora acknowledged this with a weak smile. It wasn't unusual for her mother to nod off during the course of the day. Accepting the proffered cup and saucer, she waited until the care assistant withdrew, thankful for a quiet few minutes to herself, even though the tea was tepid and much too milky for her liking.

If you asked Flora to sum up her character in a single word, 'collected', she might have said. She'd had to be. Working out of Aboyne Health Centre, her remit covered the GP practices of Aboyne, Ballater, Banchory, Braemar and Torphins, with a total practice population of over twenty-three thousand. The multi-disciplinary, multi-agency team bore twenty-four-hour responsibility for patients in their own homes: organising and preventing admissions, anticipating care needs and managing long-term conditions. In addition to service delivery, Flora had been responsible for the recruitment, training and personal development of district and community nurses, healthcare support workers and admin staff. And that was discounting the administrative aspects of her job: computer systems, time and mileage sheets, off-duty rotas, equipment and pharmacy orders and stores.

So how was it, she agonised – with a degree in district nursing and decades of clinical experience – she hadn't sussed her own mother was presenting with the early indications of Alzheimer's?

Flora looked around. The room was well appointed: spacious, south-facing, with a view not dissimilar to that of Albert Villa – the reason she'd jumped at it, despite what she deemed an exorbitant price. But for all its amenity, the hospital-style bed and locker gave it an institutional look. Her fault. She was engulfed by another wave of guilt. The move into full-time care had happened so fast, she hadn't got around to choosing the small items of furniture that would lend familiarity, the pictures that would break up blank walls.

She'd had the presence of mind, at least, to pack a favourite pillow, a few family photographs. Still, she cursed herself for her inaction. Losing her husband after all those years must have been a body blow to Kate, without the further loss of her mental faculties. And, now, to leave her home, with all its memories …

In that moment, Flora saw for the first time how bleak might be her own future: single, middle-aged, impecunious. She was even losing the sense of humour that had first attracted Allan, seen her through the many crises in her long career.

Allan. Her mind jumped back to their first date. He'd been so nervous, standing in the doorway of her student digs—

Resolutely, Flora wiped the image from her mind.

Still, she couldn't escape the unvarnished truth: she missed him. Was reminded every day in some small way of their … not love, so much as shared experience.

Draining her cup, Flora made a mental resolution: she'd been wallowing in self-pity long enough.

Time she got her act together.

Found new purpose in life.

And fast!

Fifteen

Chatty MacIntyre poured tea for a new arrival. The welcome cuppa was a cornerstone of the five-star tourist board rating Castle View aspired to. It also offered a golden opportunity to establish her guests' spending potential and general usefulness.

Across an inlaid tea table in the guest lounge, Mark Outhwaite took a tentative sip. Late forties. Tall. Toned, judging by the sit of what looked to be a brand new tweed jacket. Chatty eyed the garment with asperity. PPOs were supposed to blend in with the local community, but stood out like a sore thumb. Still – she appraised the groomed hair, the chiselled jaw – this one was an improvement on the officers she'd hosted thus far.

Personal Protection Officers, she'd learned, protect select members of the Royal Family, both at home and abroad. A Google search produced more information: following a merger of the Royalty Protection Command with the Specialist Protection Command in April 2015, Royalty and Specialist Protection (RaSP) is responsible for guarding the Royal Family and associated residences and consists of a number of sections: Personal and Close Protection, Residential Protection and the Special Escort Group. The senior police officers – each with ten to fifteen years' experience – are trained in firearms and unarmed combat, advanced driving and emergency first aid.

With a suggestive glance, Chatty bit the glacé cherry off an empire biscuit. She chewed languidly, lips puckered in a scarlet moue. Then, swallowing, enquired, 'This your first tour?'

'No. I've been doing the job for a couple of years, but this is my first on Deeside.'

Her eyes dropped to his chest. No lumpy armpit.

She checked his lapel. No telltale badge, the giveaway he was carrying. Armed Protection Officers – by dint of having to be contained – were billeted in staff quarters, where possible, on the Balmoral Estate and at Birkhall.

'Where do you call home?'

'South of the Thames: Clerkenwell.'

She clocked his wedding finger. No ring. 'Must be difficult, living so far away.'

'You'd think so. To be honest ...' Leaning forward, he lowered his voice. 'I'm enjoying the change of scene. It's so quiet up here. Peaceful.'

Lasciviously, Chatty licked a slick of jam from the side of the shortbread biscuit.

'And,' with a wink, 'the digs aren't half bad.'

It's all right for you, mate. Mark Outhwaite wasn't lumbered with a great mausoleum of a house. Didn't have to get up at the crack of dawn. Be at everyone's constant beck and call.

On the table, his phone rang.

Reaching out, 'Better take this.'

Standing, he crossed to the window, his back to her.

One eye on his pleasing physique, Chatty weighed her options. The Royal Protection Officers were a godsend, but she'd only landed the contract due to another bed & breakfast being flooded. She couldn't rely on it being renewed. Deeside was chock-a-block with boarding establishments, many better appointed. If Chatty couldn't raise the capital to upgrade Castle View's outdated facilities and attain a good star rating, the officers might go elsewhere. And now the Queen was dead, would Balmoral continue to draw the Firm, as the Royal Family had first been christened by George VI? Charles and Camilla were settled at Birkhall. They'd spent only three weeks at the castle in summer 2023, and the King was – reportedly – planning to make the royal palaces more accessible to the public.

Might be worth a go at achieving a sale. The publicity generated by the late Queen's death had given the local property market a welcome boost. But, unlike Ballater, where a clutch of royal warrants lends cachet to the retail trade, or Braemar, which has a lively cafe and music scene, Ballochbrae was something of a backwater. That said, didn't Royal Deeside have cachet? If Castle View were to achieve a full price, Chatty could go back to Edinburgh. And if it didn't attract a buyer, she could always take it off the market. Her heart sank at the prospect.

Checking Mark Outhwaite was still talking into his phone, Chatty debated how to go forward. She could try to secure a bank loan to fund the upgrade necessary to generate more business. But the bank would demand security. Castle View was only entering its first full season and the accounts wouldn't currently satisfy close inspection. Nor would they ever, unless a high star rating was achieved. And that would only happen if she spent money on the place. Maybe she could take out a mortgage? But if she got a quick sale and found somewhere to buy, that might complicate things.

Caught between a rock and a hard place.

Chatty chewed her lip. Best hang in. Build up the business. But how long would that take? Her spirits sank even further.

A movement caught her eye.

Looking up, she saw Mark Outhwaite stride towards her, pocketing his phone.

Chatty's thoughts crystallised: *What I need is a man.*

Giving Mark a cursory glance, she found him wanting: presentable enough, but below an – admittedly – already low bar.

Her imagination took a leap: the fisher, might he be a potential meal ticket? Bit on the short side, but given her present circumstances …

Catriona Calthorpe-Drummond-Smythe.

She pictured herself back in the Scottish capital, being introduced at a smart luncheon: The New Club, perhaps. Founded in 1787, Scotland's oldest private members' club occupies a prime position on Princes Street, with panoramic views of Edinburgh Castle, and is patronised by the upper echelons of Scottish society.

'Sorry about that.'

Chatty's reverie was shattered when Mark Outhwaite resumed his seat.

'More tea?' she asked, making doe-eyes.

No harm in a practice run.

Sixteen

PC MacDuff set a half-drunk pint of beer on the red Formica counter of the Clachan Inn. Letting out a loud burp, he turned and lumbered through the door leading to the gents' toilet.

A stocky figure in a navy windcheater zipped against the draught from the front door, landlord Archie Kinnear lifted the hinged flap at the end of the bar. Crossing to the far wall, he stooped and set another log in the grate. The bark caught and flared, sending licks of flame up the narrow chimney.

'Aye, aye,' nodded the only customer. The old fellow with silver mutton-chop whiskers was seated at the corner of the cast-iron fireplace, an empty glass coated with creamy foam on the round table in front of him.

Archie pointed. 'Pint of Guinness?'

'Think I could manage.'

'Not like you're driving,' said MacDuff, fumbling with his flies as he came back into the bar. He'd given Dodd Benzie a caution the month before.

Dodd ignored this. Addressing Archie, 'I'll nip out for a ciggie first.' He struggled to his feet.

'Okay.' Retracing his steps, Archie took up position behind the bar. Turning to the constable, known locally as Big Eck, he asked, 'Off-duty?'

He nodded. 'Couldn't come soon enough.'

'Any excitement on your watch?'

'I should be so lucky.' Picking up his pint, MacDuff took a long swallow. 'Nothing but traffic offences and anti-social behaviour. Kids nowadays.' Morosely, he studied the dregs of his beer. 'No respect for the law. In my day, a village copper doubled as a social worker. All it took was a quiet word with a kid's mum and they never crossed your path again.'

'True enough,' said Archie. 'Same goes for licensees. You'd refuse to serve someone and that would be the end of it. These days they're arguing the toss: flashing fake ID, shouting the odds about being disrespected and how it will affect their mental health.'

'Bunch of snowflakes.'

'Who are you calling a snowflake?' demanded Stuart Thom, pushing through the entrance.

'Well,' said Eck. 'If it's not ghillie of the year.'

Running a weary hand across his forehead, Stuart said, 'Don't even go there. I've had a bad day.'

'No fish?'

'Wasn't the fish,' he grumbled. 'It was the punters: three of my regulars and one total idiot.'

'How come?'

'Guy mouthed off about every last thing: the rod, the waders, you name it. And that was before we even left the hut.'

Draining his pint, Eck held up his glass. 'Win some, lose some. Speaking of which, your timing's spot on. I'm ready for a refill.'

'You're out of luck,' said Stuart. 'I've only cash for a half-pint.'

'Use a credit card.'

'Sorry. Left them at home.'

'Lying sod,' scowled Eck. From past experience, Stuart Thom was tight as a fish's arse.

'It's the God's honest truth,' Stuart protested. Indicating the multiple pockets of his tweed jacket, 'Empty. Or near as.' He winked, as his phone sounded. Drawing it out, he swiped to accept the call. 'Who? Oh, okay. Didn't recognise the number. No, there's no particular reason …' Casting a wary glance around the bar, 'I've been tied up with work. I'll see to it right away.' A pause, then, 'In the Clach.' Another pause. 'No. I'll come to you.'

MacDuff said, 'That sounded interesting.'

'I wish,' shrugged Stuart, sliding his phone back into an inside pocket. 'Just some nonentity pushing paperwork.'

'Total nightmare, admin.'

'Too true,' he concurred, looking shifty.

'Half pint?' Archie enquired.

'Later, maybe. Something's come up. Got to run.'

Archie turned to MacDuff. 'Same again?'

'Not tonight. I've a ton of stuff to catch up with. Best be on my way.'

'It's not like you've far to go.'

He grinned. The police house was only a short walk from the pub.

With a nod to Dodd Benzie, MacDuff followed Stuart out the door.

*

Archie looked up from rinsing glasses. 'Evening.'

Doffing a wide-brimmed hat to reveal thinning fair hair combed in a precise side parting, the newcomer responded with a grunt.

'What can I get you?'

He scanned the shelf of single malt whiskies behind Archie's head. 'Laphroaig. Make that a double.'

Taking in at a glance the tweed fishing jacket over thick sweater and corduroy trousers, Archie said, 'Good choice. That's the King's favourite.' Getting no reaction, he took a tumbler from a shelf and set it on the bar. Then, reaching for the whisky bottle, unscrewed the cap, poured a stream of amber liquid into a measure, emptied it into the tumbler and slid it across. 'Water?'

'Just a drop.'

When Archie had decanted water from a crested china jug, the man picked up the glass and held it aloft. Looking over his shoulder, 'Tight lines!' He acknowledged the only other drinker in the room.

'Slainte.' Dodd Benzie uttered the Gaelic drinking toast from his seat by the fire.

Taking a mouthful, the man swilled it around and swallowed. 'That's better!' He smacked his lips. 'Bastard of a day.' Thrusting out a hand, 'Christopher Calthorpe-Drummond-Smythe. You can call me Chipper.'

Archie grasped the soft flesh. A townie, then. 'Archie Kinnear. Fish not biting today?'

Colour suffused Chipper's pallid cheeks. 'It wasn't the fish that was the problem. It was the ghillie.'

'That so?'

'Didn't like the cut of his jib from the get-go.' Taking another mouthful of whisky, 'We were late getting started. I was tackled up with a full floater and a size twelve Crathie on the end. The Suspension Bridge failed to hold a taking fish. Fifth cast I had a fish on briefly, and later a splashy rise.'

'Water's peaty. Fish can be hard to spot.'

'Garlum produced nothing but a small grilse. Stirred up lots of brownies, but not a solitary salmon. McLaren I could see fish lying in the pools but never got a touch.'

'That's salmon for you,' said Archie. 'Things don't always go to plan.'

'"Professional dedicated guidance", the organiser promised. In my book, that means accessing the best beats, and giving fishing parties up-to-the-minute knowledge of the river, making their experience as rich as possible.'

Archie kept his counsel. Stuart Thom might be thrawn, but he knew his job.

'Accepted, our guide was on hand at the start to give casting tips and suchlike, and his suggestions for sink tips and flies seemed well informed. It's his attitude I take issue with. Didn't help the other guests were old hands and monopolised the fella. At my expense. That's the whole point of a ghillie: to guide you to the best spots.'

'There's twenty-five pools on the Crathie beat. You can't expect to fish them all on day one.'

Chipper ignored him. 'To add insult to injury, one of our party landed a whopper: fifteen pounds, near enough, measurements indicated. DNA, scale samples and photographs to prove it. What really gets me: that fish should have been mine. If the ghillie had been paying attention instead of talking on his mobile …'

'I doubt—' Archie began.

'When he finally got off the phone, he was so surly, had we been on a shoot, he'd have been on the end of my gun.'

Whoa! Archie took a surreptitious step back.

Squaring up, Chipper continued, 'I've a good mind to report the blighter to the bailiffs.'

'Fishing might be better tomorrow. Yesterday, one of my regulars had two. Last week, Monaltrie and Lower Invercauld produced five. Plus, we've had rain overnight. River is up a few inches.'

At Archie's back, the connecting door to the house swung open.

'Your dinner's on the table,' announced his wife, Janet.

'I'll be right there.' With a nod to Chipper, 'If you'll excuse me,' he squeezed past her.

Janet took his place behind the bar. 'Come far?'

'London. Flew up yesterday.'

'That your home?'

'Chelsea. Do you know it?'

'Haven't had the pleasure,' said Janet, who'd never ventured further south than Selkirk. 'Where are you staying?'

'Castle View.'

'That right?' She ducked below the bar in a show of fetching more glasses. Her sister-in-law was neighbours with Chatty MacIntyre's cleaner. She'd get chapter and verse in due course. 'Fishing trip?'

'Three days.'

'Enjoying yourself?'

'As I was telling your husband,' Chipper groused, 'got off to a bad start.'

Janet raised her head. 'How come?'

'Missed out on a whopper.'

'Bad luck.'

'Luck had nothing to do with it.' His face darkened. 'I'd kill for a fish that size.'

Seventeen

Heather asked, 'How's your coffee?'

'On the weak side,' answered her companion, Dulcie Elphinstone.

Dulcie lived alone in a small rented flat above an Aboyne charity shop, and the two had been introduced at a performing arts concert at the Deeside Community Theatre. For several weeks afterwards, Heather was tempted to follow up what had been a rather guarded introductory conversation with an invitation to tea. Her nerve failed her. Until one rainy Saturday night when, feeling especially solitary, she'd imbibed a small glass of the Edradour whisky cream liqueur she kept in the sideboard for emergencies. In a rush of blood, she'd reached for the phone.

Now, Heather said, 'Never mind, dear. Think of the view.'

They were perched on high stools in the Golf Road window of Bean for Coffee, which occupies a prime corner site in the dead centre of Ballater. Dead, because in the middle of a large, open grassy square stands Glenmuick Parish Church. Erected in 1873 to replace a smaller building, it forms the focal point of the planned village laid out by brothers Francis and William Farquharson in the late eighteenth century to accommodate visitors to the healing waters of nearby Pannanich Wells.

That Saturday morning, the large square pink sandstone building was playing host to a funeral, offering the two ladies a rolling loop of entertainment, as mourners trickled under the impressive gable of the double-height entrance, to the left of which a square tower culminating in a pointed steeple displayed a gilt-numbered clock.

'Would you look at that hat!' Dulcie exclaimed, through a mouthful of chocolate-and-cherry scone. 'Have you ever seen the like?'

Spooning froth off her cappuccino, 'Bit roary for a funeral,' Heather concurred. 'And that young thing's skirt! Doesn't leave much to the imagination.' Suddenly self-conscious, she tugged her own hem over her knees. She'd been brought up to preserve her modesty and had a horror of letting 'things' show. The window shelf was narrow, the stools precarious. Had the weather been more clement, she'd have opted for a pavement table.

'I've seen worse,' said Dulcie. 'Aboyne has gone to the dogs: the way they let students attend with pelmets for skirts and ties at half-mast.' The year before, she'd moved north from Edinburgh to teach chemistry at Aboyne Academy.

'I'm thankful my lot haven't reached that stage.'

Dulcie sniffed. 'It's symptomatic. Slippage at every turn. Talk about Curriculum for Excellence: helping children and young people gain the knowledge, skills and attributes needed for life in the twenty-first century. What a joke!

Educational standards have gone down the drain: pass rates falling, grade boundaries lowered. In our day—'

'There's not many faces I recognise,' Heather interrupted. Dipping into her handbag for a clean hankie, she set to wiping condensation off the window for a better look.

Dulcie said, 'I thought you'd know everyone in these parts, you being Deeside born and bred.'

Sighing, Heather responded, 'Sign of the times. Ballater's so busy these days. Too many incomers. They—'

Her words were drowned by the skirl of bagpipes, as the coffin was piped into the church.

When the heavy wooden shouldered-arch doors were closed, 'Retirement heaven,' she ran on. 'That's how they see it: beautiful countryside, good shops and restaurants, sports and leisure facilities. You only have to look at the rash of new-build bungalows along Craigendarroch Walk. And it's safe, compared with other places.'

'Not as safe as Ballochbrae, I'll warrant.'

'That's true.'

Dulcie said, 'Retirees bring money to Ballater, I suppose.'

'And their prejudices. Take the row over the barracks: when the Royal Regiment is in residence, the morning pipes have been pushed back from six o'clock to seven. And,' Heather added, her expression outraged, 'Johnny Cope a fifty-year tradition.'

'Read about that in the *Deeside Piper*. "Complaints from local residents", it said.'

'Local, my foot. Second homeowners, more like. Them and holidaymakers. Piper can't even play at weekends.'

'I gather the real locals are none too pleased.'

'Goes to prove my point: between incomers and tourists, Ballater's way too busy. Look at the place.' Heather indicated Church Square, where laden backpackers pored over maps and huddles of visitors peered in shop windows. 'It was bad enough before. But that September after the Queen died …' Her voice shook with suppressed emotion. 'Us locals bare had space to draw breath.'

Dulcie nodded. 'Wasn't that something?'

'Never seen so many visitors in my entire life: locals, tourists, TV crews. Not to mention their means of transportation: cars, coaches, motorbikes, you name it. Parked everywhere you looked and all, with no regard whatever to—'

'I believe the police had to draft in reinforcements from all over.'

'London, Manchester,' Heather rattled off. 'I was even speaking to a nice young officer from Wales, who—'

'Mutual aid,' Dulcie chipped in.

Heather blinked. 'I beg your pardon?'

'That's what police call it when they pool resources. Operation Unicorn they named it in Scotland.'

'Police even commandeered Crathie School as a comms centre. Put the kids on a bus and sent them to Aboyne.'

'Doesn't look like the footfall has let up much since.'

'I couldn't agree more.' Polishing off the last of a pancake, Heather said, 'Easter weekend, the crowds, you wouldn't believe. At Crathie, when the ballroom reopened to visitors, the car park was overflowing and the roads jammed. And now, with the new attractions in the castle and grounds, I can't see that changing.'

Dulcie said, 'Aboyne's not much better.'

'Give me Ballochbrae any day,' Heather asserted with a superior smile. 'There's not a lot happens in our village.'

Eighteen

Loose-limbed, the two boys leaned on the handrail, their eyes fixed on the river. Beneath the iron span, it pooled deep, dark, impenetrable. Downstream, the water flowed peat gold, glinting where boulders broke the surface.

It was the weekend. School was out and the boys were back for a second attempt. Accessing the Victorian bridge had been easier than it looked. Lachie took the lead, the latticework supports either side of the gate providing useful footholds, the rusted paintwork offering his trainers purchase. Once he'd climbed clear of the spiked top of the gate, he edged sideways around the supporting column. For long moments he clung, before launching himself backwards and dropping with a triumphant whoop to a crouch on the walkway.

Ruaridh was more cautious, closely following his friend's progress before attempting the climb. More than once, he slipped back, white-knuckled, free arm flailing for a hand-hold. Reaching the top, he hung, midriff bared, legs scrabbling.

'Jump,' urged Lachie.

'In a minute,' Ruaridh panted.

He looked down at the studded surface of the metal walkway. Tightened his grip.

Lachie called, 'Come on.'

Inside his boxers, Ruaridh felt his bowels loosen. Prayed he wouldn't shit himself. 'Great view from up here,' he joshed, buying time.

'If you're going to sit up there all day,' grumbled Lachie. 'I'm off.'

'No,' Ruaridh said. 'Wait.' Cautiously, he released one hand, then the other, and dropped with a clatter.

Lachie reached into the pocket of his jogging pants. 'Here.' He held out a fistful of small stones.

Ruaridh grinned. 'Ta.'

One by one, they dropped the pebbles into the river, watching ripples widen as fish broke the surface.

When their supply had run out, Ruaridh asked, 'What are we going to do now?'

'Dunno.'

The afternoon stretched ahead. A weak sun warmed the backs of their necks, as they scanned the horizon. Trees – Scots pine, larch, rowan and silver birch – lined the banks. Sitka spruce clad the hillsides. Gorse bushes flared yellow amidst the heather. The air was still, save for the occasional low rumble of a vehicle on the road behind or the squawk of a bird disturbed from the bracken.

'We could go over the gate at the far end, see what's doing.'

'Nah,' said Ruaridh. 'Take up too much time.'

Lachie said, 'Right enough. We'd have to do the climb twice to get back to our bikes. And we better not be late. I've to be home by five o'clock.'

Ruaridh nodded agreement. He'd been in trouble twice that week already.

'C'mon then.' Turning away from the handrail, 'Last one over's a poofter.' Lachie made a dash for the gate.

Ruaridh grabbed hold of his sleeve, and they grappled with one another until Lachie prevailed and Ruaridh dropped, winded, to a crouch on the walkway.

Clutching the metal fretwork tightly with both hands, he stuck his head through a gap in the railing, gulping greedy mouthfuls of sharp, clean air.

Behind him, 'Dah, dah, dah, dah-da,' Lachie chanted, as he started to climb.

Mesmerised by the winding river, Ruaridh ignored him. He struggled to remember what his teacher had told him about it in class: the river Dee's source on Braeriach is the highest of any major river in Britain, 140 km long from the Cairngorms to the North Sea. He was trying to recall what else Miss Garden said, when his eye was caught by something snagged on the rocks. Bulky and white, it looked – to him – like a builder's rubble sack.

As he squinted in the sunlight, it swung around with the movement of the water.

Ruaridh froze.

Sticking out was a human head.

Nineteen

In Castle View's kitchen, Chatty sat at a long scrubbed-pine table, stockinged feet resting on the slatted base. On the scarred and pitted surface, lay an open notebook with entries crossed out.

What a bore! Chatty wasn't used to doing for herself. Throughout her marriage, domestic chores had always fallen to some servant or naval rating, and she hadn't cooked a meal in years. Why would she? Either Roderick ate in the wardroom or, when he was onshore, they ate out. She salivated at the very thought: steak, seafood, fine wines. She'd taken them all for granted, without a nod to the preparation involved, far less the cost. And look at her now: reduced to little more than a housekeeper. Plus, she hadn't the foggiest how to work the ancient cream Aga, which looked as old as the house. Instead, she'd had to fall back on a slow cooker, microwave and fryer, limiting her Aga use to the hotplate and warming cupboard.

Now, struggling to come up with the following week's dinner menus, she wished she'd followed her mother's advice and studied domestic science, instead of leaving Mary Erskine in a teenage huff and jumping at the first job she'd been offered.

Chewing the top of her pen, Chatty tried to recall Roderick's preferences. None came to mind. Indeed, she didn't remember a great deal about Roderick. Except for The Incident. Banishing the thought, Chatty turned her attention back to the task at hand.

When she first started up in business, she'd availed herself of the delivery service from Sheridan, the Ballater butcher, and the neighbouring deli. Royal warrant holders both, they supplied venison, lamb and game in season, cranachan and oatcakes and Strathdon cheese. The fish van from Gourdon came on Tuesdays and an upmarket fish shop had opened on Netherley Place. But quality came at a price, and Chatty soon had to rein in her spending.

Aberdeen's Mastrick Cash & Carry had been a lifesaver. Aside from buying dry goods in bulk, Chatty plundered the frozen foods, Chef's Larder Premium range in particular. Back in Ballochbrae, she added her own tweaks: with croutons (made from the morning toast bread ends), diced vegetables, a dash of dry sherry, a swirl of cream, a soup could pass as homemade. Button mushrooms to bulk up a beef casserole. A handful of prawns added to a fish pie.

When she'd exhausted Booker's range, she reverted to the Aboyne Co-op. (Wouldn't do to be seen buying ready meals in Ballater). Tesco and Morrison in Banchory were another fallback. She'd even, in emergency, resorted to ordering a curry from the improbably named Lochnagar Indian Brasserie in Ballater's Church Square and eking it out with a cauliflower. So long as the meal was well presented and garnished – a wedge of lemon, a few sprigs of coriander, a handful of rocket – who was to know? She'd had a few questioning looks, to be sure, but so what?

'Bedside lightbulb's out in Glen Muick,' grumbled Etta, shouldering her way through the door.

'I'll replace it later.' Chatty rued the day she'd got a local craftsman to make bedroom door names: they served as a daily reminder how far she was from civilisation. 'When you're finished upstairs, you can top up the toiletries.' She indicated a couple of large containers by the sink. Another tip she'd picked up: decanting cheap shampoo and shower gel into smart Crabtree & Evelyn bottles.

'Okay.'

Looking askance at Etta's wraparound apron above feet shod in wide-fit, vinyl shoes, Chatty said, 'Don't suppose you've any supper ideas?'

'Venison casserole?'

'Forget it. I'm sick of looking at the stuff.'

'Fish pie?'

'Too much of a fiddle.'

'Coronation chicken?'

'We've done that to death.'

'There's been a coronation not that long ago.'

'Granted, but not everyone likes curry powder.'

'Balmoral chicken, then.'

'Chicken breasts are too expensive.'

'Use thighs.'

'Chicken thighs stuffed with haggis?' Chatty scoffed. 'Not exactly fine dining.'

'Bung them in a sauce and whack a pastry lid on top.'
'Really?'

Etta nodded. 'Twice the taste for half the price.'

Wondering if she could rope the woman into extra kitchen duties, Chatty scribbled a note. 'Anything else?'

Etta dipped a hand into the front pocket of her apron. Nose wrinkled, she extracted an object, held it at arm's length. 'Found this down the back of Glen Tanar's bed.'

Chatty couldn't meet her eyes.

'Reckon one of them Met boys has a bidey-in?'

Cheeks burning, Chatty said, 'How should I know?'

The corners of Etta's mouth twitched. 'What do you want me to do?'

'Don't just stand there?' Chatty shrilled. 'Get rid of it.'

Twenty

Hunched low over the handlebars, Lachlan propelled his bike at breakneck speed towards the village.

Cheeks puffed with exertion, Ruaridh struggled to keep up. He'd failed to persuade Lachie to come back down onto the bridge and have a look. It was all he could do to tear himself away from the grisly sight and make it back to his bike in one piece. 'I'm telling you,' he panted, now, fringe plastered to his forehead, sweat dripping from the end of his nose. 'It was a dead body.'

Legs going like pistons, Lachie called over his shoulder, 'A sheep, most like.'

'Was not,' Ruaridh protested. 'We better tell someone.'

'No way.'

'Why not?'

'Because, daftie, we weren't supposed to be there.'

'Oh,' said Ruaridh, reality dawning. 'Except, won't we get in trouble if it is a dead body and we don't let on?'

'We'll get in a sight more trouble if we're not home for dinner time.'

'But—'

'Who would we tell, anyhow?' Lachie cut in, standing as he cruised downhill. 'Not my stepdad. He'd have my guts for garters.'

Ruaridh eased back on the pedals. 'We could tell your mum.'

'Who would go straight to my stepdad.'

'We could call 999.'

'On my mobile? What if they trace the call?'

'Can they do that if you hang up quick?'

'Their techies can do most anything.'

'We could find a phone box.'

'Like where?'

The only public phone booth for miles was a red one on the B976 near Abergeldie Castle, and that had been bought by the then HRH Duke of Rothesay and converted into a book exchange.

'How about we tell the teacher, then?'

'Lady Garden?' Lachie's head swivelled. 'Don't be a dork.'

With a startled look, Ruaridh warned, 'You'll get in trouble if you call her that.'

'Everybody does. All the big boys at any rate.' He turned to look ahead.

Changing tack, Ruaridh said, 'We could kid on we weren't sure what we saw. Leave it up to her.'

'To do what?' Lachie interrupted, head back down on the handlebars. 'Go running to Big Eck?'

'If she did, he could call the police.'

'He *is* the police.'

'Right enough. So, what do you reckon?'

Coasting once more, Lachie pronounced, 'We do nothing.'

The village came in sight.

Handlebars in mid-air, Lachie performed a wheelie, bumped his bike back onto the road. Voice lowered, he said over his shoulder. 'Can you keep a secret, wee man?'

Vigorously, Ruaridh nodded.

'Then, keep your head down and your mouth shut.'

Twenty-one

'If I leave a pan of stew on the stove,' Morag asked in a casual voice. 'Are you okay to heat it up?'

Straddling the rear end of a pregnant ewe in Cairnshiel's steading, Fergus McCracken straightened. 'Going somewhere?'

'There's a film showing in the V&A Halls.'

'What's the matter with the television?'

'Damn else on but old movies.'

'They're a sight better than the garbage you get nowadays: nothing but four-letter words an' naked women.'

Struggling to hold on to the beast, Morag said, 'So will you heat up your dinner or not?'

He cocked his head. 'I might be needing the car.'

'To do what?'

'Deal with an emergency. The Mitsubishi's in for repair.'

Only the previous month the vehicle had sustained bodywork damage following his unfortunate brush with a German motorcyclist.

'Go to the pub, more like. That game's over, Da. From now on, either I drive, or you stay put.'

For just a moment, Fergus looked lost for words. Then, 'Going on your own?'

'Why wouldn't I be?'

'Answer the question.'

She turned her head away.

Fergus said, 'I knew it. It's that Kelman.'

Morag let go of the sheep. Drawing herself up, 'It's the cinema in Ballater we're talking, not a dirty weekend.'

'We both know what he's after.'

Flushing scarlet, she retorted, 'You would know about that.' Her dad's long-standing relationship with one of the Aboyne school dinner ladies was an open secret in the village.

'Wasn't born yesterday,' Fergus persisted. 'Fella's got his eye on ma land.'

Morag said, 'You're talking off the top of your head. Duncan has plenty land of his own.'

'Acreage that marches wi' mine.'

'So?'

He sniffed. 'You wait. He'll have it all worked out.' Waving an arm, 'The house an' all. The minute he gets his foot in the door, he'll have the place let an'—'

Morag cut him short. 'Like anyone would want it.'

The starkness of the long, low farmhouse with its thick, stone walls and deep-set windows was redeemed only by the addition of a rudimentary glazed storm porch, devoid of ornament save for a rusty horseshoe nailed above the door.

'Sell your mother's antiques for a song.'

'"Antiques?"' she parroted. 'There's not a thing worth having, and you know it.'

'That grandfather clock, for a start.'

'Pfft! It's had it.'

'Still keeps good time.'

'True. But how about the rest of it? The face is discoloured. The case is cracked, and it's peppered with woodworm.'

'There's your ma's ornaments in the china cabinet in the parlour,' Fergus persisted.

'Which nobody would give you tuppence for.'

'Says who?'

'I've had enough of your nonsense.' Turning, Morag headed for the byre door. 'Skye? Mull?'

Two black-and-white sheepdogs leapt to her command and trotted at her heels.

'I'm going out tonight,' she threw over her shoulder. 'You can heat up that stew or you can go hungry.'

Twenty-two

MacDuff had just sat down in his recliner and bent to unlace his boots when he remembered the washing machine. It hadn't been emptied for days. If he didn't do something about it, he'd have no socks or underwear to see him through the following week.

Unfolding himself from the chair's yielding depths, he lurched through to the kitchen. That morning's porridge bowl and spoon stared accusingly from the sink. In front of dated white melamine units, a blue plastic washing basket sat on the wood-effect lino floor.

The washing-machine door swung open with a clunk. Muttering under his breath, MacDuff bent to the task. Scooping out armfuls of sodden clothing, it dawned he must have overloaded the machine. He picked up the basket and walked through the connecting door to the old police office, where an extendable clothes rack still bore the remnants of a previous wash.

Cursing, he slung shirts and pants and socks at random over the plastic-coated wire rails. Pausing to disentangle a knot of dripping items, MacDuff judged it would almost be worthwhile sending Moira a wee text. Then again, maybe not.

Job done, he shut the door behind him and crossed the kitchen to the fridge. In line with his latest healthy eating plan, it contained only white meat, fish and green vegetables.

He checked the time on his watch: five minutes. If he got his skates on, he'd just about make it.

MacDuff picked up a pack of chicken thighs. Put it down again. Same with the cod fillet.

A row of ice-cold cans of beer beckoned from the fridge door.

He hesitated, outstretched hand hovering in mid-air. His shift still had twenty minutes to go. No point tempting fate.

Lifting a can of sugar free Irn-Bru from a shelf, he slammed the fridge door shut. Then, reaching up to a cupboard, fished out a tub of Pot Noodle.

He set it down beside the kettle, retrieved his porridge spoon from the sink and laid it alongside.

MacDuff walked back into the living room.

Pulled the ring on his can of Irn-Bru.

He'd flicked the remote and sat back to watch *Scot Squad* when his Airwave radio burst to life.

Muting the TV, 'MacDuff.'

Bushy eyebrows knitted as the handset crackled.

'When was this?'

His face darkened. 'Where?'

More crackling, then, 'Who called it in?'

Killing the TV, MacDuff leapt from his chair.

'I'm on it.' He bolted from the room.

Twenty-three

Flora sat in front of the breakfast room television, as she did most Saturday nights. On a tray by her side, the remains of her supper: shop-bought macaroni cheese.

She'd seen it often enough: old folk elect to eat off a tray rather than sit down to a solitary place setting. Never thought it would happen to her. Not yet. It was the thing she missed most about the marital state: the to and fro across the table. That, and the solid presence of another body in her bed.

She checked the time: 19:53. The Lotto results would be on STV anytime now.

Fingers drumming restlessly on the arm of the chair, Flora muted the TV and let heavy eyelids droop. Since she returned to Ballochbrae, she'd lost many a night's sleep, torn between responsibilities as her mother's sole carer and anxieties for her own and her children's futures. But where previously she'd been a model of professionalism – clear-headed and proactive – a messy divorce had shattered her confidence. Add to that, after the home she shared with Allan had been sold and the proceeds disbursed, she'd imagined she could live in relative comfort. Kate's diagnosis and her own forced early retirement had put paid to that.

Returning to work was the most obvious solution. There was no shortage of nursing jobs. The question was where? Aberdeen would entail a long commute, and a full-time post impact Flora's visits to Darroch View. Even part-time or agency work meant she couldn't respond quickly if the care home needed her to attend. And wild horses wouldn't drag her back to Aboyne Health Centre.

She'd kept a watchful eye on the local job market, in case something came up in Ballater or Braemar. Finding nothing other than low-paid work, she'd even flirted with the idea of online poker. Flora had played a mean hand of cards in her youth. But poker called for patience, a quality she sorely lacked. No harm, though, in a modest flutter. She'd held premium bonds for decades. Won the occasional tenner. Placed an annual bet on the Grand National. Now, she was on tenterhooks, waiting for the winning Lotto numbers to be announced.

Her phone rang.

Flora's eyes snapped open.

19:59. The screen flashed a FaceTime call: Isla.

Flora was tempted to ignore it. Her daughter had rung a few days previously. There couldn't be anything pressing.

She hesitated, finger poised in mid-air.

A niggle of doubt worried at the back of her mind: *What if there's something wrong?*

Muting the TV, she took the call.

Isla: Hi Mum.

Flora: You okay?

Isla: I've broken up with Sam.

Flora: Again? Oh.

Isla: Is that all you've got to say?

Flora: What did you expect me to say?

Isla: Thought you'd show a bit more interest.

Flora: I'm concerned, of course. Look, I'm sure, given time, things will work out. Meantime, look after yourself, pet. Eat properly. Get enough sleep. Your health comes first.

Isla: Talking of health, how's Granny?

Flora: Settling in. Have you heard from Scott?

Isla: Not for a while. Does he know about Granny?

Flora: Sent an email. Haven't had a reply.

Isla: He'll never believe you'd stick her in a place like that.

Flora: We've been through this already. Sadly, your Granny is no longer able to live independently.

Isla: Thought that's why you gave up work.

Flora: It wasn't viable long-term. And she's not stuck. I take her out several times a week. She can sit in the garden. Take part in social activities. With the right support, she can still enjoy a good quality of life.

Isla: How would you know?

Flora: I've been working with Alzheimer's patients for years.

Isla: We're not talking about any old dementia patient, we're talking about my grandmother.

Flora: Look, I'm really sorry about you and Sam, but where your Granny is concerned, we have to accept there are no happy endings.

Isla: Got to go. Bye.

Mothers and daughters! With an exasperated sigh, Flora set down her phone.

It had been on the tip of her tongue to ask if Allan had been in touch. Were his living arrangements okay? Was he eating sensibly? He never was much of a cook.

Then, what business was it of hers?

Heartsick, she tore up her losing Lotto ticket.

Twenty-four

Morag McCracken sat upright on an upholstered banquette. Across a black marble-effect table, Duncan Kelman sprawled on a faux-leather chair. After the credits rolled, they'd taken the short walk from the Victoria and Albert Halls to the Balmoral Bar on the corner of Ballater's Bridge Street and Netherley Place.

'What did you think of the film?' she asked, now.

Shrugging, he replied, 'Seen better.'

When nothing else was forthcoming, Morag made a show of studying her surroundings. The pub had undergone a refurbishment since her last visit, which she realised must have been several years previously. Tied to the farm, she didn't have much opportunity to socialise. Now, she saw the L-shaped pine bar had been repainted in soft grey, the original dark red wallpaper replaced by striking black-and-red plaid to match the new carpet. Above prints of Balmoral Castle and old street views of Ballater, brass wall lights had been replaced by trendy industrial fittings.

Over the rim of her half-pint glass, she cast a surreptitious glance at Duncan, whose eyes were glued to a football match playing on one of half a dozen giant television screens. Shifting in her seat, Morag tried – and failed – to catch his eye.

She whiled away another few minutes studying the bar menu. The usual pub grub was supplemented by dishes chosen to appeal to the tourist trade: Haggis bonbons, North Sea haddock. Her stomach grumbled. After an early start and a long day working outdoors, she'd spent way too long agonising over her choice of outfit and run out of the house with no time to eat.

Morag's eyes widened when they lit upon the gin menu. She was working her way down it when Duncan spoke: 'How are your ewes?'

Her eyes dropped to his. 'Okay.'

He set down his beer. Contemplatively stroking his stubbled chin, he pondered for a few moments. Then, 'I've a trailer o' neeps for the takin'.'

Dunc sure knows how to give a girl a good time!

The corners of her mouth twitched. 'That so?'

'What are you sayin' to it?'

'"Refuse nothing but blows", my granny used to say.'

He nodded. Switched his attention back to the football.

Morag studied the drinkers perched on stools at the bar. Recognised not one. Same went for the young lads thumbing their phones on her left, or the older couple sitting in silence to her right. Time was, she'd have known everyone, and everyone known her.

She looked back at Duncan. When they'd met up earlier, she'd been gratified – given the effort she'd put in – to see he'd changed out of his usual workday denims into a pair of brushed cotton jeans, and the holed shooting sweater been replaced by a check flannel shirt and V-neck pullover. Now, she noticed the front of the pullover was spattered with food stains.

Man needs a wife.

'Penny for them?' His voice brought her back to the here and now.

Morag shook her head. 'Just daydreaming.'

'Fancy sharing a pizza?' he said.

Twenty-five

Upstream from the suspension bridge, Police Constable Alexander MacDuff drew himself up to his full height of five feet, eleven and three-quarters. Legs spread, he tucked his thumbs into his high-vis jacket. 'Righty-ho!' He glowered down at the two small boys. 'Show me exactly where it was.'

'There,' pointed Ruaridh, rapidly withdrawing his hand to cover the other clutching his crotch. Arriving home – a two-bed semi-detached council house at the back of the village – he'd run straight to his mum. Who'd messaged his dad. Who'd called 999. Between the grilling he got from his parents, the ride in the police car, and the evils he was now getting from Lachie, he was fair bursting to pee.

'Stay right where you are,' MacDuff barked. Scrambling down the bank, he anchored his size-twelve regulation boots in the long grass and strained towards the river. In places, the water ran crystal clear, but he knew from long experience how deep and treacherous its many pools.

Slipping, MacDuff reached out a panicked hand and grasped hold of a tussock, wishing he'd first taken the precaution of carrying out a risk assessment. Seeing nothing untoward midstream, he stooped to scan the boulders clustered below the bank, almost losing his balance in the process.

Gingerly, he turned. 'You sure this is the place?'

'S-sure,' stuttered Ruaridh, close to tears by now.

'Dummy.' Lachie aimed a vicious elbow to the ribs. 'Told you it was a sheep.'

'Was not.'

'Lachlan's right, most like,' nodded MacDuff. 'I've seen a fair few things in this stretch of river, but a dead body's not among them.'

'Do you mind thon caravan,' asked Lachie, 'was on the television?'

'Aye.'

In December 2015 Deeside was shell-shocked at the sight of a residential caravan swept from Ballater Caravan Park by the raging flood waters of Storm Frank.

'Could happen again,' said MacDuff portentously. 'Forty caravans were evacuated after the flash floods in November 2022.'

'Even if it was a sheep,' Ruaridh ventured, 'and it was snagged on the rocks, wouldn't it be there, still?'

'Movement of the water could have taken it downstream. I'm going to have a look-see under the bridge. Don't move an inch, you two.'

Higher up the bank, Lachie and Ruaridh nodded in unison.

MacDuff picked his way along the riverside until he neared the bridge. Cautiously, he moved sideways, steadying himself by holding on to tufts of grass. Gaining the bridge's stone supporting wall, he stopped. Between that and deep water was nothing but a narrow ledge, what little footing it afforded slimy with lichen.

Conscious of the two small boys standing unsupervised on the riverbank, MacDuff rued he hadn't taken more time to assess the intel before charging off on a one-man mission. If he screwed up, his superior officers would have his guts for garters.

He was debating his next move, when his eye was caught by a flash of white. Back pressed to the wall, MacDuff inched into the gloom, arms outstretched. Against his spread palms, the granite slabs were ice-cold to the touch, damp and smelling of decay.

Mind buzzing: what were those kids up to? Why hadn't he radioed for assistance? How would he explain his actions to his DI? His eyes scanned the river's surface for anything out of the ordinary.

MacDuff had almost reached the other side when he saw it: an amorphous mass corralled by giant boulders.

Heart pounding under his heavy uniform, he leaned forward as far as he safely could.

Fought to focus in the fading light.

Beneath him bobbed a bloated human body, the face identifiable only by an obscenely engorged tongue.

Twenty-six

'Praise, my soul, the King of heaven,' Heather's sweet soprano rang out. A favourite hymn of her mother and of the late Queen, it had been sung at the 1947 wedding of the then Princess Elizabeth and Prince Philip and at Queen Elizabeth's 2022 state funeral.

It was Sunday morning. In Ballochbrae Kirk, Heather's thoughts turned to the monarch's sudden death. It had come as a coup de foudre to the United Kingdom. To Scotland, a country the Queen held in high esteem. And to Deeside, where she'd found in Balmoral a tranquil retreat replete with memories of milestone family events. First visited with her grandparents, King George V and Queen Mary in the late 1920s and 30s, it was there in 1946 Prince Philip reportedly proposed marriage. Where the newlyweds spent part of their 1947 honeymoon, as did Prince Charles and Princess Diana in 1981. The Queen was at Balmoral when, in 1992, Heather had been among the crowd at Crathie Kirk to see Princess Anne marry former equerry Tim Laurence, and in 1997, when news broke of Diana's tragic death.

'… ransomed, healed, restored, forgiven …' The text of Anglican clergyman Henry Francis Lyte's 1834 free paraphrase of Psalm 103 had been imprinted on Heather's memory since

early childhood, the music as instinctive as drawing breath. She said a fervent prayer that – after seventy long years of unswerving service – her dear Queen was resting in perfect peace.

Which conjured a rather more febrile mental image: a body dragged, lifeless, from the icy waters of the River Dee. At the end of his sermon, the minister had referenced the incident and invited the congregation to join him in a short prayer. An Edinburgh man, Murray Chalmers had come late to the ministry after a career in academia: philosophy, Heather had been led to understand. Given to dramatic gestures and florid turns of phrase, he was too High Church for her taste.

Feeling a sneeze coming on, Heather fumbled for a handkerchief in the pocket of her Harris Tweed coat. Raising it to her nose, she blew softly, one eye on the minister lest she cause offence. Then, from behind cover of the embroidered lawn square, took covert stock of her neighbours. Across the aisle, local laird, Torquil Auchterlonie, and his wife, Venetia, occupied their customary places in the front pew. A few rows behind sat Jessie and Angus MacTavish. He looked to be asleep, she beady-eyed, missing nothing. The village minimart would likely have closed by the time emergency services left the riverside on Saturday evening, but would have opened well before the 11 a.m. Sunday kirk service. If there were any details to be had, Jessie would have them. Whether she would share them was another matter.

Seated on the pews between the Auchterlonies and the MacTavishes, Heather identified several local business owners. Chatty MacIntyre wasn't among them, although if ever there was a service laid on for the great and the good of the county, Heather would stake her life upon Chatty being front and centre.

'... *slow to blame and swift to bless ...*' Her gaze lighted upon Minnie MacSporran, proprietrix of the Bide a Wee tearoom, another one wouldn't give you tuppence. Glancing towards the pulpit, Heather found the minister's eyes upon her. Chastened, she stuffed the hankie back in her pocket and bowed her head, saying a silent prayer for God's forgiveness of her lack of charity.

With a flourish Heather deemed superfluous, Reverend Chalmers brought the service to a close.

Grasping the twin handles of her Sunday handbag, she rose and stepped out of the pew. Patience was a virtue. And Heather had it in spades, born of decades sitting through her own father's sermons. But that morning the service had been especially long-winded. And on the very day she was itching for it to be over.

Joining the slow-moving queue of worshippers shuffling towards the entrance, Heather strove to contain herself.

Then her patience snapped.

With unbecoming haste, she shouldered her way down the aisle until she gained the vestibule.

Giving the minister's outstretched hand a body-swerve, Heather shot through the double doors.

From her vantage point at the top of the steps, she scanned the small clusters of worshippers dotting the forecourt.

Zeroing in on her quarry, she tripped down the steps. 'Can I have a word?'

Turning, Jessie MacTavish said, 'Make it quick. I've a business to run.'

'That's just it,' puffed Heather. 'I wondered if any of your customers had information on that business last night?'

Jessie's eyebrows met the brim of her plum felt hat. 'I'd have thought you'd be the authority, given your loons were front and centre.'

Heather's jaw dropped. 'My loons?'

'Pupils,' Jessie snapped. 'Students. Whatever you call them nowadays.'

This was news to Heather, who had spent her Saturday night watching *Strictly Come Dancing*, before retiring with a cup of hot milk and the latest Mills & Boon romance.

'If there's nothing else,' Jessie continued, 'I've to get back to the shop.'

Heather laid a restraining hand on the sleeve of Jessie's burgundy wool coat. 'Hang on,' she gasped, still fighting to get her breath back. 'Are you saying it was students of mine …' She broke off, inhaled another long draught of cold air. 'Primary school pupils—' her eyes came out on stalks, '—who found the body in the river?'

Jessie's lips thinned. 'That's what I said the first time.'

'That's what I thought,' Heather squeezed out, feeling ready to faint. If the students in question were the two lads she had in mind …

'Now, if you'll excuse me.' Shaking her off, Jessie added, 'Can't stand here gossiping all day.'

And off she marched, leaving Heather marooned in front of the kirk, cheeks flushed in embarrassment.

Twenty-seven

In the bay-windowed sitting room of Albert Villa, Flora sat at a fall-front bureau. Her mother's desk, it was where Kate MacPhee sat most days after breakfast dealing with her correspondence: the thank you notes she was meticulous in sending, the birthdays she carefully listed in her New Year's diary, the letters she still made time to write on cream vellum in a cursive hand. Flora had sat there two years earlier after her father died, filling in the forms, picking over the bones of a loved one's life. Little did she think, then, she'd be back at this very desk a single woman and her mother in care.

She wished she hadn't committed to taking her mother for a run out in the car. If she were to go down the village, she'd get chapter and verse on the body the police had recovered from the river. Chewing the cap of her pen, she weighed her options. She could easily postpone the outing. It was not as if her mum would know the difference. Kate could no longer tell the day of the week or time of day. But still. Already, Flora beat herself up every minute of every day: her marriage, her kids, her job. Or lack of. No point piling on the guilt.

She focused on the open laptop. The entries danced before her eyes: council tax, electricity, car insurance, petrol, groceries. And then one: the direct debit for Darroch View.

Her mind boggled at the figure, hugely inflated by top-up fees: the premium room, the extra nursing hours needed by dementia patients, activities to keep Kate's mind stimulated. Things Flora would have factored in had she not been mired in her own problems.

If Kate were to survive for a number of years, Flora's reduced pension benefits wouldn't be sufficient to prevent Albert Villa being sold. And in an uncertain property market. Who knew what would happen to the economy? Elbows splayed, she let her head drop onto her hands.

It takes two to make a marriage. Her mother's words, that first row she'd had with Allan, rang in Flora's head. *Two to break it.*

They'd been a good team. Rubbed along with scarce a harsh word: money worries, like everyone else; minor disagreements. But until that fateful day, Allan hadn't put a foot wrong. Was committed to the practice. Devoted to her and their children.

If Flora hadn't been so wrapped up in her work …

If she'd stopped to catch a breath instead of charging at life head-on …

If she hadn't let herself go …

Casting a downward glance at her comfy old jeans and sensible flat shoes, she allowed herself a wry smile.

False pride, that was the nub of it.

She'd thrown Allan out the house that very same day.

Refused point blank to enter into dialogue.

Looking back, they might have patched things up, given time.

Reached an accommodation, for the kids' sake at least.

*

Flora was still trying to square the accounts when a FaceTime call flashed on the screen: Scott.

Her spirits soared.

Scott: How's things?

Flora: Fine. You?

Scott: Sorry I haven't been in touch. Been up to here. What's new?

Flora: Other than a man drowned in the Dee?

Scott: Wow! When did that happen?

Flora: Yesterday. Got it from Shuggie who delivers our oil. Emergency services passed his tanker on the road.

Scott: Anyone you know?

Flora: No idea.

Scott: How's Gran?

Flora: As well as can be, given the circumstances.

Scott: How about you? Must be a relief not to be living on your nerves.

Flora: It is, of course. But I miss her, rattling around this house on my own. Have you spoken to Isla?

Scott: Couple of days ago. Told me she's broken up with Sam again. Seems it's not only Sam. This past while, she's been out of sorts: not the old upbeat, can-do Isla.

Flora: Is it down to her job?

Scott: Not from what she's said. I think London's getting to her: the commute, the long working hours, the exorbitant cost of everything …

Flora: That surprises me. I thought she was there to stay.

Scott: I think she's hankering for home. Except … she doesn't have a home, not really. Sorry, Mum. Don't take that the wrong way.

Flora: I won't. And you're right. That's why I'm so desperate to hang on to Albert Villa.

Scott: It's not at risk? I mean, there can't be a mortgage, not after all these years.

Flora: No. But it takes a fair bit of upkeep.

Scott: If you need any help—

Flora: I'm perfectly capable of managing my own affairs.

Scott: Wonder Woman! Coming back to Isla, it's Sam's flat. If they split up, she'll have to find somewhere else to live.

Flora: Let's hope it doesn't come to that.

Scott: Fingers crossed. Sorry, Mum, got to go. I've a conference call lined up.

Flora: No probs. Speak soon.

Ending the call, Flora reappraised the room's Regency-striped wallpaper and pale green Wilton carpet. A handsome carved oak fireplace was framed by a pair of cream brocade sofas. Walnut side tables displayed framed family photographs and cherished ornaments. In one corner stood a pretty Victorian button-back chair upholstered in apple-green velvet. It had belonged to Flora's great-grandmother, long deceased.

A thought occurred: *something to add interest to Kate's room at Darroch View?*

And was summarily dismissed: *don't be ridiculous. No one will ever sit on it.*

Turning her attention back to her laptop, Flora couldn't help but wonder how long Kate had left. Five years? Ten? Fifteen? From experience, she knew the life expectancy of Alzheimer's patients could vary widely.

And when the money ran out, then what?

Twenty-eight

On a discoloured white fascia board, black letters – picked out in italics – spelled 'MacTavish Grocer'. A scarlet Spar sign jutted at a right angle. Below, twin display windows were crammed to bursting. On a bed of sun-bleached crepe paper, tins of lentil soup and sliced peaches in syrup jostled with bottle openers and vacuum flasks and tartan souvenirs.

Heather pushed against the door's brass fingerplate.

Above her head, a bell jangled on its curved iron bracket.

After Jessie had given her the brush-off, she'd lingered in front of the kirk, shamelessly soliciting information. In the process, she'd gleaned random titbits relating to the discovery and retrieval of the dead body, but not – critically – the names of the students involved. And there was no question: if Jessie MacTavish was party to the information, she wouldn't have let up until she'd extracted those very names.

Stepping inside, Heather's eyes darted out of habit to the Post Office in the near corner, where, on weekdays, Jessie occupied her station behind a glass screen.

Predictably, there was no one there.

She scanned the interior.

The minimart – that was what everyone called it these days – was Ballochbrae's one remaining retail outlet. The village butcher and baker and hardware emporium had been driven out of business by the growth of supermarkets and internet shopping. It was laid out like any corner shop: narrow aisles bisected by multi-tiered gondolas, wire dump bins at intervals holding special offers. Green plastic crates defined a small fruit and veg section. A bank of freezers took up half of one wall. On the other – closest to the checkouts – beer, wines and spirits were displayed.

'Hello?' she called in a shaky voice, nerves frayed to breaking point. After charging out of the kirk in an unseemly fashion under the critical eye of who knew how many of Ballochbrae's great and good, she'd no doubt offended the minister by failing to accept the hand of friendship. And in Heather's opinion Murray Chalmers' sensibilities already bordered on the edge of vain-gloriousness.

'Hello?' Heather called, again. When Jessie was otherwise occupied, her husband, Angus, known locally as Gus, was usually on hand.

No reply.

Tiptoeing down the nearest aisle, her ears picked up muffled noises.

Following the sounds, she spied the stockroom door standing ajar.

Heart in mouth, she gave it a push.

Jessie was kneeling on the floor by a stack of cardboard boxes, Stanley knife in one hand.

'There you are!' Heather exclaimed. 'I've been searching all over.'

Jessie looked up. 'What do you want?'

'Cat food. I've run out.' She offered up mute contrition for the untruth.

'I'll be right with you,' said Jessie, waving the knife alarmingly in the direction of the front shop.

'Thanks.' Heather beat a hasty retreat. UnChristian it might be to so determinedly chase gossip, but it wasn't as if she was doing it out of idle curiosity. The sooner she could identify the students who'd come upon the body in the river, the faster she could take steps to stem any potential fallout.

Standing alongside a display of toilet tissue, Heather steeled herself for the battle of wits she suspected was forthcoming. From past experience, she knew – when pressed – Jessie could be thrawn.

She'd have to stand firm.

But stand firm she must.

Heather dared not lose another student.

Her career depended upon it.

Not only her career, her entire life.

Twenty-nine

There are four major towns and villages on Royal Deeside – the valley of the River Dee, which rises in the Cairngorm Mountains and flows down through the surrounding hills, eastwards to the North Sea at Aberdeen. From west to east, these are Braemar, Ballater, Aboyne and Banchory.

The most westerly of Royal Deeside's villages, Braemar, nestles on a sheltered plain six miles from Balmoral Castle. Host to the annual Braemar Gathering, which since 1848 has been attended by the reigning monarch and members of the Royal Family, it attracts visitors from around the world.

A number of pretty wooden houses give the village an almost alpine feel. Standing in stark contrast are a handful of dour Victorian granite hotels: The Invercauld Arms, currently closed for refurbishment; Braemar Lodge, destroyed by fire in 2022; and The Fife Arms. Built in the nineteenth century by the Duke of Fife, the hotel was purchased out of bankruptcy in 2015 and sensitively restored by Swiss international art dealers, Iwan and Manuela Wirth. Furnished with many thousands of antiques, curios and artefacts, it reopened at the end of 2018 as an upmarket boutique hotel.

In the Brae Room, one of the hotel's function suites, Chatty thrust out a hand. 'Catriona MacIntyre.' She'd wangled an invite to the lunchtime event in the hope of making useful connections.

'Esme Dunbar. Dreadful business, that drowning. I take it you've heard the news.'

'Hasn't everyone?'

'News travels fast in these parts.'

'Doesn't it?' Chatty offered up a prayer her past never came to light. 'You wouldn't have the victim's name?'

'Sorry.'

'Speaking of names,' Chatty confided. 'I'm connected with the Farquharsons. On my father's side.'

'Really? Farquharson is your maiden name?'

'Chattan,' came the practised reply. 'The Farquharsons are a sept of the clan. Badenoch MacIntyres were a constituent group of Clan Chattan,' she expanded. 'An alliance of clans headed by the Mackintosh chief which fought on the Jacobite side in the risings of 1715 and 1745.'

'I hadn't realised. Must be nostalgic to be back in Farquharson country.'

'Absolutely,' said Chatty, preening. 'Invercauld.' (Referring to Invercauld Castle, until 2021 the seat of the late 16th Laird, Captain Alwyne Farquharson.) 'Braemar.' (Braemar Castle is on a long lease to the Community of Braemar.) 'And, there's my own home, of course. Been in Roderick's family for generations.'

'You've changed the name, I believe.'

'Needs must. People can't cope with words they can't pronounce.'

'I suppose.' Esme didn't look convinced. 'Did I hear you're taking in boarders?'

'Paying guests,' Chatty corrected. 'Gives me something to occupy myself now I'm on my own.'

'How long is it since …?'

'The Commodore passed? Coming on a year.' She pulled a tragic face. 'Such a wonderful life we had in the Royal Navy: the overseas deployments. The glamour, I can't tell you.'

What Chatty didn't say: she wouldn't have wished Roderick dead, but the marriage hadn't been a success. All the effort she'd put in and look how it ended: stuck in the back of beyond with no money and fewer prospects.

'Sounds fabulous.'

'It was. Seeing the world, and at such a young age. But it's the company I miss most: educated, sophisticated. One can't expect the same standard—'

'Do you have children?' Esme cut in, her face a picture of discomfort.

'One: Sholto. Darling boy. A man, now, of course. But I always think of him as a toddler. Such a beautiful child: a mop of blonde curls, and those eyes—'

'Where is he now?'

'London. He's director of a major gallery.'

'Really?' said Esme. 'Then he must know Princess Eugenie. After gaining her Art History degree from Newcastle, she worked for a London auction house before becoming a director at Hauser & Wirth.'

'Of course,' fibbed Chatty, realising her faux pas. The Wirths were also owners of The Fife, as the hotel is known locally, and of the Fish Shop and restaurant in Ballater. As for Sholto, true, he'd been briefly employed by an auction house. Last she'd heard, he was jobless, yet again.

'Didn't you think of settling in London to be near him?' asked Esme, not altogether kindly. 'City life might have been less of a culture shock.'

Chatty said, 'I did consider it. That, or Edinburgh. It's where I was born. Went to school. Mary Erskine.' She waited for the implications to hit home. Was disappointed. 'The school was founded in 1694 as a hospital for the daughters of Edinburgh burgesses,' she explained. 'Anyhow, it's where my career began.' Lowering her voice, Chatty confided, 'I was PA to the Douglas Millers.'

Esme looked none the wiser.

'Jenners department store.'

'I'm with you. Such a loss to Princes Street.'

'Isn't it? Did you know it was Scotland's oldest independent department store?'

'I didn't.'

'One hundred and twenty-nine years old. Harrods of the North, we Edinburgh folk used to call it.'

'It's being redeveloped as a hotel, I believe.'

'That's right. Anders Povlsen, the Danish billionaire. Plan is to restore the retail space, create a hotel in the disused rooms above. That's where I used to work. Though when I say PA …' Chatty raised her eyes to the ceiling. 'I was the Douglas Miller family's go-to for just about everything.' Registering the scepticism in Esme's eyes, 'With my looks, I could have been a model, but Papa was dead against it. Not that it matters, now. Roderick came on the scene and swept me off my feet.'

Chatty had trotted out this line so often she almost believed it. The truth of the matter: Xanthe MacIntyre had been less than welcoming to her only son's intended. From the moment the two crossed swords, Xanthe made clear she'd rather Roderick had chosen some local girl, ideally from the landed class. To compound matters, Roderick's father hadn't contributed a penny piece to the wedding.

'We were married shortly after: St Giles, naturally. So atmospheric, and absolutely *steeped* in history.' With a theatrical sigh, 'Poor Roderick. My husband died so suddenly …'

'In rather mysterious circumstances. Or so I've been led to—'

Chatty cut her short. 'Tragic accident.'

'I'm sorry.' Laying a hand on her arm, Esme said, 'I didn't mean to upset you.'

'No, really,' said Chatty, deflecting the gesture. 'The family home was lying empty. And there was so much to see to. Between the two of us …' She leaned in close. 'I've been looking for a city bolthole.' In her mind, Chatty conjured a vision of Edinburgh's New Town. Saw herself installed in an elegant Georgian home. 'Nothing grand,' she added, lowering expectations. 'Just big enough for a weekend shopping expedition. It's an age since I had a trip to Harvey Nicks.'

'Never been there.'

'It would need to have a drawing room,' Chatty ran on. 'And a second bedroom, so I can have friends to stay. Goes without saying it must have a good address. So important, don't you think?'

Ann Street was way beyond her budget. Heriot Row she discounted. Ditto Moray Place. In the years since Chatty had left home, traffic volumes had escalated, and with them parking restrictions. But Stockbridge had come up in the world, Danube Street having long shrugged off the notoriety of brothel madam Dora Noyce. St Bernard's Crescent or Saxe Coburg Place might fit the bill. If push came to shove, she'd even settle for a mews.

Quirking an eyebrow, Esme said, 'In Edinburgh, perhaps.'

The inference was lost on Chatty.

Deciding there was no more to be had from the conversation, she scoped the room. Spotting a likely target, 'Lovely to meet you, Esme,' she turned away. 'I've so enjoyed our chat.'

Thirty

Heather was on the cusp of heading home when she took herself in hand: bested she may have been by Jessie MacTavish, but – given the portent of the matter in hand – she was hell-bent on sourcing the information elsewhere.

But where? Pointless calling at the police house. Constable MacDuff was likely still embroiled in the incident. Even if he was off-duty, it was unlikely he'd be forthcoming. The Clachan opened at noon, but Heather deemed it unseemly for a single woman to darken the door of a public house, leastways on the Lord's Day. The Ballochbrae Arms hotel had lain empty since the last tenant called time.

That left the Bide a Wee, Ballochbrae's only surviving café, the village takeaway having morphed from fish and chips to Chinese before ultimately giving up the ghost. Beneath a louring flannel-grey sky, Heather bent, pressed her nose against the ice-cold sash window and peered inside.

Perched on a stool at the rear of what had once been Granny MacSporran's parlour, proprietrix Minnie MacSporran locked gimlet eyes.

Raising a tentative hand in greeting, Heather straightened. Turning, she took a few hesitant steps and pushed through the half-glazed inner door.

The stripped-wood floor was crowded with small tables covered in polyester-lace cloths. She threaded her way to the counter running the length of the back wall. In the interest of economy, Minnie had dispensed with most of the long-serving waiting staff and gone self-service.

'What are you doing here?' she asked, now.

'Well, um …' Heather prevaricated. The tearoom catered almost exclusively for tourists. How to explain she was trying to find out which of her students had been involved in the drowning incident without telling an outright lie? 'Fancied a change of scene.'

'That so?'

'Yes. I …'

Through pursed lips, Minnie added, 'Not like a Christian schoolmistress to be out gallivanting on the Sabbath.'

Colour flooding her face, Heather could do nothing but bow her head in shame.

'Now you're here, what can I get for you? Tea? Coffee?'

'Um …' She'd planned to nip in. Engage Minnie in conversation. Throw in a few casual questions. Be out and home in time to give Darcy his lunch.

'Something more substantial?' Minnie asked hopefully. 'Soup? Sandwiches?'

'Tea would be lovely.'

'Nothing like a pot of tea to keep the weather at bay.'

With an ingratiating smile, Heather said, 'All the better when it's made for you.'

She watched as Minnie dunked a single teabag into a stainless-steel pot and topped it up with boiling water. 'Milk?'

'Please.'

She plonked a prefilled jug on a tray. 'You'll have something to eat. Must have worked up an appetite after this morning's sermon.'

Heather shook her head. 'Plucked one of my bantams for Sunday luncheon only yesterday. Speaking of which …' Confidentially, she inclined her head. 'You'll have heard what happened.'

'Bad business.'

'Got word students of mine may have been involved.' She looked to Minnie for confirmation. Found her expression unreadable as the Sphinx. 'And I was wondering—'

Minnie waved a hand at the counter-top spread. 'You'll have room, still, for a wee something.'

Behind glass, an array of cakes – Victoria sponge, chocolate and raspberry, lemon drizzle, coffee and walnut – sat on china comports. In front, scones rubbed shoulders with empire biscuits and millionaire's shortbread.

Heather chewed on a fingernail. 'Doubt I could manage.'

'Our fruit slices are affa fine.'

'Just tea, thanks.'

Minnie's mouth turned down. 'Sure I can't tempt you?' She indicated a plate of Balmoral shortbread. 'Made to the late Queen's secret recipe. Passed on by her private chef.'

Not according to prize home baker Heather, who'd been told by a reliable source that if ever she were challenged, Minnie had her answer ready: at Balmoral, the chef added not only cornflour, but vanilla paste.

'No thanks.'

'Three pounds ninety-five.'

Heather blanched. Mentally calculating the price of a teabag, she fumbled for her purse and counted out the coins.

'Take a seat.' Minnie retreated behind the till. Hoisting corned-beef legs onto a high stool, 'Sugar's on the table.'

Heather made a beeline for the nearest seat. On the table, a posy vase of plastic white heather and meagre bowl of sugar sachets bookended a well-thumbed laminated menu.

She set down the tray and lowered herself onto a varnished hard chair topped with a tartan seat pad. Desperately, she cast around, searching for something – anything – that would give her a lead-in to the questions jostling in her head.

Over her shoulder, a reproduction Jacobean dresser dominated one wall. Souvenir plates and mugs crammed the shelves, alongside jugs and jam-pots and butter dishes and tea strainers. On the cupboard top, wicker baskets, each lined with a curling paper doily, held bookmarks and keyrings and fridge magnets and tiny tartan hipflasks. Nor did the Bide a Wee retail offering stop at the dresser. Every inch of available wall space had been harnessed to maximising sales opportunities. Custom-made wooden racks held miniature china teapots and thimbles and commemorative teaspoons. Varnished plaques broadcast clan names. A plastic-coated wire display unit offered Bide a Wee recipe books and postcards.

Heather took a deep breath. 'The body in the river,' she began.

From her elevated position, Minnie wagged a cautionary finger. 'Drink up your tea, or it will be as cold as that corpse.'

Thirty-one

MacDuff fumbled in an inside pocket for his debit card.

'On the house,' said Archie, sliding a pint of Caledonia Best across the Clachan counter. 'Gus Moir was in earlier.' Gus was one of the local roadmen. 'Saw police activity down by the suspension bridge last night. Sounds like you could use a drink.'

'You might say.' Reaching for the glass, MacDuff raised it to his lips. 'Cheers!' He took a long draught. 'Did I need that.'

'Photos are all over social media. Been the talk of the Clach.' Indeed, word had swept through the village like the annual muirburn, the traditional heather burning which allows the plants to regenerate and provide food for red grouse, deer, mountain hares and livestock.

MacDuff puffed his chest. 'I was first responder.'

Archie whistled through his teeth. 'That right?'

Sneaking a glance over his shoulder to make sure no one was listening, MacDuff confided, 'Couple kids came on it. Was the parents phoned in.' Cupping a hand over his mouth, 'Challenging situation. But employing' —he cleared his throat— 'skills of detection built over a lifetime of policing, I managed to achieve a positive outcome.'

'Hero of the hour,' said Archie, drily. 'The fatality, anyone we know?'

Lifting a hand to his lips, MacDuff made a zipping motion. 'Couldn't rightly say.' Taking another swig, he added, 'Wasn't a pretty sight. Between you and me ...' He leaned across the bar. 'Crows had taken the eyes. And that was the least of it. Plus, by the time Banchory raised the troops, it was dark.' And hours after his shift ended. But MacDuff had been pushing his luck. And if he wanted to protect his pension ...

'Come on,' pressed Archie. 'You must have some idea.'

Straightening, 'What I can tell you: the deceased was an adult male.'

'Local?'

'Wouldn't like to say one way or the other.'

'Clothing must have told you something.'

'Wasn't much left to go on.'

'An accident?'

'Hard to tell. When the other agencies recovered the body from the water, it wasn't in great shape.'

'Where is it, now?'

'Once the duty doctor pronounced life extinct, he sent the deceased to Aberdeen for a post-mortem.'

'When will you get identification?'

Sighing, MacDuff said, 'How long is a piece of string? City Mortuary was bad enough before they sold Queen Street.'

Police Scotland's North East Divisional headquarters – an ugly 1970s' concrete multi-storey – had been sold to the city council.

Archie said, 'I read in the *Press & Journal* the building's going to be demolished.'

'Aye. Part of the council's so-called urban regeneration.'

'"To cut police operating costs", the paper said. "Work more efficiently and integrate more closely with local services".'

'Meaning do more with fewer bodies. They claim the idea's delivering benefits already. Could have fooled me. Although the public counter and some police staff have moved into Aberdeen City Council's headquarters at Marischal College, there's other folk gone all over the shop. Nobody knows their arse from their elbow.'

'Doesn't affect you, surely.'

MacDuff tapped an open palm on the bar. 'Touch wood. Tough luck on Joe Public, though.'

'Just as well we've still got a local bobby,' said Archie, deadpan.

'Aye.' Draining his glass, MacDuff asked hopefully, 'There wouldn't be another where that came from?'

Thirty-two

Rushing between Castle View's kitchen and dining-room in the run-up to the evening meal, Chatty almost collided with Brett and Marvel.

Affecting interest, she enquired, 'How was your day?'

'Wet,' Marvel complained.

Chatty's eyes dropped to the hall floor. Planted on the Victorian encaustic tiles, Marvel's trainers – she was gratified to note – were no longer pristine.

'Started off sunny,' Brett compensated.

'That's Scotland for you: four seasons in one day. Did you make it to Balmoral?'

'We did,' he replied. 'What a pile!'

'Constructed from granite quarried at Invergelder,' parroted Chatty, straight from one of the tourist brochures which graced a carved oak console table in the vestibule. 'In the Scottish Baronial style. At the southeast is an eighty-foot-tall clock tower topped with—

Marvel cut her off, mid-flow. 'Place was smaller than I thought.'

'Really?' said Chatty, with a show of disbelief. 'The castle is actually much enlarged from the original. Purchased in 1852 from the Farquharson family by Prince Albert, the husband of Queen Victoria, it was found to be too small to accommodate their growing family and the quarters required for visiting friends and official visitors such as cabinet members. The current building was then commissioned and the old castle demolished.'

Marvel said, 'We've larger homes in the USA. LA, Palm Beach, you wanna see the real estate. A close friend of ours has—'

'They don't have the history, hun,' Brett countered.

'Indeed,' crowed Chatty. 'The building was completed in 1856.'

'But as I was saying—'

'Those battlements,' Brett interrupted, 'aren't they something? And that covered entrance.'

'Porte-cochère,' Chatty corrected. 'At the southeast, you'll have observed an eighty-foot-tall clock tower topped with turrets. Other Scottish baronial features are crow-stepped gables and dormer windows and the battlemented porte-cochère.' She took perverse pleasure in repeating the phrase. 'Crenellated battlements are a feature of Scots Baronial architecture, not unlike the turret you may have observed here.' She finished with a satisfied smile.

Marvel said, 'Another disappointment: I was expecting to see your Highland cattle.'

Chatty couldn't help herself. 'They're not kept in a petting zoo.'

'The flowers were pretty,' Marvel grudged. She pronounced the word 'purty', which made Chatty wince. 'One thing I lurrved,' she ran on. 'The pet cemetery. Hang on.' She delved into a pocket, extracted a scrap of paper. 'I wrote down the corgi names: Minnie, Flash, Kris, Holly, Pheonix. They spelled that wrong. Should be like our Phoenix in Arizona.'

'Take your word for it,' Chatty snapped. She'd dashed back from Braemar and was feeling decidedly squiffy.

'Spark, Flora,' Marvel concluded. 'Darling names, don't you agree?'

'"*Darling*",' echoed Chatty, ready to throw up.

'Queen Elizabeth was mad for them.'

'An acquired taste, if I may say so. Pembrokeshire corgis are scatty, noisy, and known for their disobedience. Prince Philip wasn't at all keen on them. Nor, indeed, is King Charles. He much prefers Jack Russells. He and Queen Camilla had two, Beth and Bluebell, rescued from Battersea Dogs & Cats Home. Sadly, Beth has since died.'

Ignoring these nuggets of information, Marvel ran on, 'It says in my guide book Susan was an eighteenth birthday present from her father, King George. Queen Elizabeth even took the dog on honeymoon.'

Bad idea.

'She had over thirty corgis in her lifetime, don't you know.'

At Chatty's back, a venerable longcase clock chimed the hour.

Turning, she exclaimed, 'Golly, is that the time!' She had tons to do, and Marvel was getting on her tits.

She turned back. 'You're in for supper tonight, I see.' She had seven covers, Mark and Chipper among them. (Tourists mostly chose to eat out, but the Royal Protection Officers boarded on a dinner, bed and breakfast basis). Was thankful she was dressed to kill.

'That's right,' said Brett. 'Looking forward to some good Scotch cooking.'

Scots!

Chatty offered up a silent prayer there wouldn't be any cock-ups. 'Then, I mustn't keep you,' she oozed, inwardly spitting blood.

With a pointed look at Marvel's ravaged maquillage, 'You'll want to get upstairs and freshen up.'

*

In the room her in-laws called The Library, Chatty lay full length on a battered leather Chesterfield sofa. Heavy wool curtains in MacIntyre Ancient Hunting tartan were drawn against the draughty windows. On a side table by her elbow, sat a dinner plate heaped with leftovers and a brimming glass of white wine. At her feet, a small television balanced on another table. It was showing the ten o'clock news.

What with her early start and Marvel making her feel like something the cat dragged in, Chatty's day had been tiresome. Truth to tell, since she took possession of Castle View, every day was a struggle. From the minute she rose – breakfast was served between seven and nine – until the dinner guests had retired and the tables cleared and set for the next day, Chatty worked non-stop. After her guests had gone out, there were rooms to be cleaned, beds to be made, provisions to be garnered, menus to be planned, dishes to be prepared. Plus, she had to do it all virtually unaided.

Even if she could have run to employing staff, they were near impossible to come by. Not for the first time, Chatty wished she could poach one of the hard-working East Europeans employed at Craigendarroch, Hilton's hotel and timeshare complex on the outskirts of Ballater. But, by all accounts, even they were having difficulty recruiting. There was Etta, but she only worked part-time. Except on Mondays, when she staffed the kitchen and Chatty – paying pin money to a plain, but personable village housewife to wait table – had a precious evening off.

Raising her eyes to the ceiling, she thanked whoever was up there for the recently installed dishwasher, a Gumtree find. Then, levering herself onto one elbow, reached for a ragged piece of cold chicken and stuffed it in her mouth. She chewed hungrily, chasing the meat down with a fragrant swig of Sauvignon Blanc cleared from a table (opened bottles of wine were marked with a guest's name and set aside for the following evening, but anything under half a bottle was fair game), assiduous networking earlier in the day having precluded eating.

Eyeing the roll of fat that hung over the waistband of her leggings, she thought, *I'm getting so thick around the middle. Thank God I've still got my legs!* Swiftly followed by her umpteenth resolution to eat proper meals and cut back on the booze. Take more exercise, too. Her bingo wings had burgeoned, along with her double chin.

Nibbling on a limp broccoli floret, Chatty flopped back on the sofa and let her eyelids droop. She'd made a career of living by her wits, bolstered by striking good looks and Scots resilience. Still, she wondered how long she could keep it up: this cycle of food preparation and bed changes and having to be civil to people she wouldn't normally give the time of day. Not only her paying guests. Ballochbrae was home to some pretty unappealing characters.

Which led her to the body in the river.

Life's too short.

If she let things run on, she'd suffocate in this God-awful place. Lose her face. Her figure. Her sanity.

In the hallway, a door banged.

Chatty's eyes blinked open.

Anticipating another demand on her time, she struggled to a sitting position.

Stooping to retrieve the shoes she'd kicked off to relieve her swollen feet, she noted the already threadbare Turkey rug was holed in places. Something a Health and Safety Inspector was bound to pick up, along with curtains held together by decades of dust, and a long list of other things she had neither time nor money to address.

Footsteps passed the door and receded.

With a sigh, she slumped back on the sofa.

What wouldn't I give to be shot of this place?

Chatty knew she'd inherited a poisoned chalice.

What she hadn't realised until that moment was just how toxic.

Thirty-three

If you'd asked Morag McCracken what kept her in Ballochbrae she'd have said the soil. She was as rooted to the landscape as any rowan tree. As the seasons slid one into the next with relentless surety, so Morag went about her daily tasks with grim stoicism. Her mother had done so before her, and her mother's mother before that, stretching back through the generations with little deviation. The tools employed might have been refined, but the days were as long and the work as monotonous.

There were moments, when she was out on the hill – the sun warm on the back of her neck, sheep grazing contentedly – she'd close her eyes and imagine another life: one where she lived in happy domesticity with a hard-working husband. She'd be in the kitchen, everything spick and span. The kids – boy and girl – would be doing their homework at the table, and Brodie (she'd always liked the name, and Duncan didn't cut it) would come in for his tea, sneaking up behind her to drop a kiss on the nape of her neck.

Now, Morag stood in front of the Cairnshiel bathroom sink. Overhead, a fluorescent light tube fizzed, its deflector dotted with dead insects. Behind her, the bathwater gurgled and coughed down the drain from a rust-stained steel bath.

She wiped condensation off the age-speckled mirror with a greying towel and studied her reflection.

Where did that come from?

She leaned over the basin for a closer look. Sure enough, a wiry black hair sprouted from her chin. Catching it between two fingertips, she gave a sharp tug. To no effect. Then, shaking her head, pulled a frayed toothbrush from a plastic beaker, squeezed a dot of toothpaste from a tube, and vigorously brushed her teeth.

At her feet, dirty dungarees formed a hillock on the lino. Morag scooped them under one arm, switched off the light and padded through the kitchen and up the stairs. Reaching the landing, her dad's whisky-fuelled snores emanated. from behind a treacle-varnished door. Her mouth twisted in a satisfied smile. Maybe she'd get a night's sleep.

Coming from the fug of the bathroom, her own bedroom felt chillier than ever. Shivering, Morag dropped her soiled clothes into a Lloyd Loom linen basket and reached for the fleece pyjamas lying at the foot of the three-quarter oak bed. About to step into the bottoms, she hesitated. Then, crossing to the double oak wardrobe that stood against the far wall, steadied herself with one calloused hand on the carcass and rose on tiptoe. Reaching over the pediment, fingers spread, she fumbled for her prize.

The glossy high-end carrier with its silken cord handles fell in a flurry of dust bunnies to the floor. Stooping, Morag gave it a shake before carrying it across to the bed and setting it down on the polyester duvet cover.

Dipping inside, she extracted a wrapped package and peeled back the tissue paper.

The lace-crusted silk bra and matching French knickers were the apogee of femininity.

She ran her fingers over the luxuriant fabric.

Picked up the knickers.

Shook out the folds.

Was bending to put them on when a clatter caused her to jerk upright.

'Morag?' a voice roared.

Her shoulders slumped. If he wasn't wanting something from downstairs, her dad would be needing his bedclothes changed.

Morag took one lingering last look at the undies.

Gently, she tucked them back into their wrappings.

Crossing to the wardrobe, she reached up and stowed the carrier safely back in its hiding place.

Then, shrugging on her old pyjamas, 'Coming,' she yelled, and headed for the door.

Thirty-four

Behind the Ballochbrae School toilets, a tight circle of boys clustered shoulder to shoulder, bent heads close together.

'What are you lot up to?' called Heather, rounding the corner.

The boys sprang apart. 'Nothing, miss,' replied their spokesman, guilt written all over his face.

Heather's eyes zeroed in on Lachlan Burnett. He was standing with his back to the wall, chin down, arms crossed protectively across his thin chest. 'You all right?'

His chin came up. Arms dropped to his sides. 'Course.'

'How about you?' This addressed to Ruaridh Shirras, who was cowering in Lachlan's shadow.

Lachlan volunteered, 'He's fine.'

Heather dismissed him with a stern look. 'It's Ruaridh I'm speaking to.'

Goggle-eyed, Ruaridh looked to Heather. Then to Lachlan. Then the other boys, who had rearranged themselves in a loose semicircle. Pointing, 'They said we'd to tell what happened with the police.'

Her heart plummeted to the pit of her stomach. 'And how did you reply?' she continued, in what she hoped was a dispassionate tone, though she was gagging for the answer.

Lachlan jumped in. 'I never said nothing. Can't speak for him. Police put us in different rooms.'

Heather scanned the faces of the onlookers. 'I should hope not,' she said briskly. 'Whatever information you were able to provide must remain strictly confidential. Do you understand?'

Lachlan shrugged. 'Okay.'

'Ruaridh?'

Nodding vigorously, 'Yes, miss.'

Heather said, 'Good lad.' Privately, she determined to extract a full account in the course of the school day. Struck by a sudden pang of conscience: it was unbefitting a Christian schoolmistress take such prurient interest in someone else's tragedy. Then again, hadn't this been brought to her door? And didn't her future hinge on the possible ramifications? Her gaze swept the small group. 'Otherwise, it might hinder the police investigation.'

Investigation! The word conjured in Heather's mind all sorts of frightening scenarios: what if the two lads had not only committed trespass, but been caught doing so? What if they'd given their accuser lip? Lachie, especially, wasn't backward in coming forward.

Her imagination ran riot: what if they'd gone so far as to push someone into the river?

A voice at her elbow. 'Can I go, miss?' Ruaridh jerked his head in the direction of the toilets. 'I'm bursting.'

Heather nodded. 'Off you go, the lot of you. But, remember, there's to be no further discussion in class on this subject.' Brow furrowed, she singled out Lachlan and the ringleader. 'Or it may lead to severe consequences.'

Severe consequences! As she uttered the words, Heather experienced a chilling frisson of fear.

Thirty-five

'Good of you to walk me round,' said Chatty, with a stiff nod of acknowledgement.

'Nae bother,' said the estate worker, who had introduced himself as Rabbie.

Mark Outhwaite had offered to facilitate a guided tour. Chatty jumped at the chance. Since launching the business, she'd been deluged with questions about the local area and its attractions. Chatty had scant interest in either, but – what with the buzz around the coronation and her first full season approaching – saw the need to satisfy not only her paying guests, but VisitScotland. Add to which the castle's official Expedition Tour cost three hundred and sixty pounds for a private two-hour tour of the estate by Land Rover, albeit for up to six persons. Chatty couldn't afford to look a gift-horse in the mouth.

That morning, after clearing breakfast and seeing her guests off for the day, she'd driven the short distance to Crathie in the Mazda MX-5 she'd sourced from Bain's garage. Disregarding Bandy Bain's advice, she'd passed up a low-mileage silver Astra in favour of the snazzy sports model. Soul Red. The colour was the clincher. Accelerating across Brunel's iron bridge, she'd bypassed the visitor car park and proceeded through Balmoral Castle's tall iron gates to the designated meeting place.

Now, Rabbie asked, 'It's a while since you were here last?'

'Years.' Indeed, it had been upwards of three decades since Roderick – in the first flush of his courtship – had proudly escorted her to Balmoral.

'Big changes since then.'

'So I believe. Huge estate,' Chatty remarked, for lack of anything better.

'Covers an area of approximately fifty thousand acres.'

'Must take a lot of managing.'

'Aye. As you'll know, it's a working estate, including grouse moors, forestry and farmland. There's around a hundred and fifty buildings on the estate. Takes in the region of fifty full-time and between fifty and a hundred part-time staff to keep on top of it.'

'It's beautifully maintained, I must say.' Chatty's first impression was of orderliness: crisp tarmac roads, manicured verges, tidy cottages with understated taupe paintwork and picket fences. Pointing to a green plastic box on a post, 'What's that?'

'Security camera. There's another one up there.'

Chatty followed Rabbie's finger. Sure enough, nestling discreetly in a stately Scots pine, was another camera.

Strolling on, he indicated points of interest: Estate Office, Mews Gift Shop, Café, staff accommodation, golf clubhouse (constructed in 1925, the nine-hole course has limited tee times for visitors), greenhouses. Statues of Queen

Victoria and Prince Albert stood close to one another. That of the Queen's close companion, John Brown, was on a less conspicuous site, moved from its original position on the orders of Victoria's son, Edward VII.

Passing the gamekeeper's cottage, barking dogs heralded their proximity. Reaching the bijou building that was the dairy, Chatty pulled up short. 'Enchanting,' she breathed.

Rabbie said, 'It's no longer in use, but you'll be able to see inside the larder.'

Sure enough, the door to the circular building – decorated with antlers – stood ajar.

Chatty stuck her head inside. 'Yuk!' She recoiled at the reek of hung deer.

'That's Craigowan Lodge,' Robbie was saying, now.

Set back from the estate road behind a wire fence and grassy slope and backed by dense forest, Chatty eyed a substantial granite property with crow-stepped gables and fronted by twin bay windows.

'The English newspapers call it a cottage,' Rabbie scoffed. 'Seven bedrooms and all mod cons. My missus wouldn't turn her nose up at it, I can tell you.'

'Isn't that where Princess Diana spent her honeymoon?'

'Part of the honeymoon. The King and the young princes were staying there when they got news of Diana's death. The late Queen often stayed there and all before moving into the castle.' Doffing his cap, he bowed his head. 'God rest her soul.'

Chatty cleared her throat. 'So sudden.'

'Not to them as knew her. When she received outgoing Prime Minister Boris Johnson and his successor Liz Truss, she'd been so poorly her doctor, Douglas Glass, was in the next room. Did you know he held the title Apothecary to Her Majesty's Household at Balmoral, and had served her for thirty-four years?'

'Very interesting,' Chatty lied.

'There had been talk of doing the handover remotely,' he continued, 'but the Queen insisted. Doing her duty to the last.' He leaned in close. 'Once Philip went, we reckoned she wouldn't be long after. Whatever it says on the death certificate, I'll tell you straight: she died of a broken heart.'

'You think?' But if she thought she was going to be party to some salacious gossip, Chatty was disappointed.

'They'd not long finished upgrading Craigowan, more's the pity,' Rabbie ran on. 'Installed extra security: gate, intercom, CCTV, you name it. Place is like a fortress.' Waving a hand, 'Try going near that hedge and see what happens. They even put in a state-of-the-art lift. Twenty thousand pounds it cost, according to *The Sun*. But you can't believe everything you read, can you?'

'No, indeed,' said Chatty, with an inward shudder. If her past should come back to haunt her she'd be done for.

'Still, better she passed away up here on Deeside among her own folk. Queen Elizabeth II was half Scottish, you know. Her maternal lineage can be traced back to the Thane of Glamis, and on the paternal side from the Stuart King James VI, so it's fitting she spent her last days at Balmoral.

You'll know you won't see around the castle,' Rabbie ploughed on. 'Except for the ballroom.'

Tartan and taxidermy. Chatty had hazy memories of a cavernous space, dark beams criss-crossing a vaulted ceiling, walls hung with stags' heads. Of Highland landscapes in ornate gilded frames. Silver statues also featured, alongside Minton china. More vivid were the furtive kisses in dark corners. As she recalled, they'd had to stop themselves rushing outside to find cover for Roderick, as he quaintly put it, 'to have his way with her'.

'Probably most famously known as the setting for the annual Ghillies' Ball. Highlight of the year. Eileen Pike and Frank Thompson used to play piano and accordion. Gives folk like me the chance to socialize and even dance with the Queen and her family. Did, anyhow, before …' His voice cracked.

It was, Chatty knew, where the late Queen's coffin had been placed, so household staff could pay their respects.

'Not that it was anything like as rowdy as what they showed on thon TV series.' The corners of his mouth turned down. 'Alcohol wasn't served until halfway through, for a start. Not like at Birkhall. It's much more relaxed. Plus, what they haven't taken into account, the squaddies would have rehearsed the dances – Dashing White Sergeant, Strip the Willow, Eightsome Reel and the rest of the programme – until they couldn't put a foot wrong.'

Chatty scoped the flower border in front of the castle. Phlox, at a guess. Wondered if it was worth copying at Castle View.

'There's talk of King Charles giving the public more access, but there will be alterations needing made. There's been a planning application submitted, and the building crew has taken on extra labour: joiners, plumbers, masons, electricians ... Plus, there's big changes already underway: lots of tree planting, new fencing and signage. The King wants more flower beds an' all. But where Queen Elizabeth liked them neat and tidy, he prefers a more natural look. There's to be a yew maze in the form of a thistle,' he chuntered on. "A childhood indulgence", the King said.'

Chatty smothered a yawn.

'You'll have read about the cattle fold.'

'Say again?'

'The Highland cattle and pony stud are to be moved down to London: Hampton Court Palace. It's a sad day.' Puffing his chest, 'Our star bull, Gusgurlach of Balmoral, won top prize at the 2022 Royal Highland Show for the second year running, and there have been Highland ponies at Balmoral since 1852. The late Queen—'

She cut him short. 'You'll have heard about the suspension bridge incident.'

'Aye.' He nodded sagely. 'Bad business.'

'You wouldn't have the victim's name?'

'Not a clue.'

Chatty couldn't hide her disappointment. 'Thanks so much for the tour,' she said, oozing insincerity. If there was no gossip forthcoming, no point keeping up the pretence.

Plus, she hadn't expected to walk so far, and her feet were killing her. 'This has been invaluable, but I really must fly.'

As she limped back to her car, Chatty said a fervent prayer she'd move back to the city.

And soon.

Thirty-six

Flora nosed the car out of Darroch View's entrance onto the main road.

'Are we going home?' Kate MacPhee asked in a hopeful voice.

Flora felt a sharp stab of guilt. 'We're going to Bridge of Feugh,' she replied.

'Where?'

'Bridge of Feugh,' Flora repeated. 'I asked you the other day if you'd like a run out.'

'You sure?'

'Quite sure.'

Kate's face clouded. 'Where did you say we're going?'

'Bridge of Feugh,'

'Why are we going there?'

'Just for a run.'

'A run?' Kate echoed.

'That's right.'

'What's at …?' She knitted her brow. 'Tell me the name of the place again.'

'Bridge of Feugh,' Flora said for the fourth time. Not that she wasn't used to it, but she was trying to concentrate on the road. 'There's the Falls of Feugh. The bridge has a separate walkway so you can safely watch the cascades, and see the salmon leap as they travel upriver to spawn.' Getting no response, she continued, 'Do you remember Dad always liked to watch the fish from the viewpoint on the footbridge?' As she spoke, Flora cursed herself for asking a direct question.

Brightening, Kate answered, 'That I do.'

Flora's grip on the wheel relaxed some.

'Jock never tired of seeing how the salmon fought their way to their spawning grounds upstream.'

'Not surprising. You wonder how a fish could get up those rocks, never mind against those waterfalls crashing down.'

With a sigh, Kate said, 'I miss your dad something terrible.'

'So do I.'

For a few minutes they sat in silent contemplation. Then, 'Where did you say we were going?'

'Bridge of Feugh. It's not the best time to watch the salmon. That's the autumn months. But we can stand on the footbridge for a wee while, if you feel up to it, enjoy the views. Then we can have a cuppa in the tearoom.'

'What tearoom?'

'The one right by the bridge. We used to go there a lot.'

Kate shook her head. 'Don't remember.'

'There was a wishing well in the middle, and home baking to die for.'

'Is that right?'

'It has gone upmarket since then. And been extended. The Falls of Feugh Restaurant & Function Room it calls itself, now. Caters for weddings. There's a proper chef, not the wifies who did the baking and served tables when it opened first. But you can still get a good pot of tea and a fine piece: lemon drizzle cake, isn't that your favourite?'

'Is it?' Kate puzzled.

'You know it is.'

'Take your word for it.' She clutched at Flora's sleeve. 'Are we going home?'

'We're going to Bridge of Feugh,' Flora repeated in a level voice, although she could have screamed.

Kate said, 'Me and Jock were married in the kirk.'

'Yes,' said Flora, 'I know.'

'The whole village came out.'

'So you said.'

'Did I ever tell you the funny story about our honeymoon?'

'I think you might have,' Flora replied, tongue in cheek. She'd heard the story countless times before. 'But I'd love to hear it again.'

Thirty-seven

'Fit like?' Janet broke off from polishing glasses when MacDuff came through the pub door.

'Bit under the weather, to tell the truth. Caught a chill during the recovery exercise. Haven't been able to shake it off, and now it's gone to my chest.'

'Sorry to hear that,' Janet responded, without letting up. 'Pint of Caledonian?'

'I'll stick with Diet Coke.' Tapping a forefinger to his temple, 'Lot going on. Need to keep the old brain cells sharp.' He looked around the empty pub. 'Archie at his tea?'

'Gone into Aberdeen.'

'Right,' said MacDuff, voice betraying his disappointment. He was putting off his return to the empty police house and had been counting on an hour or two's dalliance.

When the tumbler of Coke was in front of him, Janet enquired, 'Any more on the suspension bridge body?'

MacDuff groaned. 'Don't ask. When we'll get answers from the mortuary, who knows. Since reorganisation, Aberdeen's gone to the dogs. As for Banchory, no point having a public counter if the door's locked. Plus, the custody cells are non-operational, both there and Ballater. Time was, if a bam needed locked up for a lower-level offence, he could be dealt with locally. Now, I've to drive him to Kittybrewster. Takes up most of my shift.'

Janet said, 'Must be frustrating.'

'It's soul-destroying. Folk think a village bobby's a cushy number: free hand to organise your workload, nobody looking over your shoulder. What they don't understand'—he gazed morosely into his glass— 'you're a one-man band. When you come on shift, you've no idea what you're going to be hit with. Nobody phones the police when they're having a good day, do they?'

'I suppose not.'

'When they call you out, folk look to you to fix their problems,' MacDuff ran on. 'And you have to carry authority.' Squaring his shoulders, 'It's a heavy weight of responsibility.'

'I hear they've appointed a replacement for Ballater.'

His ears pricked. 'Where did you get that?'

'Couldn't rightly say.'

He threw her a suspicious look. Behind that bland exterior, Janet Kinnear was a shrewd woman. 'Not before time. Must be two years, at least, since Donald Macleod retired.'

'Woman, by all accounts.'

MacDuff choked on his drink. Setting down his glass, 'Bubbles caught the back of my throat.'

Janet eyed him serenely. 'Does that sometimes.'

He pulled a crumpled tissue from his pocket and blew his nose.

Woman. Mind racing, MacDuff speculated where the cop was being transferred from. She'd be keen as mustard, he didn't doubt. Anxious to prove herself. And where did that leave him? He was already living on borrowed time.

For years MacDuff had been expecting the call. They'd been closing rural police offices up and down the country: around a hundred and forty since 2013, when eight regional forces had merged to form Police Scotland. But the call hadn't come. Why, he couldn't fathom, unless he'd fallen below someone's radar.

The latest reorganisation in Aberdeen had really put the frighteners on him. If he were to put a foot wrong—

'Get you another?' Janet's voice broke his train of thought.

'I won't, if it's all the same. Things to do. I'll be on my way.'

He was halfway out the door when Janet called, 'What are you saying to the new constable?'

MacDuff turned. 'Good luck to her,' he lied.

Thirty-eight

'Mwah,' said Chatty, waylaying Flora in the hall.

She'd let herself in. Castle View's house rule was to leave the front door unlocked until 10 p.m.

Instinctively, Flora backed off. Not that she was fooled for one minute by Chatty's affectations. Rather, a lifetime of nursing had taught her to maintain an empathetic distance.

'We're in the Library this time.' Steering her by the elbow, Chatty ushered Flora into a side room. 'Business is picking up. My guests will need exclusive use of the Drawing Room.'

Bagging one of the battered leather club chairs, Flora eyed the magnificent flame mahogany breakfront bookcase. 'What have you done with the books?'

With a careless shrug, Chatty replied, 'On the bonfire, most of them.'

'Isn't that a bit rash?'

'Nothing else for it.'

'How so?'

'They were rubbish: Scott's Waverley Novels, that sort of thing. Nobody reads stuff like that these days.'

'Couldn't you have sold them?'

'Pfft!' scoffed Chatty. 'You can't even give them away. Same with gazetteers, books that are yonks out of date. Charity shops don't want to know.'

'Really?' said Flora, unconvinced. 'I thought they were happy to take everything, so long as it's in good condition.'

'I've hung on to anything decent: bindings that will sit well with the new decor, embossed leather, bit of gilding. Anything ...' She struggled for the right word. 'Tonal.'

'"Tonal"?' echoed Flora, uncomprehending.

'Works with the new paint colours.' Another tip Chatty had got off Mumsnet: you can get cheap emulsion mixed to match the upmarket Farrow & Ball paint chart. 'Of course,' she rattled on, 'when it comes to interiors, one can't compete with The Fife. Or even Banchory Lodge. But, then ...' With a self-satisfied look. 'They haven't got my location.'

'Hello?' Heather's voice rang out from the hallway.

Chatty called, 'In here.'

Heather stuck her head around the door. 'This is a change.'

'Yes,' snapped Chatty, who had a low boredom threshold and couldn't be doing with repeating herself. 'Take a seat.'

Gingerly, Heather dropped onto the clapped-out sofa and set a twin-handled calf handbag on the floor.

Indicating a metal ice bucket on a side table, Chatty said grandly, 'I've a bottle of Prosecco chilling.' She'd been given it as a freebie, hoped it was drinkable. 'Might as well open it.'

'How kind,' said Flora, lowering herself onto the sofa alongside Heather. 'It's ages since I had a treat.'

Heather said. 'Not for me, dear.'

With insouciance born of long practice, Chatty eased the cork from the bottle with a gentle pop. 'Sure I can't tempt you?'

Heather shook her head. 'I shouldn't.'

'Come on,' urged Chatty, bottle tilted at a precarious angle. 'One glass won't kill you.'

Coyly, 'Just a soupçon, then.'

Chatty poured fizz into flutes and handed them around. Then, eyes drilling into Heather, 'What are you saying to the body in the river? Rumour has it was two of your pupils found it.'

Taking a tentative sip, she replied. 'I doubt it would be prudent to divulge information that isn't in the public domain.'

'Come off it,' scoffed Chatty. 'It's the topic du jour.'

Flora said, 'Lachlan Burnett and Ruaridh Shirras. Correct me if I'm wrong.'

Heather dropped her eyes. 'I wouldn't like to say.'

'Don't be such a killjoy. We're gagging for the details.'

Heather looked up. 'Much as I'd like to help, I've professional standards to consider. 'What I can tell you …' Setting down her glass, she drew her knees together and folded her hands in her lap. 'Two of my students were interviewed by the police in the presence of appropriate adults.'

Chatty asked, 'Was it Constable MacDuff took the boys' statements?'

'No. A sergeant drove out from Banchory.'

Pink-faced and visibly perspiring, Morag barged through the door. 'Heard your voices.' Her eyes zeroed in on the bottle. 'Pour us a drink, quick.' Then, collapsing onto the nearest seat, 'Feckin' sheep, I swear they'll be the death of me. Marking, dipping, lambing, shearing. Never lets up.'

Chatty passed a brimming glass.

'Lifesaver!' breathed Morag, glugging it back in one. 'Have I missed anything?'

Flora said, 'Heather was about to give us chapter and verse on the body her pupils found in the river.'

'Who was it? Anyone we know?'

'Banchory cops aren't saying, and according to Dodd Benzie, MacDuff was in the Clach right after. Wasn't giving much away.'

'He didn't recognise the man?'

'Not that he's letting on. Can't be a local. Big Eck knows everyone from here to yonder.'

'Face might not have been recognisable,' said Chatty. 'Depends how long the body was in the water. Those stones are sharp, and fish can do a lot of damage.'

'How would you know?' Flora jibed. 'I've never seen you out of high heels.'

'Years married to a Royal Navy Commodore, darling.' Clocking Flora's disbelieving expression, she added, 'Don't take my word for it. You can check on Google: fish have been known to strip a corpse in twelve hours.' Then, brightly, 'Who's for a top-up?'

While Chatty replenished their glasses, Flora said, 'In any event, if the man was local, MacDuff would have been able to recognise him from other identifiers: build, hair, clothing …'

'Shirt and trousers,' Morag volunteered. 'Lad from the Fire Service helped recover the body. His mum was in the minimart yesterday, said as much.'

Chatty asked, 'No jacket? Mobile phone? Credit cards?'

'Not that she mentioned.'

'Fisher,' Flora suggested. 'Walker, maybe.'

Morag said, 'For all we know it could be some random tourist. There's a spot by the bridge with steps down to the riverbank and a wooden bench. Good place for a picnic.' Turning to Heather, 'What did your kids have to say?'

Her lips thinned. 'Even were I privy to such information, it's not something I would broadcast.'

'Suit yourself. Who was the duty doctor, anybody know?'

Flora said, 'MacSorley from Braemar. Leastways, that's what Jessie told me in the Post Office.'

'You must be well in,' Morag grumbled. 'I never got a thing out of her when I was there yesterday.'

'Can't have gone about it the right way. Anyhow, knowing Speedy, he'll have arrived at the scene, dispatched the remains to Aberdeen City Mortuary, and whizzed back to his warm fireside in short order.'

'Why would the body go to Aberdeen?'

'Unexplained death.'

'This is all conjecture,' Heather complained. 'And not what we're here for. Now, acting on Flora's suggestions, I've drawn up a shortlist of book club picks. I've even'—she gave a disparaging sniff—'thrown in a couple of thrillers.'

Morag said, 'Who needs a crime novel when we've the real thing?'

Chatty nodded vigorously. 'Couldn't agree more. And the incident certainly raises questions.'

'But,' Heather protested. 'My shortlist—'

'While we're considering our future direction,' Flora interrupted, looking to lower the temperature, 'why don't we do some digging?'

'A fact-finding mission,' Chatty enthused.

Heather said, 'That's a job for the police.'

'It would give our meetings focus.'

'No offence, dear, but we're patently not qualified to play detective.'

'I don't agree,' Flora argued. 'Between us, we've a range of skill sets: my medical background, your facility with IT, Morag's technical know-how, Chatty's … um …' She struggled for a tactful phrase. 'Networking skills. Plus,' Flora rushed on before Chatty could react, 'many of the earliest detectives were women.'

Morag said, 'Don't think so.'

'Trust me. In 1857, the Matrimonial Causes Act provided a path to divorce. But divorce on the grounds of adultery required evidence, leading to an upsurge in private detectives, many of them women. Not surprising, when you think about it: who better to double as a chambermaid or confidante?'

Chatty said, 'I get you: our perceived weakness is also our strength.'

'Spot on!'

Preening, 'I'm not just a pretty face.'

'Quite!' Flora struggled to maintain a neutral expression. 'We'll be able to pursue an investigation under the guise of idle chit-chat.' Her eyes swept the room. 'Whose turn is it to host our next meeting?'

'Mine,' said Morag. 'But the old fella's playing up. Anyone mind if I pass?'

'No problem. Albert Villa has plenty space and – more important – no distractions. Plus, there's no point waiting a week. If we're going to do this, we need to crack on, be in constant touch: phone, text, email, doesn't matter so long as we keep the communication channels open.'

'A live investigation,' marvelled Chatty. 'What sport.'

Heather said, 'Hardly the word for a soul gone to the hereafter.'

'Where he's gone,' said Flora, sagely, 'is a moot point.'

Thirty-nine

Morag was shovelling muck off the steading floor when her mobile pinged.

She fumbled in her overalls, checked the caller display: message from Duncan. She hadn't seen him since their outing to the cinema, had planned to ghost him. Not that he'd probably notice. Their relationship was more off than on.

DUNCAN: Fancy eating out tomorrow night?

MORAG: If you like.

DUNCAN: Meet up in Ballater?

MORAG: The Balmoral?

DUNCAN: How about The Barrel?

MORAG: Does it do food?

DUNCAN: We could have a drink, pick up a fish supper from the Phoenix.

MORAG: I'd rather sit down.

DUNCAN: We can sit in Church Square.

MORAG: I can sit in Church Square any day of the week.

DUNCAN: Beside the river, then. Or maybe you'd prefer Chinese.

MORAG: Forget it.

She was finger poised to end the message when a thought occurred: Dunc was a regular in the Clach. He'd likely have the lowdown on the dead body. And where better to open the conversation than by the riverside?

MORAG: The river will do.

DUNCAN: Five o'clock?

MORAG: See you then.

As she pocketed her phone, Morag shivered with expectation. Not in anticipation of seeing Duncan. Her hopes of a romantic relationship had withered on the vine. Rather – if she played her cards right – she'd get the book club investigation off to a flying start.

Forty

'The body in the river,' Flora began. 'Anyone manage to find out who it was?'

'Not me,' said Chatty.

Morag shook her head. 'No joy. What I did establish: Stuart Thom was heard complaining in the Clach about travellers down Dinnet way.' Following her rendezvous with Duncan, she'd gone hotfoot to the pub to interrogate Archie. 'Had to take one of them to task.'

'Could be a promising line of enquiry. Anything from you, Heather?'

She shook her head. 'Sorry.'

It was Thursday afternoon, and the ladies had dropped in to share their findings: Morag in dungarees and work boots, Chatty from prepping that evening's supper, Heather – flushed – straight from school. Now, they were in Albert Villa's conservatory. Prior to his retirement as Senior Roads Engineer with Aberdeenshire Council, Flora's father James – known locally as Jock – had built the extension on the western side of the property in the happy expectation of leisure time to enjoy the views and catch the afternoon sun. Sadly, he hadn't lived to reap the benefit.

'What about the police?' asked Chatty, dropping into a capacious cane armchair. Then, kicking off her shoes, 'Am I glad of a seat! I've been on the trot all day. So, tell me, anyone hear anything?'

'I was hoping *you'd* tell *us*,' Heather complained, eyeing askance the plate of shop-bought biscuits set on a matching cane-and-glass coffee table. Able as she deemed Flora MacPhee in many respects, she'd be mortified if she didn't have a square McVitie's biscuit tin in the pantry with home-bakes layered on sheets of waxed paper. 'If there was anything to be heard, I'd have expected you'd be first, with Protection Officers under your roof.'

'My PPOs,' Chatty opined haughtily, 'are retained for their discretion and not given to idle chit-chat.'

Morag fanned herself with the sheet of kitchen roll Flora had offered in lieu of a paper napkin. Bright and welcoming as the conservatory was, she found it, if anything, too warm. Or maybe it was a hot flush. 'What's MacDuff saying?'

'Haven't seen him about,' Flora replied, taking a sip of instant coffee from a Denby pottery mug. 'Probably taken to his bed. Weekend's excitement will have been too much for him.'

'Duff by name and duff by nature.'

Heather said, 'The man does his best.'

'You must be living in a parallel universe,' Morag countered, grabbing a handful of biscuits. 'If he's not blagging a fly cup of tea somewhere, he'll be up a back road, asleep in his car.'

'If the recovery team weren't able to identify the body,' said Flora, 'they'll have followed standard protocols: checked with Missing Persons, issued an appeal on social media.'

'How about Banchory?'

'They'll be waiting on the outcome of the post-mortem. And I wouldn't count on Big Eck to display anything approaching initiative, so it's up to us.'

'Anything come out of Aberdeen?'

'Radio silence. And don't expect the PM report anytime soon. Mortuary has staffing problems. There's already a backlog of post-mortems.'

'How would you know?' demanded Chatty.

'I've an inside contact. The only folk left in the Queen Street building are the Court and Tribunals Service and the Mortuary.'

'Imagine. Bodies piling up, like bin bags during a strike.'

'They won't be piling up,' Morag argued. 'They get put away in sliding drawers in a big fridge.'

'"Big" being the word,' added Flora. 'Did you know they have bariatric fridges these days, with doors up to two metres wide to take corpses up to seventy-two stones?'

'In Queen Street?'

'No. Theirs are standard 750 mm. Larger folk are sent up to the Infirmary.'

'All very informative,' said Heather, sipping tea from a mug. 'But, somewhat superfluous, if I may say.'

'I thought we were on a fact-finding mission,' Flora argued. 'If the deceased is at Queen Street, it testifies to the fact he wasn't oversized.'

'Doesn't give us height or build,' said Morag. 'Or facial description.'

Chatty said, 'Can't the police find the man's identity through DNA?'

'Not unless he has a criminal record.'

'I thought they just needed your toothbrush or something.'

'Which they have to send to a lab for testing,' said Flora irritably. 'Takes time, and costs money.' Then, mindful of her resolve to get her act together, she softened her tone. 'If we're serious about investigating this incident, we need to get ourselves organised.'

'But,' Chatty puzzled, 'where do we start?'

'Same way the cops do: set up an incident room, divvy up tasks, collate feedback.' Drawing herself up, 'This can be our headquarters. I'll head the team.'

'Why you?'

'I'm best qualified. Analytical and decision-making skills aside, in my professional capacity, I've experienced death at close quarters.'

Heather said, 'I'm sure we've all seen a dead body.'

'Regardless,' argued Morag. 'Flora's proposal makes sense. Me and Chatty are too pushed for time. Your life experience is …'

'Compromised,' Flora rushed to add. 'By dint of your relationship with key witnesses.' She threw a nod to Heather, who looked suitably mollified. 'Add to which, from decades of community nursing, I have knowledge of policing which the rest of you lack.'

'You don't say.' Chatty sat forward, interest piqued. 'Give us the gory details.'

'A man is dead,' Heather huffed. 'This is no time to be facetious.'

Flora said, 'Who is the likely victim? Let's start by trying to narrow the field. First off: Chatty, do you have fishers staying?'

'Did have. Only one. But he's gone.'

Flora said, 'See if you can confirm his travel arrangements. And smooch your Protection Officers: find out if they've had any intel from the local cops.'

'Another thing,' said Morag. 'According to Archie, Stuart hasn't been in the pub these past few days. Maybe he's been the victim of an assault.'

Chatty's eyes narrowed. 'Either that or it was him threw the guy in the river.'

'He's owing Archie for a carry-out, more like,' said Flora. 'Jumped ship to Coilacreich.'

'That the place midway between Ballater and Crathie?'

'Yes. Coilacreich Inn. Great wee pub. Don't tell me you've never been there.' Catching Chatty's disdainful expression, 'On second thoughts, it's probably too authentic.'

Morag said, 'Roadman told me Stuart was spotted that way in the middle of last week.'

Chatty sniped, 'Which tells us what, exactly?'

'Nothing, other than he was seen up by the forestry houses. Story goes—'

Flora cut her short. 'Stick to the facts.'

'If you'll let me finish.' Eyes dancing with mischief, Morag said, 'He was scrambling backwards out a window, bare-arsed.'

Lips compressed, Heather said, 'Disgusting. Wife still away?'

'At her mother's in Perth. And Hector Pirie doesn't get on with Stuart. I heard they had a fistfight a while back. So …'

'Way I heard it,' Flora interrupted. 'Stuart was fighting with squaddies from the Royal Regiment after a dance in the village hall.'

'When was that?' asked Chatty eagerly. 'I thought the hall was only used for the occasional concert or sale of work.'

'Ages ago. Don't worry, you haven't missed anything.'

'Do you remember,' said Heather, 'when we had regular Saturday night hops?'

'Don't I just.'

'Villagers young and old used to dance to piano and accordion accompaniment,' she expanded, for Chatty's benefit. 'The men would line up their quarter bottles of whisky on the dyke outside, in the certain knowledge they'd remain untouched.' She shook her head. 'Changed days.'

'Changed, indeed,' said Flora. 'Now, getting back to Stuart Thom, last time I saw Stuart he was due leave. He might have nipped down to Perth to see his kids. Or gone to Aberdeen. There's a fishing tackle supplier he buys from in Bon-Accord Terrace. He could have got plastered and found a bed somewhere.' She scoped the room. 'Any other names in the frame?'

With a dramatic sigh, Chatty replied, 'Don't ask me. I've been so snowed with booking requests I haven't had a minute to call my own.'

'There was a story in the *P&J* couple weeks back,' Heather volunteered. 'Walker reported missing in Glen Gairn. Could he have—?'

'Old news,' Morag broke in. 'Eejit changed his route. Didn't think to tell anyone.'

'Regardless,' said Heather, 'this is nothing but so much hot air. If you'd only agree on a book to read …' Looking superior, she allowed, 'I'd even settle for Tartan Noir.'

Flora said, 'Books are off the table. But you have a point: instead of talking in circles, let's try to establish when and where these individuals were last seen. Using your connections, find out if anyone is missing, has been behaving oddly, had an altercation—'

'Won't be difficult,' Morag interrupted. 'They're all paranoid in the farming community.'

'Heather, I know we can count on you to keep eyes and ears open, whether in school, in the community or the kirk.'

Heather ducked her chin. Her earlier attempts at eliciting information had fallen short.

'Whilst maintaining the utmost probity,' Flora added, looking to massage Heather's ego. 'In your teaching capacity, you bring skills the rest of us perhaps don't match: a facility with IT systems and familiarity with social media. See what you can find: Missing Persons posts on Facebook, that sort of thing. Anything of interest, get back to me.'

'I'll do my best.'

'Morag, follow up on those leads.'

'Will do. But, right now, I've got to run.'

'Me, too,' sighed Chatty, 'or my guests will go without their supper.'

Morag said, 'I'm out of here. My pa will be screaming blue murder.'

Forty-one

Flora calls an old colleague at Aberdeen City Mortuary.

Flora: Can you speak?

Contact X: If you make it quick.

Flora: I'm chasing an update on the mortuary situation.

Contact X: Nothing to report. Situation here is getting worse: of the two pathologists, one has already left. The other is planning to leave. She's only doing on-call at the moment, so there are no actual post-mortems happening.

Flora: None at all?

Contact X: Correct. Wouldn't have happened under James Grieve's watch. Add to that, the contractor is due to start a soft demolish of the Queen Street interior.

Flora: What? Knock the place down around them?

Contact X: Looks like it. And now there are rumblings from Strathclyde about sending PMs south.

Flora: You're kidding.

Contact X: Dead serious. Forgive the pun.

Flora: How could that work?

Contact X: Your guess is as good as mine. They're talking the more complex cases. Power grab, if you ask me.

Flora: Like Strathclyde with Police Scotland?

Contact X: You said it. Politics. Got to go.

Flora: Thanks for your time. Okay if I keep in touch?

Contact X: Of course. But I wouldn't raise your hopes.

Forty-two

Chatty ran down Mark Outhwaite in a corner of Castle View's drawing room. The magnificently proportioned space was crowned with a deep plaster cornice and elaborate ceiling rose, from which hung a dusty multi-armed chandelier. The bay window was shrouded in faded velvet drapes. Above the imposing oak fireplace, in which a reproduction Georgian fire basket held a clutch of unconvincing electric coals, a tall over-mantel was carved with the MacIntyre clan crest: a cow either side of a shield, itself surmounted by a silver helmet, and above that a hand clasping a dagger and the motto PER ARDUA (Through difficulties).

Summed up her situation, Chatty thought with some rancour. Making a mental note to replace the sad-looking coals with more realistic logs soon as, 'Hi there,' she called.

Mark looked up. 'Mrs MacIntyre.'

She flashed a perky smile. 'Enjoy your supper?'

'Up to your usual standard,' he replied, without a trace of irony.

Modestly dipping her chin, 'We do our best.'

'I believe you took me up on the Balmoral tour.'

'I did. Thanks *so* much,' she gushed. 'Fascinating! Enjoyed every minute.'

'No problem.'

'Mind if I join you?'

'Not at all.' He set his coffee cup in its saucer and laid them on a mahogany pedestal side table.

Chatty plumped down next to him on the Knole sofa, a tasselled monster of a thing, upholstered in brocade trimmed with heavy bullion fringing. Tugging her top over her bulging stomach, she crossed her legs above the knee. 'How was your day?'

'Pretty full, actually. Been quiet this past while, but the pace is stepping up.'

Making a show of uncrossing her legs, Chatty shuffled sideways on the feather cushions, so there was scarce an inch between herself and the Met officer. 'The body in the river,' she began. 'You involved in that?'

'Not directly.'

'Bet you know chapter and verse all the same.'

With a shrug, Mark responded, 'It's my job.'

'Are the police any closer to identifying the body?'

He quirked an eyebrow. 'That would be telling.'

Chatty threw him a come-hither look. 'Mark Outhwaite, you're such a tease.'

'Takes one to know one.'

'Ooh.' her lips formed a suggestive pout. 'But, seriously ...'

'It's taking a bit of time,' he admitted.

'The corpse ...' Swiftly, Chatty scoped the room. There were no other guests within earshot. Nonetheless, she dropped her voice. 'Was it disfigured?'

'Not so much that as …' He broke off. 'I don't suppose it's giving anything away to tell you Banchory have encountered difficulties reaching the next of kin.'

'I wondered what was taking them so long.'

'These things …' A shadow crossed his face. 'Take as long as it takes.'

'Still,' Chatty deliberated, 'you'd think in this day and age …' Getting no reaction, 'Who would be hard to trace?'

'You tell me.'

Lips puckered, 'Let me guess: a tourist?'

Mark shook his head.

She puzzled for a few moments. Then, 'I've got it: an itinerant.'

'Not even close.'

For a well-judged interval Chatty kept her counsel, all the while observing him out the corner of her eye. 'It wouldn't be somebody foreign?'

'Not unless you'd call Perth foreign.'

'Perth?' she repeated, mind working overtime.

Cupping a hand to his mouth, Mark whispered in her ear.

Chatty sat bolt upright. 'Really?'

'You didn't get that from me.'

Eyes wide, she said, 'Won't breathe a word.'

'Care to join me in a nightcap?'

'Tomorrow, maybe? Things to do.'

Chatty leapt to her feet.

She couldn't wait to tell the girls.

Forty-three

Flora charged through Darroch View's entrance. Made straight for Reception. 'What happened?' she asked, signing in.

'Mum's had a fall.'

Flora's heart beat even faster. She'd been ready to turn in when she took the call. Tugging a baggy jumper over T-shirt and tartan pyjama bottoms, she'd slipped her feet into sheepskin boots, run out of the house and driven at speed. 'Is it serious?'

The receptionist reached for the phone. 'I'll get someone to come down.'

Flora shifted from one foot to the other while the woman punched in numbers.

She looked up. 'Take a seat.'

'I'll stand, thanks.' Through the murmured conversation that ensued, her fingers drummed impatiently on the desk.

'Ms MacPhee?'

Flora whirled.

'Sheila Moir, Night Nurse Manager. If you'd care to come with me.' She led Flora down a corridor and into an unfamiliar side room, sparsely furnished with two armchairs either side of a coffee table.

Flora clocked the depleted box of tissues. Speculated this was where they broke the news of a loved one's demise. 'A fall, is that right?'

Before she went into care, Kate had suffered a number of falls. Put them down clumsiness. Now, looking back, Flora cursed her lack of attention.

Sheila nodded. 'We think Mum got out of bed and became disorientated. Tried to find the door, possibly. Walked into things.'

'Did she sustain any injuries?'

'She's badly bruised. Suffering from shock.'

'Has she been examined by a doctor?'

'We called one out straightaway, as a precaution in case Mum needed hospitalised. He gave her a very thorough examination, let me assure you.'

Flora made to rise. 'Can I see her?'

'Of course. She was sleeping when I last looked in. Even if she's awake, you won't get much out of her. Doctor gave her a sedative.'

'I don't get much out of her anyhow,' Flora said with a rueful smile. 'But now I'm here, I'll sit with her for a while. Put my mind at rest.'

'I should warn you, even with our best efforts, falls are difficult to prevent.'

'I understand.' From experience, Flora knew only too well how susceptible the elderly were: loss of vision, low blood pressure, long-term conditions such as heart disease were all potential contributory factors. Knew people with dementia to be at greater risk because of mobility and balance problems and muscle weakness, on top of having difficulties with their memory and finding their way around.

Sheila's voice broke her train of thought. 'Going forward, despite all the safety measures in place, it's likely there will be more episodes of one sort or another.'

Flora nodded.

'Can I get someone to bring you a cup of tea?'

'Thanks. Milk no sugar.'

When she had gone, Flora looked around.

A glass of water sat on the bedside chest alongside a bottle of hand cream. On the windowsill, a book Flora had fetched from Ballater Library.

And – over all – the sweet, sickly smell of old age.

Forty-four

For Heather's convenience the Book Club, as the ladies still styled themselves, were assembled in the parlour at Thistle Cottage. The meeting had been convened at short notice. No china cups on this occasion, nor fire in the grate.

'I've something to tell you,' Chatty announced in her best Mary Erskine voice.

Flora said, 'It will have to wait. We'll kick off with feedback from our last meeting.' Turning to Heather, 'What did you get off social media?'

'Not much from Banchory Police Facebook page. They haven't put out a Missing Persons appeal, just the standard request for information.'

'Anything else?'

'The usual mindless chatter on Twitter, or X as they're calling it now. Photos of the recovery scene on Instagram. Nothing we don't already know.'

'Picked up any intel from the mainstream press?'

'I haven't seen anything in the papers, and there's been nothing on TV or radio since that first newsflash.'

'How about those two young lads? Have they—?'

'Can I say something?' Chatty interrupted.

'When it's your turn,' Flora said firmly. 'We need to conduct this in a systematic fashion. As I was saying, Heather, your students, have they divulged any more details?'

'Nothing that will move us forward.'

'Come on,' Morag urged. 'Don't be such a Miss Priss.'

'Before you speak,' said Heather, shoulders rigid with affront. 'I urge you to consider your choice of words.'

'I'm not afraid to call a spade a spade. Unlike some.'

Flora said, 'Moving on—'

Chatty cut in. 'Now, am I allowed to open my mouth?'

'In a moment.' Turning to Morag, 'Have you come up with anything?'

'Not a lot. MacDuff hasn't been in the Clach much since this kicked off. 'I've had more luck on the forestry cottages.'

'Go on, then.'

'It's rumoured Hector Pirie's wife, Jean, has been putting it about.'

'With Stuart Thom?'

'Haven't got that far.'

Flora turned. 'Chatty …'

'Now we're getting to it,' Chatty said, with a look that could have stripped paint.

'Did you check your fisher's whereabouts?'

'Tried. Didn't have much success.'

'How about your Protection Officers? Did you manage to winkle anything out of them?'

'With great difficulty.'

'Well,' said Flora. 'Are you going to sit there, nursing that mug, all night? Or are you going to tell us what you found out?'

'I was trying to. Before you pulled weight on me.'

'It's not about pulling weight. It's about—'

'Eek!' Chatty shrieked as the cat rubbed his flank against her leg.

'Darcy!' Heather shot out of her chair. Scooping him up, 'Naughty boy!' She headed for the door.

'Fearsome-looking thing,' Chatty muttered. 'And ill-tempered with it. I swear it gave me the snake-eye.'

Morag said, 'Child substitute, my best guess.'

Brushing herself down, 'With a name like Darcy? Lover more like.'

'That's cruel.'

'It's not wide of the mark,' Chatty insisted. 'Heather spends a fortune on that cat. Plus, she's constantly petting and pawing at it. I bet she lets it in her bed at night.'

'So what?' said Flora. 'You'd be surprised how many people let their pets sleep on the bed.'

'Not "on",' countered Chatty. '"In".'

Morag pulled a disbelieving face. 'No.'

'What you have to bear in mind,' Flora intervened. 'Heather has devoted her life to caring for other people. That cat is a small price to pay for companionship.'

'If it's companionship we're talking,' Chatty sulked. 'I can think of better ways—'

Morag said, 'Don't even go there.'

'And that shaggy coat: full of fleas, I'll bet. I'd think twice before sitting on that old settee. You never know what you'll pick up.'

'We've all got old furniture,' said Flora, looking to head off another argument.

'Some better than others. It's one thing having to buy your own furniture, quite another exhibiting such execrable taste.'

'Give the woman a break. She'd give you the coat off her back. Plus, she's running that school pretty much single-handed. She probably doesn't have a minute in the day to think about herself, never mind interior design. Which begs the question: how are your renovations coming along?'

Swimmingly,' fibbed Chatty, who'd spent the best part of the day touching up threadbare carpet patches with a pack of Tesco fibre pens.

'You were about to tell us what you found out,' said Heather, coming back into the room.

Hitching her bra straps, Chatty straightened in her seat. When she had everyone's attention, 'I have it on good authority the body recovered from the river is that of Stuart Thom.'

'You sure?' said Flora.

'Hundred percent.'

Heather bowed her head. 'God rest his soul.'

'What took them so long?' Morag asked.

'Stuart's mother-in-law had moved house. Took the cops a while to track her down. Plus, they'd have had to bring his wife up to Aberdeen to identify the body.'

Flora said, 'Good work. Now Stuart has been positively identified as the deceased, we need to establish …'

'... who killed him.' Breathlessly, Chatty finished the sentence.

Morag asked, 'You think he was murdered?'

'Don't you? He's the last person you'd expect to end up drowned, given what he does for a living.'

Flora said, 'It's critical we don't make baseless assumptions. We should proceed with caution. What's more, teamwork is of the essence.' Turning to Heather, 'I'm relying on you to monitor TV, press and social media. Morag'—she turned back—'see if you can put flesh on that rumour about Jean Pirie. Not someone I've ever met. Do you know the woman?'

'We used to go to the same evening class. Lately, we've only spoken in passing.'

'Anyone else come across her?'

'Name rings a bell,' Heather replied. 'But I can't put a face to it.'

Morag said, 'Tall. Slim. Long dark hair.'

Heather shook her head. 'I've had so many kids through my hands. Them, and the parents ...'

'Forget it,' said Flora. 'Any detail these boys of yours can add to what we already know may prove invaluable. You'll be our eyes and ears on that front. Chatty, follow up on your fisher. Draw on your police source. See if we can move the investigation along.'

A lascivious smile playing on scarlet lips, Chatty said, 'I'll do my very best.'

'Of that,' said Flora, with thinly veiled irony, 'I've no doubt.'

Forty-five

'Wasn't expecting you,' Archie said, when MacDuff ambled into the bar. 'Something going on?'

'I wish.'

'No developments yet on Stuart Thom?'

'If Banchory have any, they're not saying. And to get over my disappointment, I'll have a pint of Caledonian, thank you very much.' When Archie had pulled and served the pint, he said, 'Talking of goings on, any idea what Flora MacPhee is up to: her and Heather Garden and thon dame from Dalnacreich?'

MacDuff took a long draught of his beer. 'Castle View, Mrs MacIntyre's calling it, now. Daft cow.'

'Wheesht!' With a surreptitious look around, Archie lowered his voice. 'Better watch your language.'

'Och,' said Eck. With a yank of his head towards the other drinkers, 'They'll agree with me. Thon place has no more view than the hin end of a beast. And when it comes to running a guesthouse, you want to hear the Protection boys' stories.' He rolled his eyes. 'Hallyracket.' He used the local term for chaotic.

'He's right,' said Dodd from his seat by the fire. 'Woman's no' all there.'

Archie said, 'Give her a chance.'

'A chance!' MacDuff exclaimed, eyes cast upwards to the tobacco-coloured ceiling. 'Wide berth, more like. Mouthful o' marbles an' more sides than the church clock.'

'You have to hand it to her, she has guts, taking on a place like that.'

'Guts? She'd eat you alive, that one. Talk about a cougar: *Living Doll* meets *Whatever Happened to Baby Jane*.'

From behind him, came a ripple of laughter.

'Fair fancies herself, right enough,' Dodd chipped in.

'I wouldn't say no, mind you,' said Eck, his fat face splitting into a grin.

'Me neither.' Dodd's hands made an hourglass shape. 'Sex on legs.'

Archie said, 'Heather Garden, now, she's a different story: polar opposite of Catriona MacIntyre.'

'Aye,' said Eck, with a stage wink. 'In every department.'

At his back, this was met by more laughter.

MacDuff took another swallow. 'But to answer your question, their so-called Book Club have been stirring it. Noses are bothering them, that's the long and short of it. Women.' He made a show of looking around the bar. Was met by nods and cackles. 'Wouldn't have thought that lot would agree on anything, mind. A more ill-suited bunch you couldn't conceive.'

Dodd said, 'What brought them together, anyone know?'

'Flora and Morag aren't that far apart in age,' Eck observed. 'They'll have rubbed shoulders at school. But they're neither of them churchgoers, so how they got in tow with Heather Garden is anyone's guess.'

'She likely roped them in. Heather's aye looking for stray souls in need of redemption.'

'She is a bit of a Holy Joe,' Archie conceded. 'That said, she's kindness personified: wouldn't let the wind blow on you. Flora, now, she's a nippy sweetie. Wouldn't have thought she'd give Catriona MacIntyre the time of day.'

'I'm with you on that one,' said Dodd. 'She's good at her job, mind. When my old pa was dying of cancer, Flora couldn't do enough for him. Passed away in his own bed a happy man.'

'And Morag McCracken calls a spade a spade,' Archie ran on. 'I'm told she's in on it and all.' He gave the bar a wipe. Rinsed the cloth and wrung it out.

'Can't see where she'd find the time,' MacDuff observed, 'Fergus being the way he is.'

'Way I see it,' argued Archie. 'They don't have to get on. They only have to like whatever book they're reading.'

MacDuff puzzled, 'A sewing bee I could understand. Or a knitting circle. But books? Doesn't ring true.' He paused for a beat. 'Having said that, anyone can understand how a woman's mind works, they're a better man than me.'

Forty-six

'Sorry,' said Morag, clipping the woman's heels with her trolley.

The woman looked over her shoulder. 'That's okay.'

'Jean!' Affecting surprise, 'Haven't seen you in ages.'

They were in the Co-op supermarket in Ballater's Golf Road, Morag having shadowed Jean Pirie from her cleaning job and halfway around the village before she had the chance to strike up a conversation.

'How's life?'

'Okay. You? I heard your marriage …'

With a dismissive shrug, Morag said, 'Water under the bridge. Hector, is he well?'

'Suppose. What with our jobs and his sport …' Colouring, she allowed, 'We rarely get the chance to talk.'

'And your kids: two, if I remember right. They must be well up by now.'

'Lewis has another year at the Academy. Gemma's left school. She's nearly nineteen.'

'She must be a big help to you.'

Jean grimaced. 'Not a bit of it. Kids, nowadays. Takes me all my time to keep the house straight and the pair of them fed. No matter I do a big shop every week …' She gestured to the contents of her trolley. 'I'm forever needing to top up.'

'You won't have time spare for evening classes, then.'

'You kidding? How about you?'

'No chance. I'm running the farm and playing housekeeper to my old da. He's another one needing fed all day long.' As if the thought had just occurred, 'I could fair use some caffeine. Do you fancy a coffee?'

Jean hesitated. 'I should be getting home.'

'Just a quick one?'

She shook her head. 'By the time I'm done here and get up the road, Hector will be looking for his dinner.'

'Shame,' said Morag. 'It's not every day you bump into an old friend.'

'True.'

'Especially one you have a lot in common with. Must be years since we had a good chinwag.'

Looking discomfited, Jean said, 'I'd love to catch up. Only …' She pulled out her phone. 'Give me your number. We can maybe do it another day.'

Morag rattled off her contact details. Then, looking to prolong the conversation, 'Must say, you don't look a day older.'

'You think,' said Jean, cheeks flushed with pleasure. Loosening her grip on the trolley, she rearranged a mane of dark hair.

'Always thought – with your looks – you'd end up as a model,' said Morag, getting desperate. Then, registering Jean's dubious expression, 'Something artistic, anyhow.'

Jean laughed. 'It was you had all the talent in that painting class. I just went along for the company.'

'Good times,' said Morag.

A loud voice in her ear. 'Excuse me.'

She whirled to see a well-upholstered woman with a laden trolley and two small kids in tow.

'Can I get past?' the woman mouthed.

'Sorry.' Morag squeezed up close to Jean.

Throwing a nervous look around, Jean said, 'Best crack on. We can't stand here all day blocking the aisle.'

Morag's mind raced. 'You sure you don't have time for a coffee?'

'Less, after standing gassing.'

'Twenty minutes,' she pressed, desperate to maintain contact. 'We need only go as far as the corner.'

'Well …'

Jean looked down at her trolley.

Looked back at Morag.

'Beat you to the checkout,' Morag said.

Forty-seven

Flora hosts a Zoom call.

> She opens the call: Who wants to go first?
>
> Morag dials in: I got back to the Estate Office. They confirmed Stuart Thom had a fishing party Tuesday, Wednesday, Thursday that week. He had the Friday and the following Monday off.
>
> Flora: Anything else?
>
> Morag: Put the feelers out. Rumour mill has it right, for once. Stuart Thom has been seen going in or out of the Pirie house two or three times a week for the past month or so, always when the husband was at work. Most recent sighting was last Monday. My informant couldn't be sure of the time. Thought it was early afternoon.
>
> Flora: That's a starting point. This informant, they reliable?
>
> Morag: Absolutely.

Flora: What do we know about the Pirie household?

Morag: I conducted surveillance on Jean Pirie.

Flora: Get you!

Morag: Took me half the day. It's harder than you'd think.

Flora: What was the upshot?

Morag: Married to Hector since her early twenties. Two kids: one late teens, one still at school. Does part-time cleaning jobs.

Flora: Flexible hours, then?

Morag: She can suit herself, by all accounts.

Flora: Be home in the afternoon?

Morag: I suppose.

Flora: Did you get as far as her social life?

Morag: Non-existent, from what I could gather.

Flora: Lover material for Stuart Thom?

Morag: Could be.

Flora: Anyone else?

Chatty enters the room: Can confirm my fisher was booked on a Friday morning flight out of Aberdeen. More significant: one of my PPOs mentioned Stuart Thom was spotted by a Metropolitan Police officer on regular patrol on his mountain bike. According to the officer, Stuart was on the riverbank talking to another man. From the way they stood, they looked to be arguing.

Heather: Did the officer recognise the man?

Chatty: No. But judging by his clothes, he didn't think he was a fisher. In fact, the reason it attracted his attention was a report of those travellers parked up in a layby at Dinnet.

Flora: Why so?

Heather: The only authorised sites are Greenbanks at Banff and the Aikley Brae stopover at Maud. Last I heard, the travellers were up Elgin direction.

Morag: The quad bike that was nicked. Could the two incidents be connected?

Heather: That's unfair on the travelling community. They're already discriminated against. Notices everywhere you look: *Maximum Stop 8 Hours. No Fires. No Overnight Camping.* Code for no travellers, if you ask me.

Morag: It's coincidence, is it, that farm machinery goes missing and oil tanks get emptied when tinkers are in the locality?

Heather: You can't call them that. We're all God's bairns.

Morag: Some more godly than others. Maybe Stuart caught the guy poaching.

Flora: I doubt travellers would be bothered, not unless it was for their own consumption.

Morag: Still, how do we find this man?

Flora: We don't. Few travellers have passports or appear on the electoral roll, so they're difficult to pin down. Unless someone else witnessed the incident, our best chance is by way of Chatty's PPOs.

Morag: Chance would be a fine thing. They're arrogant, those Met boys. Entitled doesn't begin to—

Flora: Still, see what you can winkle out of them, will you Chatty?

Chatty: I'll try.

Flora: Speaking of bairns, anything more from your students, Heather?

Heather: Sorry, no.

Morag: Assuming Heather has nothing to contribute, can I call it a day? I've beasts needing seen to.

Flora: Okay. Before we wind up, to summarise: we potentially have a jealous husband. A thief. Any other suspects?

Heather: Let me stop you there. Since we've been unable to agree on suitable reading material, I've taken the precaution of investing in a police handbook.

Morag: You're kidding. Wasn't it you said we're not qualified to play private detective?

Heather: Not from inclination, let me assure you. Rather, to keep us on the right side of the law. It says a suspect is the person you believe committed a crime. What we're talking about is a person – or persons – of interest, who may also be a suspect, but is usually someone the police believe may have pertinent information.

Morag: If that's the benchmark, half the village will be on our list. I was at Bain's Garage the other day. Stuart Thom's car was in last week with slashed tyres. When I grilled their mechanic, he told me Stuart owes Bandy big time. Then, when

I followed up on that, I learned from various sources Stuart's in debt all over the place.

Heather: Nonetheless, if we're to mount a credible investigation, we ought to use the correct terminology.

Morag: If we were anywhere near putting a case together, I could see the point. As it is—

Flora: An investigation doesn't resolve itself overnight, if at all. It can be a slow, painstaking business. We'll just have to chip away.

Chatty: Boring. Whose idea was this, anyhow?

Flora: If you don't want to participate, I'm sure we can manage without you.

Chatty: Wouldn't miss it for the world, darling. It's the most excitement I've had since I landed in this hole.

Forty-eight

In Heather Garden's classroom, Ewan and Aileen Shirras sat on low chairs, knees grazing their chins.

Seated on a correspondingly small seat opposite, Heather inclined her head. The urgent phone summons had caught her sideways. Providing the weather was clement, she covered the half mile distance from Thistle Cottage to Ballochbrae Primary on foot. Today, she'd just come through the cottage door lugging a heavy bag of classwork. She'd been looking forward to taking the weight off her feet with a pot of tea and a Walker's Ginger Royal, a treat usually reserved for Sundays. On weekdays, she made do with dunking an Abernethy.

A sudden squall of rain rat-tatted on the slate roof and streaked the windows. Baulking at the idea of walking back to school, Heather headed for the garage. The 1967 2-door AD059 saloon had been gifted to her late father, courtesy of a bequest, by the Church of Scotland. Whilst thankful for a set of wheels, Kenneth Garden deemed the Old English White paintwork and red leather interior unsuited to his Presbyterian calling. In consequence, he used the car sparingly, relying upon an ancient black Raleigh bicycle for pastoral visits within a few miles' radius. Hence, upon his death at the age of ninety-three, the vehicle had clocked up modest mileage. Heather had seen no reason to upgrade. Not then. Not since, despite overtures made from time to time by classic car dealers.

Now, Ewan opened the conversation. 'You'll have guessed why we asked for this meeting.'

'I may have some idea,' Heather said, her voice guarded. 'But before we go any further, please be assured many children go through a difficult patch before they—'

'Difficult?' Aileen broke in. 'It's not you been up half the night trying to calm a child having nightmares. Nor you having to strip beds and wash sheets.'

'I can understand your distress.'

'Can you?' Aileen screeched. 'And you a single woman?'

Ewan threw Heather an apologetic look. 'I'm sure my wife doesn't mean to downplay your commitment to the children here. What you may not be aware of: Ruaridh has been troubled with persistent bed-wetting. It has been a struggle, to be honest, with us both working. Only stopped quite recently. We assumed he'd grown out of it. So you can imagine how alarmed we were when it started again.'

'He's had a few wee accidents in class, too,' Heather responded. 'Don't worry. It's very common: two to three times more so in boys than girls. But I understand your concerns, really I do.'

'Then you'll understand our decision to move him to another school.'

No! Heather's heart pounded in her chest. Frantic, she clamped spread fingers to the front of a mauve wool cardigan. Failed to still the churning inside. 'That's rather a drastic step,' she finally managed to squeeze out. 'From experience, I should warn you uprooting a child halfway through their—'

Ewan cut her short. 'A drastic step for a serious problem. It must have been obvious to you – as well as to us – Ruaridh spends most of his free time in the company of Lachlan Burnett.'

'So, I believe,' murmured Heather. She'd seen this coming.

'Don't get me wrong,' Ewan continued. 'Lachie's a nice enough lad. But between you and me …' He leaned in. 'The stepfather and him, they don't get along.'

'I'm sorry to hear that.'

'In consequence of which, the boy's out there, unsupervised, at all hours.'

'Plus,' interrupted Aileen, rejoining the conversation. 'He's older than our Ruaridh by a good eighteen months. Makes a difference.'

'It certainly does,' Heather concurred.

'So,' Ewan continued, 'you see where we're coming from.'

'Absolutely,' Heather squeezed out. 'But …' Desperately, she played for time. 'What you have to take into account: in no time at all, Lachlan will be leaving class and moving up to Aboyne Academy. If you'll just be patient—'

'What my wife is getting at: Lachlan Burnett is a bad influence. If Ruaridh was in a bigger school, he'd be in a class with his own peer group.'

'That's true. But there are advantages to a composite class such as we have here in Ballochbrae: continuity, smaller class size. And research has shown younger students find more opportunities for acceleration.'

'Still and all, if our lad had friends his own age and not been keeping company with an older boy, I bet none of this truanting would have happened.'

'Nor,' Aileen interjected, 'the police come knocking at our door.'

Pink-cheeked and perspiring, Heather blurted, 'You can hardly blame the school for a man falling into the river.'

'No,' Ewan conceded. 'But I blame Lachie Burnett for talking my son into trespassing on that bridge. If Ruaridh hadn't been there, he wouldn't have seen what he did.'

'Something no child should ever see,' Aileen added, stricken-faced.

Forty-nine

Flora calls her contact at Aberdeen City Mortuary.

Flora: Me again. Are you free to speak?

Contact X: Give me a couple of minutes. I'll call you right back.

Flora: I'll hold, if you don't mind.

Contact X: No worries.
(Sound of fingers tapping on keyboard)
Chasing that PM again?

Flora: Sorry to pester you. I know you're up against it, but it's been a while.

Contact X: You're in luck. Interim report landed on my desk not long ago.

Flora: What does it say?

Contact X: I've only had time for a skim read, but the gist is: your man didn't die from freshwater drowning.

Flora: What *did* he die of?

Contact X: That I can't tell you. You'll have to wait for the final report.

Flora: How about time of death?

Contact X: That old chestnut? You know as well as I do many factors come into play when a body is recovered from water, more so as the post-mortem interval increases.

Flora: Can you take an informed guess?

Contact X: What I can tell you: the lungs weren't especially heavy and there wasn't a lot of marine fauna activity present, so the deceased hadn't been in the water long: a day or two at most.

Flora: Any way to narrow that down?

Contact X: Sorry. Final report might tell you. Then again …

Flora: How long will that take?

Contact X: Who knows?

Flora: Thanks, anyhow. I'll be back in touch.

Fifty

'How can someone be pulled – dead – out of a river,' asked Chatty, 'and not have drowned?'

'Because,' answered Morag caustically, 'they were dead before they went in.'

They'd been briefed on the intel from the interim post-mortem report, and for reasons of both space and confidentiality were back in Albert Villa. No alcohol on offer. Clear heads the order of the day.

'Ooft!' Chatty's lips formed a tight circle. 'An accident, do you think? Could he have tripped on something: a branch, a stone?'

'He'd have to go some to end up in the river.'

'Maybe he suffered a heart attack.'

'Unlikely. Stuart Thom can't be much over forty.'

'I could quote you innumerable incidences,' Flora argued, 'in people of that age or younger.'

'Natural causes, is that what you're thinking?'

'Not necessarily. From the information available to us, the death could be attributed to a variety of causes, foul play included.'

'But,' Heather fretted, 'who would do such a thing?'

'Take your pick,' Morag replied, gulping down a mouthful of instant coffee. 'What with philandering and debt, Stuart Thom wasn't exactly flavour of the month.'

Flora said, 'Let's start with the basics: what do we know?'

'IC1 male,' Heather pronounced.

'Jings!' exclaimed Morag. 'Where did you get that from?'

Modestly, Heather dipped her chin. 'I've been reading up.'

'Glad you accept the book club is a dead duck.'

Her head jerked up. 'Mothballed, is how I'd describe it. And a police handbook is better than no book at all.'

'Give us a break.'

'IC1 male,' Flora repeated. 'Identified as Stuart Thom. What else do we know?'

'Employed as a ghillie. Age forty-three,' Morag added. 'Got that from the Estate Office.'

'Body recovered from the river Dee,' said Chatty, 'in the vicinity of the suspension bridge.'

Flora asked, 'Do we know *when*, exactly?'

All eyes fixed on Heather.

Colouring, 'Last Saturday,' she replied.

'Common knowledge,' sighed Flora. 'We need to know what time.'

'Can't say for sure. Must have been sometime after six. The boys were due home before five, and by the time the parents called the police and the emergency services arrived on the scene …'

Flora mused, 'What time is dusk, I wonder?'

'Half past six,' said Morag authoritatively.

Chatty said, 'Which begs the question: what was Stuart doing there?'

'What do you think? He was a fishing ghillie, for heaven's sake.'

'Teatime on a Saturday?' queried Heather. 'Doesn't sound right.'

'Fair comment. He'd more likely have been in the Clach.'

'We don't know how long his body was in the water,' Chatty argued. 'Could have gone in anytime between then and when he was last seen alive.'

Flora said, 'I can narrow that window. According to my source, the body – when recovered – was quite fresh, probably no more than forty-eight hours in the water.'

'So, Thursday or Friday,' Heather came back in. 'Was Stuart working those days?'

'He was due leave, remember,' Morag chipped in. 'I'll get back to the Estate Office and double-check.'

Flora said, 'Next question: *where* did he go in the water?

'He could have fallen from the bridge.'

'Not unless he was trespassing, like Heather's schoolkids.'

Morag said, 'He could have gone in any place from Linn o' Dee and been swept downstream. Where was his car, assuming the slashed tyres got repaired? Did anybody say?'

'Not that I've heard.'

'Nor me,' said Heather.

Chatty said, 'The vehicle has already been recovered.'

'When? Where? By whom?' Three voices spoke in unison.

'Somewhere between Invercauld and the suspension bridge.'

Flora asked, 'I take it you got that from your PPO?'

'Correct.'

'Any details?'

'That's all I'm allowed to say.'

Morag came back in, 'Even if Stuart wasn't murdered, is it possible he could have been the victim of an assault?'

'Possible,' Flora conceded. 'And since it's a death out of doors, and not witnessed – as far as we know, anyhow – Scene of Crime will have attended from Nelson Street in Aberdeen.'

Heather said, 'They'll have collected forensic evidence and sent it to the police lab for testing.'

'You *have* been doing your homework,' said Flora approvingly. 'But although the duty DI would have been made aware, SOC would most likely only have taken photos of the deceased and the locus.'

'How about CID?'

'They don't usually take the enquiry on if the cause of death was obvious straightaway as being natural.'

'We're supposed to take your word for it, are we?' Chatty complained.

'Everything points to the fact Stuart Thom died as the result of a fishing-related accident.'

'He wasn't dressed for fishing. No chest waders. No life vest.'

Morag said, 'No one from around here would be bothered wearing one.'

'Good point. He wasn't even wearing an outdoor jacket, isn't that right?'

'So, I was told.'

Flora said, 'Bodies lose clothes in water. It's a proven fact. Whether Stuart was or wasn't wearing a jacket to start with, or it got washed away, doesn't take us any further. Our best way forward is to establish the last sighting of him before his body was recovered.'

'I second that,' said Heather. 'What was Stuart doing? If he had a fishing party, who was in the group? If not, who – if anyone – was he with?'

'Have there been any incidents which could have led to a confrontation?' Chatty threw in. 'Anyone might wish Stuart harm?'

Morag said, 'Jean Pirie's husband. And that's just for starters.'

'Follow that up,' Flora instructed. 'To summarise, we know the *who*. What's still unclear is the *where*, the *when* and – most important – the *why*.'

'No pressure.'

'We did set out to challenge ourselves,' Heather chided.

Morag rounded on her. 'You've changed your tune.'

'Not so. As it says in my Bible: A man's heart plans his way, but the Lord directs his steps.'

Fifty-one

MacDuff swung the Land Rover off the A93 at Dinnet, a small holiday village approximately equidistant between Ballater and Aboyne. Said to be the gateway to both the Highlands and the Cairngorms National Park, it is also home to Deeside Gliding Club, holder of the UK wave soaring altitude record of 38,600 feet.

MacDuff's thoughts were fixed firmly on the ground as he pulled into the large layby alongside the airfield. A motley assortment of old cars bookended a clutch of shabby motor homes. On the steps of one perched a young man.

Drawing to a halt, MacDuff pulled on the handbrake and switched off the ignition. Lowering the driver's window. 'Tinsley?' he called.

The young man looked up. 'Who's asking?'

MacDuff glowered down at him. 'Don't come the daft laddie wi' me.' Reaching for his uniform cap, he opened the door and jumped down.

The lad set aside the stick he'd been whittling. 'Which Tinsley you after?'

'How many you got?'

He shrugged. 'We're a big family.'

Aye. And you all look alike. 'Kenny'll do.'

'Crivvens!' He made an exaggerated show of surprise. 'You're in luck. That's me.'

'Okay. The reason I'm here—'

'Give it to me straight: what am I supposed to have done?'

'I'm following up a complaint: you're suspected of salmon poaching.'

Kenny yawned. 'Come off it. Wouldn't waste my time. Besides, I don't even like salmon.'

'You could have sold the fish.'

'Couldn't be arsed. Where was this, anyhow?'

'Crathie.'

His eyes darkened. 'That bastard ghillie! He didn't find a thing on me. Should be *me* havin' *him* up for assault.'

MacDuff looked him up and down. 'You'd be hard-pressed. I'm not seeing any evidence. No scars. No abrasions. Not even a wee bruise.'

'So?'

'The ghillie's vehicle had its tyres slashed that very night. Bit of a coincidence, wouldn't you say?'

Kenny held up his hands. 'You can't pin that on me.'

'Maybe. But you're young and athletic. And we both know you've previous. If there was an assault, my money's on the ghillie would have come off worse.' He pulled out his notebook. 'When did this alleged assault take place?'

'Can't remember.'

MacDuff said, 'There's more than one witness will help jog your memory.'

'And say what: I was down the riverside at Crathie mindin' my own business?'

'Problem is, you weren't minding your own business, were you, Kenny? Chances are you were eyeing up opportunities: if it wasn't poaching, it would be nicking some poor farmer's gear.'

Red-faced, Kenny snivelled, 'Travellin' folk get blamed for everythin'.'

'Or mebbe you were bent on taking it out on the ghillie for cramping your style. If that's the case …' MacDuff rocked back and forth on the soles of his boots. 'I wouldn't want to be in your shoes.'

Kenny blanched. 'You talkin' 'bout the same ghillie: the one that drowned?'

'I am.'

His eyes popped. 'Hang on. You tryin' to fit me up?'

Fifty-two

'Sorry to drag you back here at such short notice,' said Flora. 'I've come by useful intel, which may well change the focus of our investigation.'

'Ooh!' exclaimed Chatty. Dressed in stained leopard-print T-shirt, baggy black leggings and old Converse trainers, she'd run straight from cooking off a beef stew. 'Let's have it, then.'

'Better make it good,' muttered Morag, picking bracken off a pair of hiking socks. She'd ditched her mud-caked boots at the door.

Flora said, 'Let's give Heather a few minutes.'

'Did she say she was coming?'

'Phone went to voicemail. I've left a message.'

'No point waiting,' Chatty insisted. 'This time of day, she's bound to be in class.'

'Pains me to say it,' Morag growled, 'but she's right.'

Flora said, 'Then I'll cut to the chase: Dodd Benzie overheard a man threatening to kill Stuart Thom.'

'Where?'

'In the Clach.'

'When?'

'A few days before Stuart's body was found.'

'How do you know?'

Flora tapped the side of her nose. 'Been asking my own questions.'

'Dodd's not your most reliable witness.'

'Granted. But the male customer was sounding off to Archie Kinnear when the threat was made, and Archie's a different story.'

'How come Stuart came into the conversation? Was he in the pub, making an arse of himself?'

'The guy in question was one of a group led by Stuart fishing the Crathie. Wasn't happy the way things were going.'

'You can't please everyone,' Chatty said, with feeling. From food allergies to pillow preferences she'd had it with paying guests.

'There's more to it than that,' Flora insisted. 'The guy alleged he'd missed out because Stuart wasn't doing his job.'

Morag said, 'That I can understand. Big bucks it costs these days to fish a beat on the Dee.'

'You think this man could have murdered Stuart?' asked Chatty.

'Maybe not murdered,' Flora replied. 'But, if there was bad blood between them, they could have got into an altercation and Stuart fallen to his death.'

'Or been pushed,' Morag added. 'Fella's not in the area, still, I don't suppose.'

'Shouldn't think so. There's not many fishers manage more than three days on a beat.'

Chatty said, 'That's that, then.' The night before, she'd knocked back the dregs of a few wine bottles from the dining room and her head was splitting.

'It's our best lead,' Flora protested. 'Surely worth following up.'

'The police will have already done that.'

'I wouldn't count on it. They're so stretched these days. I say we give it a try.'

'How?' Morag queried. 'Archie won't be keen to share a private conversation.'

'Wasn't private.'

'Okay,' she conceded. 'But it's a long shot.'

'Too long.' Chatty yawned. 'When I signed up to this, I thought it was going to be fun, but it has turned out like a boring school project.'

Flora said, 'It's early days. From what I've gleaned, an investigation can involve hours of painstaking—'

'For Heaven's sake, can you not leave off for once? I've the devil of a headache.'

'Have you taken something for it?'

'A pill you mean?' Chatty's voice dripped scorn.

'If not, I'm sure I have—'

'Plus,' she interrupted, 'I've been on a starvation diet. I'm fit to faint.'

'I could make you some toast,' offered Flora, who'd been too embroiled in the investigation to think of catering. 'You don't want to lose too much weight. Our time of life, it's a toss-up: your face or your figure.'

Dispassionately, Chatty eyed Flora's jutting cheekbones. 'You would know. However, I'm with the Duchess of Windsor: "You can never be too rich or too thin."' Seeing Morag's puzzlement, 'Words attributed to the late Wallis Simpson, the American divorcee whose relationship with King Edward VIII led to his abdication in 1936.'

Morag said, 'Who wants to look like a stick insect?'

'I could name half a dozen off the top of my head.'

'Go on, then.'

'Victoria Beckham. Brigitte Macron ...'

'Keep going.'

Chatty's brow furrowed in concentration. 'Nancy Pelosi, Meghan Markle ...'

'Now you're talking. And it's not just weight she has in common with Wallis Simpson. Prince Philip was reported to have privately called Meghan "DoW", short for "Duchess of Windsor", because she reminded him of her fellow American.'

Flora said, 'And look how things played out: Harry living in what is effectively exile.'

Chatty mused, 'I wonder if they'll every come back.'

'As a family?' Morag queried. 'No chance. I can't see Meghan playing second fiddle to Kate. Never did. But now, after Kate's cancer scare ...'

'Poor Harry!' Flora pulled a tragic face. 'Destined to live in slavish devotion until the day he dies.'

Morag scowled. 'I wouldn't waste your breath.' Turning on Chatty, 'I'm only counting four so far.'

Chewing on her lower lip, Chatty began, 'There's Kate—'

'That's cheating,' Morag cut in. 'You can't attribute Catherine's weight loss to dieting. The girl has been gravely ill.'

Flora said, 'In my view, Kate was too thin even before she went in for abdominal surgery.'

'You're talking rubbish,' said Chatty. 'She looked fabulous in that sequinned pink Jenny Packham gown at the Buckingham Palace Diplomatic Corps reception. And who can forget the white trouser suit she wore to the Christmas Carol service at Westminster Abbey?'

'My point exactly: you have to be rake-thin to pull off an outfit like that. Same with the blue Alexander McQueen coat Kate wore to the Christmas service at Sandringham. Helps she has the height, but that wrap waistline was tiny. As for Meghan, between the diet regime and the hot yoga, there's not a spare ounce on her.'

'Whatever,' Chatty sulked.

'My advice: stick to fish and chicken, eat loads of vegetables, the more colours the better.'

'In Ballochbrae? I should be so lucky. Last time I was in the minimart, aside from tatties, neeps and carrots, there was nothing on offer other than a couple of wrinkled green peppers.'

Flora ignored this. 'The weight will drop off you. And drink lots.'

'Shouldn't be a problem,' muttered Morag, giving Chatty the side-eye.

'It's important to stay hydrated.'

'Speaking of drink,' Morag continued. 'Before Weight Watcher of the Week took off at a tangent, you were telling us Dodd Benzie heard a punter in the Clach voicing threats against Stuart Thom.'

'That's right.'

'Problem is, even if we follow that up, I'd lay money on Dodd won't remember a thing.'

Heather said, 'There could have been other folk in the Clach overheard what was said.'

'Good point,' said Flora. 'Plus, one thing Dodd does remember: the man had a triple-barrelled name.'

Chatty croaked, 'Double-barrelled, don't you mean?'

'No. Dodd was tickled, apparently. Never knew there was such a thing.'

'Really?' Struggling to her feet, Chatty asked, 'Can I use your bathroom?'

'You all right?' said Flora. 'You've gone terribly pale.'

'Time of the month,' she squeezed out.

Morag hooted. 'Who is she kidding?'

'Be my guest,' said Flora, biting her lip to suppress a giggle. 'You know the way.'

Fifty-three

The bell jangled overhead on its curved iron bracket as Flora pushed against the minimart door's brass fingerplate.

'Morning,' came a disembodied greeting.

She checked behind the Post Office counter. Empty.

Her eyes scoped the interior. 'There you are!' she exclaimed.

Snug in Spar uniform's black-and-red body warmer, Angus MacTavish broke off from rearranging the green plastic crates in the small fresh veg section. 'Fit like?'

'Doing away,' Flora replied. 'Jessie about?'

He straightened. 'Nipped back to the house. We've a man coming to see to the television.'

'Oh.' Flora's mouth turned down. She'd been hoping to pick up the latest gossip on Stuart Thom.

Gus made to move. 'Needing the Post Office?'

'No. I …' She struggled for a plausible excuse. 'Just dropped in for a pint of milk.'

'You know where it is.'

Flora was reaching into the refrigerated cabinet, when Gus called, 'Did you hear they found Stuart Thom's things?'

She whirled. 'When?'

'This morning, early.'

Flora scuttled back to his side. 'Who found them?'

'Fishing party up Invercauld way.'

'You wouldn't happen to know exactly what was found?'

'Jacket, far as I know.'

'Anything else? Wallet? Keys? Phone?'

He shook his head. 'It's Jessie you'll need to ask.'

'When will she be back?'

'Dunno.'

'The television man, what time was he due to arrive?'

'Ten o'clock, but fella rang to say he's running late.'

'Okay. So what time …?'

'Could take long enough. Canna depend on folk these days.'

'No, indeed. But you must have some idea …'

He cocked his head. 'Why are you so interested?'

'Who wouldn't be?'

Eyes narrowed, he leaned in close. 'Is it true what I'm hearing about you an' Morag McCracken?'

'Don't know what you're talking about.'

'You're thick wi' her an' thon MacIntyre woman.'

Flora shrugged. 'We have a girls' night occasionally. No harm in that.'

With a wink, 'Girls' night, is it? What I'm hearing: there's a sight more to it.'

Ostentatiously, she checked the time on the Post Office clock. 'Better run.' Resolutely, she turned to leave. 'I'll catch up with Jessie another time.'

She was halfway out the door, when, 'Flora?'

She turned.

'You've forgotten what you came for.' Gus MacTavish waved a pint of milk.

Fifty-four

Flora said, 'Before the others arrive, I should mention I collared Janet Kinnear in the village today.'

'Really,' Chatty acknowledged, face the picture of disinterest.

'Thought I might get more on what Dodd Benzie saw and heard in the Clach.' She threw Chatty a hard look. 'Might not look it, but Janet's sharp as a tack.'

'What did she have to say?'

'That fisher, the one with the fancy name …' She broke off, savouring the moment. 'Turns out he was staying at your place.'

Chatty blanched. 'So?'

'When were you planning to share this information?'

'I … I …'

'Christopher Calthorpe-Drummond-Smythe,' Flora challenged. 'Correct me if I'm wrong. The very man who threatened to kill Stuart Thom. The man whose culpability we discussed at some length when we last met. According to Janet, that man was billeted under your roof.'

'Even if he did board at Castle View,' Chatty blustered. 'I don't see what—'

Her words were drowned by Albert Villa's doorbell.

*

Setting down her coffee mug, Flora said, 'Now we're all here, Chatty has something she wants to share.'

Cheeks aflame, Chatty tugged at the neckline of a clingy jersey top. Clearing her throat, 'Yesterday, when Morag and I met up with Flora, she introduced a new suspect.'

'Person of interest,' Heather corrected.

'A fisher, I believe Flora later made you both aware. At the time, I was suffering from what I can only describe as nervous exhaustion.'

Morag muttered, 'Alcohol poisoning, more like,' raising a hastily suppressed chuckle from Flora and a disapproving frown from Heather.

Chatty wrung her hands. 'As a result, I didn't make the connection between the individual Flora was referring to and a prior guest of my own establishment.'

Through a mouthful of biscuit, Morag said, 'You must be thicker than I thought.'

'Either that,' said Flora, 'or more devious.'

'Now, now, ladies,' Heather remonstrated.

Flora's voice rose. 'A man is dead. The police investigation is – at best – moribund. And we may hold the key to a resolution.'

Chatty said, 'I still don't get—'

'Then I'll spell it out: this intel puts your fisher squarely in the frame.'

'I don't see how? By the time Stuart went into the river, my guest would have been back in London.'

'Mortuary said Stuart could have gone in on the Thursday,' Flora argued.

'Accepted. But he was on the beat all day, so it would have had to be later on.'

'When did you last see Christopher what's-his-name?'

'Breakfast, Thursday.'

'How about dinner?'

'Wasn't booked. He'd have been keeping his options open.'

'Either that,' said Morag, 'or done a runner.'

'Chatty, check with the Estate Office he showed up at the hut.'

With an exaggerated sigh, 'If I must.'

'He might have caught a flight on the Thursday night.'

'He'd have had to go some,' Heather observed. 'By the time he drove into Aberdeen, passed through security …'

Flora said, 'Remind me: when was his scheduled flight?'

'Mid-morning Friday,' Chatty replied. 'But he could have had a change of plan. Happens all the time.'

'Who was he flying with?'

'How should I know?'

Heather asked, 'Did he have a hire car?'

'He did.'

'Is there any way we can check when the car was returned to the hire company? If, indeed, it has been returned.'

'We could give them a call, I suppose. Act daft.'

Morag eyed her with asperity. 'Wouldn't be difficult.'

Flora said, 'Anything else you'd care to share?'

Chatty's eyes dropped to the floor.

'Well?' Flora pressed.

'That Thursday night ...'

'What about it?'

'Chipper's bed ...' Her voice faltered. 'It hadn't been slept in.'

In the conservatory, there was stunned silence. Then, with an outward whoosh of breath, Flora said, 'You sure?'

'Saw it with my own eyes. Friday morning, Etta was late, so I had to commence breakfast service on my own. When she took over in the kitchen, I went upstairs to make a start on the rooms.'

What Chatty didn't say: after dinner on Wednesday, she'd plied Chipper with brandy and come on to him, a move which had been briskly rebuffed.

Morag said, 'Hope he paid in advance.'

Chatty rounded on her. 'Do you take me for a fool?'

'You said it.'

'Who else knows about this?' Flora demanded.

'No one.'

'How about Etta?'

'No way.'

'Your PPOs?'

'You kidding? Anyhow, I don't know why you're making such a thing of it.'

Flora threw her a withering look. 'I'll tell you. It not only puts your fisher in the frame, it puts us ahead of the police.'

Fifty-five

Flora was turning down the thermostat on the boiler when the doorbell rang. Mouthing a muttered expletive, she hurried through from the back of the house. Her heart missed a beat when she saw MacDuff's yellow high-vis jacket framed in the inner doorway.

Turning the handle, 'Alec. Something wrong?'

The constable shook his head.

'Thank God. I thought for a minute it was Mum.' Collecting herself, 'Come away in.' She led him down the hall.

'How is Kate?'

Flora turned her head. 'Up and down. I never know what to expect from one day to the next. One minute she'll be chatting away, then all of a sudden she'll be in a different place.' She showed him into the snug. 'Sit down. Can I get you something?'

Lowering his bulk into her dad's well-worn armchair, 'I won't, thanks all the same.'

Instinctively, her eyes dropped to his waistline.

'No, I'm not on a diet,' he said, with a rueful face. 'Though if you were to say I could do with losing a stone or two, I'd have to agree with you.'

Taking the chair opposite, 'Well,' Flora began. Checked herself. Dishing out dietary advice had been part and parcel of her old life.

MacDuff rearranged his features into something approaching officialdom. Fingering his lapels, he said, 'I'm calling about another matter altogether.'

'And what would that be?'

'Those pals of yours ...'

'Pals?'

'Whatever you want to call them: the women been meeting up this past while.'

Flora's antennae switched to full alert. 'Oh, that?' She said airily. 'It's nothing. Just a wee book club some of us girls formed to pass a dark evening.'

MacDuff knitted his brow. 'That so?'

She forced a laugh. 'It's not against the law.'

'Not unless the books are of a ... how can I put it ... questionable nature.'

'Really, Alec,' Flora chided. 'Can you see a pillar of the kirk like Heather Garden reading porn?'

He chuckled. 'Mebbe not. All the same, I've heard word there's a bit more to these get-togethers than reading.'

'What, for instance?'

'Matters discussed. Questions asked.'

Flora was framing a plausible explanation when a text pinged on her phone: Morag. Swiftly, she set it aside. 'You wouldn't expect a bunch of women to get together and not exchange news.'

Assuming his most threatening expression, MacDuff looked her in the eye. 'There's news,' he said. 'And there's news.'

'I'm not with you,' Flora responded, her face the picture of innocence.

'Then I'll spell it out: it has come to my attention your book club – or whatever you want to call it – has been meddling in a live police investigation.'

Flora opened her mouth to protest.

But before she could say a word, he went on, 'Not only that, but enlisting other people – members of the community, serving police officers, civilian personnel – to assist with what can only be called a covert investigation.' Pursing his lips, he sat back in his seat.

Affecting injured surprise, Flora said, 'Come on, Alec, when there's an unexplained death in a tightknit community like ours, people are going to talk, like it or not.'

'That may well be so. But—'

'From the minute the incident was called in, folk will have been talking. Not just the emergency services: worshippers at the kirk, customers in the minimart, the Post Office, the tearoom, garage, pub. Then there's—'

'I don't dispute that,' MacDuff interrupted.

'If the police had more meaningful community involvement,' she added, twisting the knife. 'There would be less opportunity for idle speculation.'

He leaned forward. 'You know as well as I do why community policing has been cut back: police numbers are at their lowest since 2004.'

'So I believe. Nonetheless—'

'We've nine hundred fewer officers than ten years ago,' he expanded. 'Plus, we're picking up the slack from other agencies, mental health for one.'

'I get that,' Flora interrupted. 'Must be frustrating. But, still—'

'If they had the resources to do their job properly. If we didn't have to carry out welfare checks on vulnerable people, we'd have the capacity—'

She cut him off mid-sentence. 'It's Ballochbrae we're talking.'

'Then there's the Court Service,' he ploughed on. 'I can sit the entire day at Aberdeen Sherriff Court waiting to be called, only to be sent home again. Did you know there are more than five hundred officers called to court on a daily basis and only a very small proportion actually give evidence? And don't get me started on the Hate Crime Bill.' He cracked the knuckles of his right hand, one by one. 'Busybody's charter. If I had a pound for every incident I've had to log, I'd be a rich man.'

Flora said, 'Returning to the case in point, you're never going to stop people talking, nor drawing their own conclusions.'

'And when it comes to the police investigation,' MacDuff countered. 'You have to understand, there's things going on we're not in a position to share.'

'Well, I can assure you we were only—'

'Whatever you were doing.' He cut her off. 'You need to stop right now.'

Fifty-six

Kate looked up from her station at Darroch View's window when Flora came into the room. 'You all right?'

'Yes,' she smiled. 'Why do you ask?'

'You look tired.'

'Do I?'

'You do far too much, I'm forever telling you. You'll make yourself ill if you don't let up.'

Flora dropped onto a chair. 'I've given up my job. What else do you want me to do?'

'Stop running back and forth to this place for a start.' Kate waved a hand around the room. 'I'm well set up.'

It was on the tip of Flora's tongue to mention the fall. She buttoned her lip. Her mum had recovered more quickly than expected, and – chances were – she'd have no recollection.

'There's no need for you to be here every day of the week,' Kate continued. 'You should be out enjoying yourself, meeting folk, now you don't have …'

'A husband?' said Flora, only half joking.

'Have you heard from …' Kate raised an anxious hand to her mouth. 'I forget.'

'Allan,' Flora supplied. 'The answer is no. Not since …' She broke off, not wanting to revisit the machinations involved in dismantling their married life. 'The kids are in touch with their dad, of course.' As she voiced the words, Flora pondered how often she'd been on the point of asking Isla or Scott how Allan was doing. Had the new job turned out as expected? Did he have a girlfriend? She'd managed to bite her tongue.

'Everything else okay?'

'Why wouldn't it be?'

'The house. Takes some keeping up, as I well know. If it's not the roof, it's the chimney, the gutters or the …' Brow furrowed, she broke off. 'Those round things come down the wall.'

'Downpipes?' Flora supplied.

'And the windows need regular attention. They—'

'The house is fine, Mum.'

'Take your word for it. But you need to keep on top of things. If you let the place run down, your dad will turn in his grave. It was in his family for—'

'I know. And I'm perfectly capable. You're not to worry about the house. Or me. I'm a strong woman.'

'Don't give me that. You're soft as putty.'

Flora laughed. 'You know me too well.'

'Your own worst enemy is what you are. You've been trying to save the world single-handed since you were knee-high.' Kate reached out. Clasped Flora's strong hand in her own frail one. 'You go at things head-on. And you're no spring chicken. Comes the time, you'll have to accept you're not able to do as much.'

'I know. But moving back to Ballochbrae, there's been a lot needing my attention.'

She gave Flora's hand a squeeze. 'Not least your old ma.'

Gently, Flora withdrew her hand. 'Are you all right? Can I bring you anything?'

'I'm fine. You're not to go worrying about me. I've lived my life. And now …'

Flora watched her mum's expression go vacant. Then confused. Then angry. 'The man,' she managed, at last. 'Can't bring to mind …'

'Dad?'

She nodded.

'James. But you always called him Jock.'

Kate pulled an embroidered hankie from her cardigan pocket and wiped a tear from her eye.

'Oh, Mum …' Rising, Flora threw an arm around her mother's thin shoulders.

Kate shook her off. 'I'm fine. I've lived my life. Now, away you go and get on with yours.'

Fifty-seven

Flora dials in to a Zoom meeting: I had a visit from Constable MacDuff yesterday. I won't beat around the bush: we've been warned off.

Chatty enters the room: Why? All we've been doing is ask questions?

Flora: That's what I told him. Didn't cut any ice.

Chatty: Did he say what stage the police investigation is at?

Flora: Just made noises about not being able to share intel.

Morag joins the conversation: Sounds like they're making progress. We better back off.

Heather: Stop now? I don't think so.

Morag: No point getting Eck's back up. He can be an awkward cuss.

Heather: But we're just getting into our stride.

Chatty: I'm with Morag. We've spent hours of our time on this so-called investigation. In my opinion, we're chasing our tails and getting nowhere.

Morag: Not helped by some people …

Chatty: I'll pretend I didn't hear that. I used to look forward to our get-togethers. But the atmosphere has got so heavy—Flora runs this club like a Stasi convention.

Flora: Someone has to be in charge.

Chatty: Granted. But you're so buttoned up.

Flora: Unlike you. If ever there was a loose cannon—

Heather: Now, now, ladies.

Chatty: As for you, Heather Garden, you've taken to the whole police thing like a duck to water. Talk about a sad life.

Morag: I can take it or leave it. I've enough drama at home.

Heather: Question is: now we've come this far, do we keep going? Or do we revert to …

Morag: If you mention books one more time, I won't be held accountable for my actions.

Flora: We're at a critical juncture. Let's take stock: what have we got in the way of leads?

Morag: The jealous husband.

Chatty: Assuming he gives a monkey's. They could have an open marriage, for all we know.

Morag: In Ballochbrae? You have to be joking.

Flora: Chatty's fisher. Where did you get to with that?

Chatty: Estate Office confirmed he joined the beat that Thursday. Another thing: they told me the fishers finished early due to the weather closing in.

Flora: So Chipper could conceivably have attacked Stuart Thom and caught a flight later that day.

Chatty: It's possible.

Flora: Did you check with the care hire company?

Chatty: I did. Got diddly-squat. Even after I shot them a hard-luck story, all they'd confirm is the car was returned to them, not the date or time.

Flora: That's a setback. Any other leads?

Morag: The traveller, if that's what he was. I drove to Dinnet the other day and checked out that layby. Whoever was overnighting there has moved on.

Heather: One of Stuart's creditors?

Flora: Keep your ears to the ground on that, everyone. Still, I think it's a long shot. Same with the altercation the Met officer witnessed. We don't even have a description. One for the cops, in my opinion. My money's on Chipper. I managed to trace three punters who were in the Clach that night. They all said, although Chipper was in his cups, the threat was made with real intent.

Chatty: Nonsense. Who'd kill for a fish?

Heather: Perhaps his intention was not to kill, but to wound.

Flora: My sources read him as an army man. Said he looked equipped to carry out his threat. Something else: they said the fisher complained he missed out because Stuart was constantly on his phone. Begs the question: who was Stuart speaking to?'

Morag: My money's on Jean Pirie.

Flora: Then again … Everything hinges on when that hire car was returned. In order to eliminate this individual, here's what I want you to do:

Chatty, have another go at the car hire people. If we can establish when Chipper returned the hire car, it might put him out of the picture.

Chatty: Okay.

Morag: Speaking of time, we've spent another hour of our lives talking in circles and we're no further forward. Way I see it, the only person with a strong motive to cause Stuart Thom harm is Hector Pirie. Why aren't we going after him?

Flora: Let's keep going, whatever MacDuff says.

Heather: I'll go with the consensus. If you can call it that.

Flora: Okay. Keep in close touch, everybody.

Flora closes the call.

Fifty-eight

Heather activated the trafficator and swung the Morris Minor right off Bridge Street into Ballater's Station Square.

Shoehorning the car into a parking space, she pulled on the handbrake and turned to Dulcie. 'Where would you like to go?' Having reflected on MacDuff's warning, she was fearful of jeopardising her job and had rung, asking to meet at short notice.

'You choose.'

Heather said, 'I chose last time. It's your turn.'

'Why don't we try Orka?'

'We were there not long ago.'

'Somewhere up the Braemar Road: The Auld Kirk, maybe?'

'Bit far. I'm tight for time, and I'll have to drop you back.' She stretched to retrieve her handbag from the back seat.

'Look,' screeched Dulcie. 'Is that not Camilla?'

Heather's head whipped around. 'Where?'

'Heading into The Old Royal Station?'

The nearest station to Balmoral Castle, Ballater railway station was closed in 1966. Reopened as a visitor centre containing Queen Victoria's waiting room and a replica royal carriage, it was destroyed by fire in 2015. In response, the then Duke of Rothesay's charity, The Prince's Foundation, initiated an extensive restoration plan to reinstate the station to its former glory.

Heather shook her head. 'It's not time, yet, for her and the King to be at Birkhall.'

'Can't be far off. And look at those suede boots. She didn't buy them in Ballater.'

'Granted. But the Queen wouldn't be on her own. She'd have protection.'

'Within sight,' Dulcie admonished. 'Not necessarily at her elbow. There's a woman coming around the corner could easily—'

'That's Isa Cowie. Cleans the public conveniences.'

Dulcie's shoulders drooped. Then, 'It *is* Camilla. I'd know that hairdo on a dark night.'

'There's nothing open in the station right now except for Tourist Information and the Library,' Heather persisted. 'And what would the Queen be wanting with a public library when she has her own at Birkhall?'

'Handed down from the Queen Mum. I don't for a minute believe their taste runs along the same lines. Plus, Camilla's a great reader. Founded the charity The Queen's Reading Room. And wasn't she at the Braemar Literary Festival in The Fife last October?'

She was,' Heather conceded. 'That, and last year, and the inaugural event the year before.'

'Look, that'll be the PPO now. Come on,' Dulcie urged, grabbing the car door handle.

Eyes wide with alarm, Heather extended a staying hand. 'What are you going to do?'

'Walk right up. Wish her a cheery good morning.'

'If it's not the Queen, you'll get a right red face.'

'And if it is,' countered Dulcie, shaking her off. 'I'll drop a wee curtsey.'

Halfway out the car door, 'Chop-chop,' she threw over her shoulder. 'If your knees aren't up to it, just dip your chin.'

*

'In here,' Dulcie hissed.

Obediently, Heather followed.

They'd crept through the double doors of the Public Library and ducked into the cover of the iCentre, where a giant wall map of the area was fronted by a rack of tourist information leaflets.

'What are we going to do now?' she whispered.

Taking a peek around one of two openings into the Library, where the woman with silver-blonde hair styled in deep wings over her ears was engaged in conversation with an assistant, Dulcie mouthed, 'Wait for our chance.'

Heather looked in vain for the Protection Officers, who'd have swept the room before taking up positions with clear sight close to the exit. The open-plan space was broken up by a tall display of souvenirs, a long double-height counter and a number of freestanding bookshelves, any of which might offer a discreet observation point.

Now, the assistant – clad in the distinctive purple VisitScotland polo shirt – was pointing in their direction.

The blonde woman turned.

Fearful they might be caught off-guard and their motive misconstrued, Dulcie tugged at Heather's sleeve and bolted through the far opening. Screened by the gift display, the two made the relative safety of the Children's Library.

Crouching behind bright blue bookshelves topped by a row of furry Highland cows, Heather – perspiring in thermal T-shirt and knitted sweater under a padded jacket – scarce dared draw breath.

They heard footsteps echo on the wooden floor.

Swing doors creaked.

The footsteps receded.

Dulcie straightened and made to follow.

Heather grabbed her elbow in a vice-like grip. 'Where are you going?'

'Need a wee.'

'You can't go in the toilets.'

'Why not?'

'If it *is* the Queen, she won't be pleased to see you when she's at her …' Propriety prevented Heather from elaborating.

'No way is she in there,' Dulcie scoffed.

'She could have been caught short.'

'In that event, Protection will have done a search and seal. Let's get out of here while we've got the chance.'

Dulcie said, 'I'm not leaving until I've eyeballed that woman.'

'Or got us both arrested.'

The swing doors creaked again.

Instinctively, Heather froze.

She watched – aghast – Dulcie drop to a squat, breaking wind as she went.

For long moments there was complete silence.

Then a low voice spoke into an earpiece and all hell broke loose.

Fifty-nine

'Hector Pirie,' Flora began. 'What do we know?'

'He's worked in the forestry all his life,' Morag replied. 'Him and Jean have been in that house since they married.'

'What does he do when he's not working?'

'He has a shed behind the house, with a lathe and stuff. Duncan goes up there once in a while if he's needing something repaired. He—'

'Thanks. That's all we need for now.'

Heather said, 'Can I just quickly show you something?'

Flora groaned. 'Not another extract from your police manual? If so, we'll give it a miss.'

'It's nothing like that.' Stooping, she delved inside a battered leather sheet-music case and produced a silver laptop. 'I've done a spreadsheet.' Clearing aside the mugs that cluttered the coffee table, she set the laptop down, flipped it open and, once it was booted up, 'See.'

Three heads craned to get a better look.

'It's pretty basic,' Heather continued. 'Timeline runs along the top.' She traced the matrix with her forefinger. 'Persons of interest listed down the side, like so.'

Chatty rolled her eyes. 'Information we're already privy to. I thought you were bringing us something new.'

'Granted, it doesn't correlate the two. What it does do is let us see at a glance where people were, and when. If you follow my finger, you'll see it places Stuart in the minimart somewhere around two o'clock the day before his body was recovered.'

In Albert Villa's conservatory, you could have heard a pin drop.

With a sharp intake of breath, Flora said, 'That puts a totally different complexion on things. Who gave you this information?'

'Can't tell you straight off. I'll have to check my notes.'

For long moments, the ladies looked, one to another, in dismay.

Then, setting down her coffee mug, Morag owned, crimson-faced, 'Now you mention it, I've a vague recollection of being in the Post Office and Jessie mentioning Stuart had nipped in for cigarettes on the Friday.'

'And you didn't think to say?' Flora seethed. 'If this can be verified, it will kibosh our entire investigation.'

'I must have told somebody at some point,' Morag protested. 'Otherwise how would Heather know?'

'Classic breakdown in communication. Have you forgotten what I said about teamwork? If we don't pull together, we'll never bring our investigation to a satisfactory conclusion.'

'And if you hadn't been so determined to do things your way,' Heather retorted, 'we'd have followed police standard operating procedures and availed ourselves of a whiteboard, which we'd have updated as enquiries progressed.'

'Typical teacher,' Morag groused. 'Don't see what difference it would have made, writing stuff on a wall.'

'If we'd done that,' Heather countered, 'we'd have established a clear timeline and wouldn't find ourselves in this position.'

Chatty said, 'I don't know why you're getting so het up. If we call it quits on our so-called investigation, the world won't stop turning.'

'No,' Flora conceded. 'But we've spent so much time and effort …'

'All the more reason to cut our losses. On a lighter note'—she leaned forward eagerly—'does anyone know, is Prince Andrew at Balmoral? My PPOs wouldn't confirm, but one of my guests reckoned he saw him leaving the golf clubhouse with a security detail.'

Heather said, 'Could be. He's been spending a fair bit of time at the castle, ever since thon …' Dipping her chin in mute disapproval, she peered over her reading glasses. 'Business.'

'Thought that was all wrapped up.'

'I wouldn't count on it.'

'I'm with you,' Morag concurred. 'Mud sticks.'

'Point a finger,' Heather warned, 'and three will point back at you.'

Clapping a hand to her mouth to stifle her mirth, Chatty mumbled, 'You don't say.'

Heather shot her a disapproving look. 'Trial by media, that's what I think. I've never met the man myself, but folk who have say he's never less than polite.'

'Talking about the media, did you all see the Emily Maitlis interview?'

'Total car crash,' said Morag. 'Unable to sweat, Pizza Express in Woking. How Maitlis managed to keep a straight face I don't know.'

'Poor man was badly advised,' Heather countered.

Flora said, 'Not so. Several well-respected people close to him argued against it, including his media adviser. But that's not what we're here to talk about. We need to—'

Chatty cut her off mid-flow. 'That's Andrew's problem: he's totally unaccountable. Nobody has ever said no to him his entire life.'

'He'd have had to get the go-ahead for the interview from his mother,' Morag argued.

'Which she was probably happy to give. Reportedly, Andrew was her favourite child: born when she'd had time to settle into her role. Handsome. Fun-loving. Falklands war hero. Plus, what mother wouldn't want to help her child out of a tight corner?'

'To the tune of twelve million?'

'That's nothing but hearsay,' Heather chided. 'And Queen Elizabeth was nobody's fool. Look at the speed with which she stripped him of his military patronages. In my opinion the man was simply naive, and unlucky to fall under the influence of a manipulative deviant.' Turning to Flora, 'Do you agree?'

'By all accounts Jeffrey Epstein was a Gatsby-esque figure,' Flora conceded. 'And Prince Andrew perhaps isn't the brightest. I think Epstein's attraction was down to entitlement and love of the high life. In royal terms, don't forget, Andrew is relatively poor. Factor in a high-end lifestyle: skiing in Verbier, the upkeep of a mansion. Small wonder Epstein's homes and yachts and private island were a draw.'

'Not to mention,' said Morag, 'the folk he rubbed shoulders with: statesmen and billionaires by all accounts. And those young girls – whether he participated in the "massages" or not – would have been eye candy for a middle-aged man.'

'Whatever his motivation,' Flora argued. 'He certainly demonstrated spectacularly poor judgement, not distancing himself once Epstein had been tried and convicted. But enough on the subject. As I was saying, we need to—'

'He's a sad case.'

Chatty said, 'I wouldn't mind having nothing to do all day but go riding or play golf.'

'Different story if you don't have a choice.'

'If it was Andrew on the Balmoral course,' Chatty speculated, 'he's as likely come up to escape from Fergie.'

'She's another one gets a bad press,' said Heather. 'The poor woman has been suffering with cancer. She's reported to have undergone a single mastectomy, and now she's been diagnosed with melanoma. That notwithstanding, if our dear late Queen was happy to walk her dogs in the company of Sarah Ferguson, that's good enough for me.'

'They say the Queen was fond of Fergie.'

Morag said, 'Unlike Prince Philip. Reportedly – after the toe-sucking scandal – he wouldn't have Sarah Ferguson under the same roof.'

'The Queen would have been lonesome, most like, after Philip went,' Heather posited. 'Nobody else around at the time.'

'Getting back to Andrew, must be a nightmare, sharing a house with your ex.'

'Not if it's big enough,' Chatty argued. 'Royal Lodge in Windsor has thirty rooms. You could lose yourself in that.'

'Seventeen bedrooms an' all.'

Chatty said, 'Bet they don't have as many bathrooms, like Harry and Meghan's place in Montecito.'

'Imagine,' said Morag. 'You wake in the night to have a wee. You wouldn't know which way to turn. Not forgetting the toilet paper they must get through, and them with two kids.'

'Never mind kids. My guests get through loo roll like you wouldn't believe. I've had to stop leaving out spare.'

Heather said, 'It's as well the pandemic is over. Remember when the minimart shelves were stripped bare and Ballater Co-op limited purchases to two per customer? Takes me back. When we had an outside privy, Mother would cut the newspaper into squares and thread them on a piece of string.'

'There's posh for you,' said Morag. 'All we had was a rusty nail.'

'That apart, Andrew and Fergie must bump into one another at some point.'

Chatty said, 'Why would they? There's a chef, housekeeping staff—'

'An indoor swimming pool,' Morag chipped in. 'Maybe they give each other a wave. A private chapel and all, if the papers are to be believed. Come in handy for Andy, should he feel the need to get anything off his chest.'

'That's completely uncalled for,' Heather complained.

'Whatever, that pair are well matched when it comes to chasing money. Jeffrey Epstein was reported to have come up with cash to save Fergie from bankruptcy. And who could forget the fake sheikh?'

Flora said, 'I, for one. If I wanted gossip about minor royals, I'd treat myself to a copy of *Hello* magazine. As it is, I understood the objective of this meeting was to progress our investigation. An investigation, may I remind you, into a tragic death.'

'I was only trying to lighten the atmosphere,' Chatty sulked.

'Consider it job done. Now, where were we?'

Morag said, 'Back at square one.'

'Not necessarily,' Heather argued. 'The discrepancy in the timeline … I'll go back. Double-check my entries.'

'Take too long.'

'It might let my fisher off the hook,' Chatty said hopefully. 'If you'll pardon the pun.'

Flora said, 'Do I take it you're no further forward with the car hire people?'

'You take it right.'

'Regardless, our first priority is to corroborate this latest piece of intel. Given how key it is to our investigation, I'd best do that myself. Heather, your spreadsheet has already shown its worth. Well done. Keep it updated, will you?'

Flushed with pleasure, Heather acquiesced with a gracious nod.

'Moving on, what's the story on social media?'

'Nothing on the police front. Hector Pirie doesn't have a social media profile. Scored a blank on Jean, too. She's on Facebook and Twitter-slash-X, but not very active on either. Last postings date from well before Stuart Thom's death.'

'Maybe because she was too busy shagging him,' Chatty suggested.

'Don't be so vulgar,' sniffed Heather.

Flora said, 'What's the state of the marriage? Anyone know?'

'Moribund, by Jean's own admission,' Morag replied. 'But they're still together.' Then, catching Flora's bleak expression, 'Must count for something.'

'Yeah,' sniped Flora. 'They're so happy together she's having a full-on affair.'

'Allegedly,' Heather corrected.

'Is the husband a drinker?'

'Not a big drinker,' said Morag. 'According to Duncan, at any rate.'

Flora asked, 'Where's Pirie's local boozer?'

'Coilacreich Inn.'

'Isn't that where Stuart goes when he's out of favour at the Clach?'

'The very same.'

'He a big chap, this Hector Pirie?'

'Caber champion. Need I say more?'

'The pair of them could have been in their cups,' Chatty breathed, wide-eyed. 'And one thing led to another.'

Heather snapped, 'Have you not been paying attention?'

'Just saying. Any chance the landlord will be forthcoming?'

'Doubt it. Willie Meston runs a tight ship.'

Flora said, 'We need to chart Hector's movements around the time Stuart died.'

'May I suggest something?' asked Heather.

'Go ahead.'

'We've been focusing on Jean Pirie's husband. But what about Stuart's wife? It says in my handbook the police always look first at those nearest to the victim.' She made quote marks with her fingers. '"TIE."'

'What are you on about?' Morag groused.

'From my police manual,' Heather expanded. 'Trace, interview or eliminate. Why is Sheena Thom living in Perth? Is it because she found out about an affair?'

'Been at her mum's place for a while. But the kids are with her. Even if she had the motive, the opportunity is lacking.'

Flora said, 'I'm in total agreement. Sheena would likely have been the first person the police interviewed in connection with Stuart's death.'

'Returning to Jean Pirie,' Morag persisted. 'Who's to say the affair hadn't gone sour. Stuart and Jean rowed. Jean accidentally—'

'Stuart might have taken compromising photos,' Chatty jumped in. 'Threatened to send them to Hector if Jean broke off the relationship.'

Morag threw her a cutting look. 'As if.'

'Don't give me that,' she snapped. 'Wasn't so long ago two local women posed as underage girls to blackmail men.'

'There's at least one problem with these hypotheses,' Flora intervened. 'We need to come up with evidence there is – or was – an affair.'

Sixty

Late for an update on her mum's care plan, Flora was just pulling in to Darroch View's car park when her mobile rang.

She was tempted to let it go to voicemail, but curiosity got the better of her. Groping in her shoulder bag, she pulled out her phone and checked the caller display: Morag.

Morag: This a good time to speak?

Flora: If you keep it short.

Morag: I was down the village, getting petrol at Bandy's, and some lads I know were filling up. I got chatting, just on the off-chance they'd heard something to our advantage.

Flora: And?

Morag: They're in a band. There's five of them altogether. They do a gig at St Margaret's, the old Episcopal church up the hill on the left as you come into Braemar. it's like, a performance, arts and heritage venue now.

Flora: Cut to the chase.

Morag: They were heading to Braemar – they go hours in advance to give themselves practice time – when one of them saw what he thought was Jean Pirie's car, parked off-road this side of Threepenny-Bit Cottage.

Flora: How did he know the car belonged to Jean Pirie? Is he familiar with the number plate?

Morag: Not sure. Said they were going at a lick, and it was screened by trees. He only caught a couple of digits, but he sounded convinced.

Flora: That it? I really have to go. Can we finish this conversation another time?

Morag: Sorry. It's just, that gig – the one at St Margaret's – it was the night before they pulled Stuart Thom from the river.

Flora: That ties in with what Jessie told Morag and I've since confirmed: the last known sighting of Stuart Thom was around two o'clock on the Friday.

Sixty-one

'Fit like?' said Archie cautiously when the two bruisers came into his bar.

Hatchet-faced, they didn't respond.

'What can I get you?'

'Diet Coke,' said the taller of the two, face pockmarked below a dark undercut. 'No ice.'

'Make that two,' said the other, shaved head book-ended by cauliflower ears.

They were dressed in matching black jackets over white shirts and black ties. Like Mormon missionaries. Only not.

Once Archie had served their drinks and taken payment – notes, peeled from a fat roll – he ventured, 'Passing through?'

Pockmark answered, 'You might say.'

'On the other hand,' Undercut began, and the two erupted in evil cackles.

When their laughter subsided, Pockmark said, 'We're looking for Stuart Thom. Heard he's a regular of yours.'

'Comes in now and again,' Archie responded.

'What sort of time?'

'Varies. Depends on his work.'

'He's a ghillie, right?'

'That's correct.'

'Dangerous job,' Undercut observed with a leer.

'Not if you have the right gear and take appropriate safety measures.'

'Say you were fishing,' Pockmark added. 'And you lost your footing. Those pools are mighty deep. Some of them,' he added with a wink, 'positively life-threatening.'

Undercut asked, 'Know where Thom's working right now?'

With a shrug, Archie said, 'Could be anywhere. There's umpteen pools on this stretch of river.'

'He never mentions which ones he'll be fishing?' Pushing his glass to one side, Undercut leaned over the bar. 'And him a regular of yours.' He stuck his face in Archie's. 'You wouldn't be trying to shoot us a line?'

Archie took a step back. 'Why would I do that?'

'You tell me.'

'What I can tell you: if you want to get hold of Stuart, you've as much chance of finding him at home.'

'Been there,' said Pockmark, rejoining the conversation. 'No one in.'

Undercut scoped Archie's display of fine malt whiskies. 'Nice place you've got here.'

'Yeah,' said Pockmark, with undisguised malevolence. 'Looks like we better stick around.'

Sixty-two

Flora hosts a Zoom call.

> Flora opens the call: You've all been updated on the sighting of a suspect vehicle. Can we pin down the location?
>
> Morag: About five hundred metres this side of Threepenny-Bit Cottage.
>
> Chatty: Where's that?
>
> Heather: By the Old Brig o'Dee. Used to be the lodge for Invercauld House. When the North Deeside Road was extended to Balmoral Bridge, it was bought by the Balmoral estate.
>
> Chatty: Funny name.
>
> Heather: It's built the shape of the old threepenny-bit coin.
>
> Chatty: Oh, right. I get where you are.
>
> Flora: What time was this?

Morag: Mid-afternoon.

Flora: Was the car still there when Hamish came back from Braemar?

Morag: No.

Flora: Probably someone stopped for a pee.

Morag: That's what I said.

Chatty: It was a red Ford Fiesta, right?

Flora: There must be dozens of red Fiestas on Deeside. What made your lad think it belonged to Jean Pirie?

Morag: He didn't, not straightaway. That's why he never mentioned it at the time.

Flora: What changed his mind?

Chatty: Must have dried out.

Morag: He was late back from the gig. Watched TV to wind down. One of those police things: *24 Hours in Police Custody*, something like that. There was this learner driver. On TV, I mean. Only he wasn't a learner anymore. He'd just passed his driving test. Anyhow, he took the car out for a run to celebrate and—

Chatty: Are we going to be here all day? I've better things to do.

Morag: Sorry. It's just, he crashed into a line of parked cars. Wrote three of them off, plus his own, and put two pedestrians in hospital.

Flora: Your point is?

Morag: He – the guy on TV – was still displaying his P-plates. Like when you've passed your test and you—

Flora: I know what P-plates are. What I don't get is their relevance.

Morag: Didn't I say? Jean Pirie's car was displaying P-plates one time Duncan saw it up the forestry houses, and so was the red Fiesta the lad saw parked at Invercauld that Friday. That's what triggered his memory.

Flora: Took long enough.

Morag: Well, as I told you on the phone—

Flora: Never mind that. What we have is a vehicle parked within walking distance of where Stuart Thom's car was found.

Chatty: An assignation?

Flora: Let's stick to the facts. Our first task is to link the vehicle to Jean. Then we'll need to verify the date, time and exact location of the sighting.

Morag: How?

Flora: You can start by asking your lad to check his calendar. Find out who else was in the car with him? Do they have anything to add? Then we can ask around the village. Between us we should manage to get what we need.

Heather re-enters the conversation: You're forgetting MacDuff. We've already been warned off once. If we go asking questions all over the place, we risk bringing Banchory down on our necks.

Flora: What's more important: solving our investigation or rubbing up some sergeant the wrong way?

Morag: There's the Banchory DI as well, don't forget. Wouldn't like to get on the wrong side of him.

Flora: Right enough. If he was to come down on us, we could get useful sources in deep trouble.

Chatty: Why don't we approach it from another angle? Morag, didn't you say Jean Pirie has two kids?

Heather: Before you ask, they're neither of them in my school. They've moved on.

Flora: Old enough, perhaps, to take a driving test? That friend of yours, teaches at Aboyne—

Heather: I'm not getting Dulcie involved in this business, if that's where you're going.

Chatty: Little bird told me you two have been up to all sorts.

Heather: Don't know what you mean.

Chatty: Way I heard it—

Heather: Nobody has the least interest in your tittle-tattle. More apposite: why don't you lean on one of your PPOs to run an ANPR check?

Chatty: No way. In any event, there are no cameras in the area.

Heather: Perhaps not. But a PNC check on both Hector and Jean Pirie's cars could come in useful.

Chatty: You must be joking. Mark could...
(Clears throat)
A Protection Officer could lose his job for less.

Sixty-three

The Mazda zipped onto Bain's Garage forecourt. Narrowly missing the single pump, it came to a halt with a squeal of tyres.

Levering herself out of the bucket seat, Chatty picked her way across cracked concrete to the office. 'Anybody there?' she called.

No answer.

She wandered around the back of the building to the workshop, where a transistor radio blared and grimy walls bore the curling remnants of magazine pin-up girls. 'Ally?' she yelled.

An oil-streaked face popped up from the inspection pit. 'Fit?'

'I'm looking for Ally.'

The mechanic cupped a hand to his ear. 'Fit?'

Chatty filled her lungs. 'Ally.'

'He's no' here.'

'Will he be long?'

'Can't hear you.' He reached to the transistor, turned the volume down.

'When will Ally be back?'

'No idea. He's a car out on a test run.'

Sod it! What with the purchase of the Mazda and its maintenance since, Chatty had put serious cash into Ally Bain's pockets. She'd expected him to be a pushover. Now, she stood for a few moments, quite at a loss.

Hitching her pencil skirt (chosen for the task in hand) above her knees, she squatted at the edge of the pit. 'You couldn't do me a tiny favour?'

The mechanic's eyes travelled up one thigh and down the other. 'Depends.'

'I've a friend to meet. Problem is, I'm not sure what car she drives.'

'That right?'

'Might be a Ford Fiesta. Or maybe a Renault Clio.' Fluttering heavily mascaraed eyelashes, Chatty affected a little-girl voice. 'I'm not good at makes. Maybe you can help.'

He scratched his head. 'I'm not with you.'

'Thing is, we've arranged to meet up in Tesco's car park.'

'Okay.'

'And you know what that's like when the schools come out.'

This was met with a blank look.

With a dramatic sigh, Chatty said, 'I'm already running late.'

Eyes narrowed, he asked, 'What is it you want, exactly?'

She bit the bullet. 'Jean Pirie, does she get her car serviced here?'

'Aye, her and the husband both.'

'You couldn't just remind me her number plate?'

'You having me on?'

Chatty made a show of checking her watch. 'Lord, is that the time?' She hitched her skirt higher. Then, 'That number plate …?'

'It'll be in the book.' Hauling himself out of the pit, the mechanic wiped his hands on a filthy rag.

Chatty followed him back around the corner to the office. Watched him lift down a hardback ledger from a dusty shelf and lay it on a desk strewn with paperwork.

He leafed through dog-eared pages.

Stopped.

Ran an ingrained finger down a column.

'Here it is.' He looked up. 'Want me to write it down for you?'

Chatty made cow eyes. 'If you don't mind.'

Reaching for a stub of pencil, he scrawled on one corner and tore it off. 'There you go.'

She snatched it from him and ran out the door.

'Oi!' he yelled. 'Don't I get any thanks?'

Chatty didn't hear him.

Gaining the Mazda, she fired up the engine and shot off the forecourt.

In her rear-view mirror, a dungaree-suited figure dwindled in a cloud of dust.

Sixty-four

'What's up with you,' Morag asked when Flora came to the door. 'You've a face on you would sour milk.'

'Mum's had another episode.'

'When?'

'Earlier this week. Can't even tell you what day. What with one thing and another, my head's a mess.' She offered a wry smile. 'To think I used to pride myself on my organisational skills …'

'Darroch View are keeping you in the picture, at least. The stories you hear …'

'A lot of it is down to staffing problems: immigrant labour has largely dried up, and there's fierce competition from hospitality and retail for low-skilled, part-time jobs.'

'So I've heard. I suppose working in a supermarket is a lot less stressful than with dementia—' She stopped short. 'Sorry. I didn't mean …'

Flora said, 'Didn't take it personally. But let's not stand gassing on the doorstep. Do you want to come in?'

'Not today. I'm on my way home from Ballater. Just looked past to catch up on developments. Any news from the mortuary?'

Flora shook her head. 'Not a word.'

Morag's mouth turned down. 'How about Chatty?'

'Hasn't got back to me.'

'Give her time. If anyone can wangle information, she can. If we can tie Jean Pirie to the car at Threepenny-Bit Cottage we're on a roll.'

'I hope so.'

Frowning, Morag asked, 'Kate okay?'

'The new medication has helped. But, to be honest, I'd hoped the move into care would make a real difference.'

'And it hasn't?'

'Not that I can tell. Add to that, Darroch View's programme of daily activities should provide stimulus to slow the progress of the disease. The reality is, many of the publicised activities are no longer on offer, either that or cancelled at short notice. Staff shortages, again.'

'That's not good. And it must be costing a pretty penny. I take it Kate's self-funded?'

Flora nodded. 'Don't get me wrong, they do their best. But I thought – once she'd settled in – Mum would mix more. There are several ladies of a similar age and background. Sadly, she's shown little inclination to socialise. I've been asking myself if I've made a huge mistake?'

Morag extended a comforting hand. 'No point beating yourself up, now.'

'Doesn't stop me wondering if the move into care will hasten her decline?'

'In what way?'

'You haven't seen what I've seen: folk lose hope, turn their backs to the wall. Now, every time I get a call, I think it will be the last. The job I've done all these years, I thought I'd be prepared. Fact is, I'm no better equipped than the next person. Worse, probably.'

Morag said, 'You and me both. I see death on the farm almost every day: lambs that don't make it. Have to put a gun to a dog's head when they can't do their job. But someone that's dear to you. Even Fergus, cantankerous old git that he is. Though I fear he'll make a hundred, just to spite me.'

'How is he doing?'

'Moans day and night. If it's not his piles, it's his waterworks, and if not that, it's his digestion. As for the business, there's not a thing I can do right, according to his lights. Talk about damned if I do and damned if I don't.'

'How did he manage before …'

'… my marriage broke up? Short answer is, he didn't. The house was a tip: dirt, mould, mouse droppings everywhere I looked. Plus, my old man's a hoarder. I had to fight my way through piles of old newspapers, dirty bottles, margarine tubs that hadn't been rinsed out, you name it. Took weeks just to get rid of the smell. And the state I was in …'

'I feel for you.' It was no secret Morag's ex was free with his fists. 'Who'd have thought, the pair of us, we'd have ended up back where we started?'

'Looking after our old folk and all. I think, sometimes, when I'm knocking my pan out to prolong my old pa's life, my own is vanishing before my very eyes.'

'I get where you're coming from. Truth be told, it's every woman's lot: to be torn in umpteen different directions. If not the parent, it's the husband, siblings, children …

'The guilt,' Morag sighed. 'Dogs you from an early age.'

Flora said, 'I can see myself, still, that first day at school.'

'Me too, as if it was yesterday.'

'Free as air and the whole world ahead of us. The dreams I had. Never got further than Aberdeen.'

'I never got that far. Swapped one set of sheep for another. Wouldn't have thought in a million years I'd be back living at Craigsheil.'

'Life takes you in circles,' said Flora, contemplatively. With a wistful smile, 'We're two bonny quines.' She used the Doric for girl.

'With nowhere to go. Fergus could live long enough. His own father lived well into his nineties.' With a shudder, Morag added, 'Doesn't bear thinking about.'

'Is there any chance you could …'

'Shack up with Duncan? Not a hope in hell. He's been too long suiting himself. How about you? Anyone in the picture?'

Colour rising under the collar of her Marks & Spencer shirt, Flora replied, 'No.'

'Last week, when I bumped into you in the minimart, I could swear I caught Struan Fyfe giving you the glad eye.'

'Pfft! Needs his head read. I've sworn off men. And before you say another word, I don't see that changing.'

Morag threw her a sympathetic look. 'Give it time.'

'Coming back to Fergus: organise a care package, I was going to say.'

'Even if I managed to get a package set up, there's not a care assistant on earth would put up with him. Short of putting a pillow over his head – and God knows I've been tempted – I'm lumbered with the old devil till he's carried out feet first.' Shrugging, 'But enough of my gripes. They're small beer compared to Sheena Thom's.'

'Too true. And seems police are dragging their feet. Fingers crossed we get some answers.'

Glancing at her watch, 'Got to go. The dogs are needing fed.'

Flora looked over Morag's shoulder. In the back of the pickup, Skye and Mull sprang to attention, eyes bright, tongues lolling. 'Thanks for looking past,' she said.

Sixty-five

Chatty teetered into the parlour.

Flora clocked the plunge top, the pencil skirt. 'Hot date?'

They'd convened in Thistle Cottage at Heather's behest. She'd been feeling poorly, she said. Put it down to a tummy upset. In truth, her ordeal in The Old Royal Station at the hands of Royal Protection still gave her palpitations every time she thought about it.

Waving a scrap of paper, Chatty crowed, 'Job done: the number plate on Jean Pirie's Fiesta.'

'How did you manage that?'

Tapping the side of her nose, Chatty replied, 'Friends in high places.'

'In Ballochbrae? I don't think so.' Chatty's arrival in the village hadn't been universally welcomed, but neither had she made much effort to ingratiate herself. 'You sure it's the right one?'

'Absolutely. Tallies with what Morag's young lad saw.' She looked around. 'Where is she?'

'On her way.' Flora cocked her head. 'Talk of the devil.'

'Sorry I'm late.' Morag lumbered into the room, collapsed into one of Heather's comfy chairs. 'Thank God for a seat!

I've been on the move since six this morning. Could sleep on a clothesline.' Turning to Heather, 'You couldn't brew us a pot of tea? I've a thirst on me you wouldn't believe.'

'Of course, dear. I'll see to it.' Rising, she left the room.

Morag waggled her backside to get comfortable. Then, frowning, dug down the side of the seat cushion. 'Look what I found!' She brandished a paperback book.

Chatty snapped her fingers. 'Give it here.'

Flora was too quick. Snatching the book from under Chatty's nose, she read out the title: '*Take Me.*'

Turning it over, '"Constance McCoy is the Good Girl of Glendorran."' She paused for a beat. '"Vicar's daughter, teacher." Who does that call to mind?'

Morag said, 'Bullseye!'

'"Charity volunteer and respected member of the community."'

Chatty tittered, 'You couldn't make it up.'

Flora said, 'If you'll let me finish: "But trouble is brewing for Constance …"' She paused for dramatic effect. '"…because Murdo McRae's roguish blue eyes and ripped body could turn Saint Constance into a sinner!"'

'I could use a ripped body this minute,' said Morag hungrily.

Chatty's eyes flicked from her to Flora and back again. 'Couldn't we all?' Not waiting for a reaction, she speculated, 'Do you think Heather has ever …' She jiggled in her seat. 'You know?'

'Doubt it,' said Flora sharply. 'And we shouldn't be bad-mouthing her when she's not here to defend herself.'

'Heather's always banging on about her highbrow taste in literature,' Chatty argued. 'I'm surprised that's what she's reading, is all.'

Morag said, 'Whatever turns you on.'

'We all have guilty secrets,' Flora cautioned. Rumours had been circulating in county circles Chatty MacIntyre was not all she purported to be.

'Sitting comfortably?' asked Heather, pushing a laden tea trolley into the room.

'Happy as Larry,' replied Morag, smothering a laugh.

Chatty said, 'Whilst you were out, we've been getting an education.' Grabbing hold of the book, she waved it in mid-air.

The teacups rattled noisily in their saucers. 'Where did you get that?' Heather shrilled.

'Down the side of a chair. The one you usually sit in, if I'm not mistaken.'

Cheeks burning, Heather said, 'I had visitors at the weekend. One of them must have left it behind.'

Morag said, 'If you believe that, you'll believe anything.'

'Are you calling my veracity into question?'

'Enough,' said Flora. 'Chatty, give Heather that book, then we'll have a cup of tea and crack on.'

*

Flora said, 'We need to tie this number plate to the car at Invercauld.'

'Easier said than done,' Heather complained, a cup of tea and a custard cream having gone some way towards restoring her equilibrium.

'Why don't we start by asking who else could have passed it that Friday evening?'

'The world and his wee sister,' Morag snorted. 'There's steady local traffic, and it is, after all, the main route through Glenshee.'

'Let me rephrase that: who might have passed who's familiar with the car and also with Jean Pirie? I'm thinking family, friends, workmates—'

Chatty cut her short. 'Not circles I move in.'

'You're so far up yourself,' Morag grumbled through a mouthful of fruit loaf. 'It's a wonder you get any business.'

'Actually,' sniffed Chatty, 'I'm doing rather well.'

'Bet if folk come once, they never come back.'

'While you're taking pot-shots at me, I notice you haven't contributed much to the investigation lately.'

'Haven't had the chance.'

Flora said, 'Lay off, you two.'

'Och,' said Morag, 'we're just having a bit of fun, isn't that right, Chatty?'

She cracked a superior smile. 'If you say so.'

'Whatever,' said Flora. 'Morag, have you anything to report?'

'Archie Kinnear told me he had a couple of goons in the Clach asking after Stuart.'

'Why does that not surprise me? Still, we'd be hard-pressed to pin a murder – or even an assault – on the likes of them, without producing any witnesses. Anything else?'

'Picked up more background on the Pirie household. The boy, Lewis, is fifteen. Gemma, the daughter, left school a few years back. She's tried a number of jobs locally: retail, hairdresser, hospitality. Never settled to anything. Currently working in housekeeping at the Fife Arms.'

'Would that explain the P-plates on Jean Pirie's car?'

'Haven't been able to establish if Gemma has had driving lessons, far less passed her test.'

'Might be irrelevant,' said Chatty, rejoining the conversation. 'If my input ties in with the intel from the Braemar Road.'

Flora said, 'All the same, it's worth chasing up. If she's working at The Fife, that's probably our best bet.' She looked around. 'Which of us is most familiar with the hotel?'

'Sorry,' Heather replied. 'Not that I'm lacking interest, but Dulcie won't go anywhere near the place. Capitalist playground, she calls it.'

'Morag?'

'Been in when they opened first to let the locals have a nosey. Haven't been over the door since.'

'How about you, Chatty?'

'Well, of course …' She graced them with an indulgent smile. 'Moving in the circles I do …'

'Have you seen the Picasso?' Heather asked eagerly.

'Naturally.'

'What did you think?'

'Could be bigger. I was at the hotel only last week, as a matter of fact. Private function,' she confided. 'Do you know the Brae Room, Flora?'

'Afraid not. Will you go along there? Speak to Gemma, if you can make it during her shift?'

'Will do.'

'Given your success in sourcing Jean Pirie's number plate, I'm sure you'll manage to find out if Gemma has passed her test without raising her suspicions. Worst case, they're a small team. Anyone in housekeeping should be able to supply that information.'

'Sure thing,' Chatty preened. 'Piece of cake.'

Sixty-six

'Good morning,' said Chatty. 'Are you ready to order?'

The nearer of the two ladies – an expensively coiffed brunette in what looked like a silk shirt, Hermès scarf knotted at the neck – glanced up from Castle View's breakfast menu. 'I think so.' She turned to her companion. 'You there?'

'Pretty much.' said the other, voluptuous auburn tresses curling to her shoulders over an intarsia knit, string of freshwater pearls at her throat. She cocked her head. 'Catriona?'

Plastering a polite smile on her face, Chatty said, 'I think you must be mistaken.'

'Catriona Chattan. Didn't recognise you at first, you've changed so much.' Giving Chatty the once-over, 'You weren't blonde for a start. But I'd know that voice anywhere.' The woman thrust out a hand. 'Fran Gilmour. We worked together in Jenners.'

Chatty's blood ran cold.

Her eyes darted around the room. Her PPOs – she was relieved to note – had departed for the day. Only two tables were occupied. 'I'm sorry,' she fibbed. 'I really don't recall.'

'On the cosmetics counter,' Fran supplied. 'This is my friend Shirley. We fancied a break. Edinburgh social round got too much, isn't that right, Shirl?'

'Non-stop action.' Shirley pulled a tragic face. 'We'd have preferred a spa, but the decent ones were booked. So …' Her lips parted to reveal a mouthful of perfect veneers. 'Here we are.'

'Catriona Chattan,' Fran marvelled. 'Who'd have thought, after all this time? And in Ballochbrae, of all places? I wouldn't have taken you for the country type.'

'This house is an inheritance,' Chatty said snootily.

'Long way from the cosmetics—'

'Beauty consultants,' she interrupted. Turning to Shirley, 'Aesthetics, they call it these days.'

Fran's eyebrows shot up, 'That's pushing it.'

'The job was a stopgap for me until—'

'I remember, now,' Fran cut in. 'You were trying to get into modelling, but they said you were too …'

'… young,' Chatty finished seamlessly. 'Plus, my parents didn't approve. Wanted me to have a profession.'

'Didn't I meet your folks?'

'Shouldn't think so.'

'I did. I'm sure of it. Let me think.' Fingers pressed to her forehead, Fran said, 'I've got it. We picked you up for a dance one time: bungalow in Craiglockhart.'

Inwardly, Chatty shuddered. 'Possibly.'

With a chuckle, Fran continued, 'Can't remember who I was with.' Throwing a wink in Shirley's direction, 'We went through men at a rate of knots.'

Chatty sneaked a look over her shoulder. The other guests had put down their cutlery, eyes fixed upon the trio.

Fran said, 'And then you met—'

'Roderick MacIntyre.'

'Right. And got engaged in short order. Though, if I remember right, he kept breaking it off.'

Chatty snapped. 'You're wrong. I was the one who broke the engagement.'

'Whatever.' Fran turned to Shirley. 'It was more off than on. It's a wonder the pair of them ever made it to the altar.' She turned back. 'You still married?'

'Widowed.'

'Oh.' She clapped a hand to her mouth. 'Trust me to put my big foot in it.'

Shirley threw Chatty a sympathetic look. 'She's had plenty of practice, believe me.'

'So,' said Fran, recovering. 'Do you run this place on your own?'

'I have staff,' Chatty replied, tight-lipped. 'It so happens several are either unwell or on leave. Otherwise' —she looked down her nose— 'you wouldn't find me doing breakfast service.'

Fran said. 'It's fate. If they hadn't been off duty, we wouldn't have met up.'

'Amazing!' Chatty breathed. Inwardly, she mouthed a scabrous curse.

'I'm still in touch with some of the Jenners' girls,' Fran confided. 'Can't wait to tell them I've seen you.'

Chatty struggled for a response, but her head was spinning out of control and her mouth bone dry. 'If you've decided,' was all she managed. 'I'll pass your order to the kitchen.'

Sixty-seven

With a squeal of tyres, Morag spun the wheel of the Mitsubishi and pulled off the South Deeside Road into the haulier's yard.

Her efforts at extracting further intel from Duncan had been met with limited success. And although she'd tried every which way to wangle information out of the wider farming community, farmers are a canny lot, North-East farmers cannier still. So she'd been buoyed when – after hours of ostensibly casual chitchat – her dad let on his haulier pal, Sandy Moir, had connections to the forestry.

Problem was, Sandy was a nightmare to pin down.

Now – after several abortive attempts – she'd managed to corner him.

'It was Jean Pirie's car, you said?'

'Aye.'

'What makes you so sure?'

'Towed it out a ditch on the Tomintoul road while back.'

The hazardous nine-mile stretch of the A939 from Cock Bridge to Tomintoul – known locally as the Lecht – is often closed in winter, due to its height and exposed location.

Morag pressed her advantage, 'Can you be more precise?'

'There was snow on the ground, so must have been the back end: November, mebbe. Or …' He lifted his cap. Scratched his head. 'Thereabouts.'

Her spirits sank. Wrong time of year.

'So,' she recapped. 'It was around November time. There was snow lying. The car had gone off the road and into the ditch, and it was you towed it out.'

'That's right.' He scratched his head. 'When ah saw the car thon night, ah thought first it had gone in the ditch again—'

'Hang on,' Morag interrupted. 'When you say "thon night" are we still talking about November?'

Sandy squinted till he looked cross-eyed. 'Naw. And there's nae ditch. No' on thon stretch o' road anyway.'

Morag drew a calming breath. One thing was clear: Sandy wasn't the sharpest tool in the box. 'We still at the Lecht?'

'Naw. Braemar road.'

Her pulse quickened. Frantically thumbing her phone, 'Can you point out where, exactly, on this map?'

'Nae problem.' He jabbed a finger.

'And it was definitely Jean Pirie's car you saw?'

'There's no many have a dunt like that.'

'The bodywork was damaged?'

'No' so anybody didn't know the car would notice.'

'So how …?' Morag began. Then, 'Was it the plates caught your eye?'

'Plates?'

'Green P-plates.'
'Naw. Windows were steamed up.'
'Like …?'
He threw her an evil leer. 'Want me to spell it out?'
She shook her head.
'Wasn't just the windows,' Sandy chuckled. Making see-saw motions with his hands, he added, 'Car was rocking an' all.'

Sixty-eight

Chatty swanned under the portico and swung through the double doors of the three-storey Fife Arms. Leaving Etta to hold the fort at Castle View, she'd dressed for the occasion – smart-casual in cashmere roll-neck and jeans under a tweed hacking jacket – and timed her arrival so the hotel would still be busy with late-breakfasting guests and her visit pass unremarked.

Taking scant heed of the watercolour of a stag's head by Queen Victoria which hangs in the lobby or the portrait of Lucian Freud by his daughter Annie she swept past the Flying Stag. Glazed doors revealed long tables flanked by wheel-back chairs on a stripped wooden floor. Above the oak bar, home to one hundred and eighty whiskies, a full-size winged stag lent the venue its name. Taking advantage of the introductory discount offered to local residents, Chatty had lunched there on the few occasions she wanted to show off her new lifestyle to friends from the city.

City living was not at the forefront of Chatty's thoughts as she passed the empty drawing room, hung with bespoke tartan taking inspiration from the local landscape, and home to the Picasso musketeer. Relieved to see a pair of guests in earnest conversation at the reception desk, she shot past, head resolutely down, and headed for the stairs.

Chatty's breath quickened as she sprinted up the first flight of a wide L-shaped staircase and turned the corner, out of sight of the lobby. From past visits, she'd ascertained there were forty-six bedrooms, some with a local theme: one dedicated to Robert Louis Stevenson, who began to write Treasure Island in Braemar. Another, named after John Brown, Queen Victoria's ghillie, featuring a carved and fretted four-poster bed. An online search the previous night informed Chatty bedrooms were graded in amenity, from the opulent first floor Royal and Victoriana Suites with village or landscape views to Scottish Culture Rooms on an upper floor and the rustic Nature and Poetry Rooms on the attic level.

Overnight stays she knew to be expensive by local standards, even the simplest room costing several hundred pounds per night. Judging a junior housekeeping assistant more likely to be employed in the less prestigious rooms, Chatty gave the empty first-floor corridor a cursory glance and crept skywards, eyes peeled, ears attuned to the least sound.

Gaining the second floor, she spied a housekeeping cart at the far end of the corridor. Tiptoeing to take a closer look, Chatty saw it was stacked with fresh linen, cleaning solutions in spray bottles and a selection of drinks and upmarket toiletries. Yielding to the temptation to pocket a few miniatures, her outstretched hand was hovering over the cart when a nearby door swung open.

'Can I help you?'

Chatty jumped to attention. The housekeeper was a good six inches shorter than she, but solid from the neck down.

'Looking for Gemma Pirie,' she replied with studied casualness.

'It's her day off.'

Chatty shoulders sagged. In her haste to get the job done, she'd failed to ask the critical question. 'What time does she come on shift tomorrow?'

'Eight o'clock. If she turns up. That girl has had more sickies in three months than the rest of my staff this past year.'

'Can't depend on the young, these days.'

'Tell me about it. Gemma's on borrowed time. When she does appear, she's never off her phone. If she goes on like this, she'll lose her job.' Her eyes narrowed, 'What's your interest anyhow?'

Chatty made a performance of rummaging for her purse. 'Wanted to leave her a tip.'

'All gratuities are pooled. You can leave it with me.'

'Oops,' she lied. 'Haven't anything smaller than a fifty-pound note.'

'Not a problem. Reception will be happy to help.'

'Thanks.' Chatty turned to leave. Feigning an afterthought, she called over her shoulder, 'You wouldn't know if Gemma drives?'

The housekeeper shrugged. 'Sorry. No idea.'

Sixty-nine

Flora was rinsing dishes at the sink when her ringtone sounded. Hurriedly drying her hands, she crossed to the kitchen table and picked up her phone: Chatty.

Flora: Hi! Been to The Fife?

Chatty: This morning.

Flora: Productive?

Chatty: 'Fraid not. Gemma wasn't at work.

Flora: Did you find out why?

Chatty: It was her day off.

Flora: You didn't think to check before you went?

Chatty: I've been up to here.

Flora: Did you get anything at all?

Chatty: Found out Gemma's shift starts at eight, finishes at three-thirty.

Flora: You could have saved yourself a car journey.

Chatty: Point taken. But that's not why I'm calling. It's about Chipper.

Flora: Let's have it.

Chatty: I went back to the car hire people like you said. No joy. Told you it was a waste of time.

Flora: Maybe I should have a go.

Chatty: If you'll let me finish. It was only when one of my PPOs was heading back south. Lovely guy, he—

Flora: I get the picture.

Chatty: It came to me: who better to get information out of someone than a police officer.

Flora: The one you have the hots for?

Chatty: Beg your pardon?

Flora: Forget it.

Chatty: As I said, lovely man. I had a wee word. And—

Flora: Give it to me straight.

Chatty: The car was returned at 10.29 on the Saturday.

Flora: They must have made a mistake.

Chatty: Trust me. No mistake.

Flora: Didn't you say Chipper's return flight was scheduled for Friday morning?

Chatty: That's right. But according to the hire company records, the car was booked for an additional twenty-four hours.

Flora: Meaning Chipper changed his flight.

Chatty: Exactly. So where did he go between leaving Stuart at the fishing hut on Thursday afternoon and catching the plane on Saturday morning?

Flora: That's the burning question.

Seventy

'Tell you one thing,' Dulcie confided. 'There's someone not far from here had a toke not long since.'

'I thought they all smoked at that age,' said Heather. 'On the quiet, I mean.'

They were in a secluded corner of The Barrel, a pub with rooms at the back of Ballater's Church Square, Dulcie having winkled from young Lewis Pirie where his sister hung out.

'Not fags. Weed.'

Heather's eyes popped. 'How can you tell?'

'I teach chemistry, for heaven's sake.'

Tilting her face to the ceiling, Heather sniffed. Once. Twice. 'I get you.'

'It's everywhere. Do you not remember the police even raided a cannabis farm in the Huntly Arms last year and arrested four men?'

'Albanians, weren't, they?'

'So I believe.'

'Disgusting!' Heather exclaimed. Then, mindful of her Christian faith, 'But who am I to judge?'

'According to the local paper,' Dulcie continued, 'the operation was on such an industrial scale police had to use wheelbarrows to fill a skip with the equipment.'

'Place like Aboyne, you'd think somebody would have noticed.'

'I quite agree. There must have been vehicles back and forth. And those men, wouldn't they have ventured outside: bought a pint of milk, smoked a cigarette?'

Heather said, 'Water under the bridge.' Eyeing the group of girls sitting in the far corner, 'Which one's Gemma?'

'Pretty one in the hoodie. Long dark hair.'

She nodded acknowledgement. 'What do we do now?'

'Sit tight. Wait for an opportunity.'

'Then what?' Her mind jumped back to the Old Station incident. 'Pity we didn't think to make a plan before we—'

'It's *me* doing *you* the favour,' Dulcie interrupted with a sour look.

Heather bowed her head over her tomato juice. 'Don't think I'm not grateful, dear.'

The heavy silence in which they finished their drinks was overlaid by non-stop chatter and the occasional squeal from the far corner.

Heather and Dulcie were contemplating their next move when, 'Miss MacPhail! Didn't expect to see you in here.'

Dulcie threw Gemma Pirie a quizzical glance. 'I could say the same about you.'

'Yes, well ...' Gemma blushed scarlet. 'We usually hang out at the public toilets, but it's too cold. And before you say anything ...' She yanked her head in the direction of the other table. 'We're over eighteen.'

'Take your word for it.'

'Right. Well, I'll be heading.'

Heather gave Dulcie a sharp nudge.

Rising to the occasion, 'What have you been doing since you left the academy?' Dulcie enquired. 'Anything exciting?'

'In this place? You kidding?'

'You in work at the moment?'

'Housekeeping at The Fife.'

'That's good. Gives you a bit of independence.'

'I wish.'

'Do I take from that you're still living at home?'

'No choice. Anyhow,' Gemma cast an anxious glance towards her friends. 'Got to get going.'

Heather's eyes flashed an SOS.

Impervious, Dulcie said, 'Good to see you. Stick with the job.'

As Gemma turned to go, Heather clutched at the girl's sleeve. 'Any hobbies?'

Turning back, '*Hobbies?*' she repeated.

'Music?' Heather ploughed on. 'Dancing?'

Gemma's mouth dropped open.

'Yoga?'

Behind her, Heather took in the huddle of girls. They were sitting bolt upright, now, ears wagging. She didn't dare look at Dulcie.

'Driving lessons?' she squeaked. Getting no reaction, 'Don't suppose you'll get those in Ballater.' She fixed Gemma with a piercing stare.

'You have to go to Banchory or Aboyne,' Dulcie chipped in. 'Either that or the instructor comes to you. Isn't that right, dear?'

'Either way,' said Gemma. 'I can't afford lessons on my wage. It was my dad got me through the test.' Lip curled, she added, 'Took him long enough.'

Seventy-one

In Albert Villa, 'Given Chatty's good work on the attribution of the number plate,' Flora began. 'And Heather and Dulcie on the P-plates, I think we can conclude the red Fiesta parked up near Threepenny-Bit Cottage the day before Stuart's body was recovered almost certainly belongs to Jean Pirie.'

'I was right all along,' Morag crowed. 'Everything points to an assignation. Add to that my witness testifying to the damaged bodywork. The steamed-up windows, that's the clincher.'

Flora said, 'It's too much of a coincidence Stuart Thom's car was located only a short distance away. And there's no disputing that. The police found the vehicle themselves.'

'Parked up a forestry track on the other side of the road from the river.'

'Where did you get that?'

'One of my farming sources. There's a layby not far off. Other places you can pull in.' Morag took a gulp of coffee. 'So why there? Looks to me Stuart knew his car would be easily recognised, so he parked it out of sight.'

'Then,' Chatty chipped in. 'He meets up with Jean. They have a quickie in her car—'

'Why do you have to bring sex into everything?' Heather grumbled. 'Even if there was a relationship, it could have been perfectly innocent.'

'Rubbish!" Morag exclaimed. 'It's common knowledge Stuart couldn't keep his pecker in his trousers. Plus, according to Sandy Moir, the car was just about lifting off.'

'There's no call for vulgarity.'

'I'm telling it like it is.'

Flora intervened. 'Heather's right. Let's keep it clean.'

Chatty said, 'Maybe they talk for a bit, then one thing leads to another.'

'He gets out the car for a fag. Jean doesn't want her car to smell of smoke …'

'She gets out for some fresh air. There's a bit of hanky-panky. He ends up in the river.'

Flora said, 'And Jean Pirie fails to raise the alarm? Doesn't ring true.'

'She's not supposed to be there, don't forget.'

'She could have come up with a perfectly credible explanation.'

'What's much more credible,' said Morag, 'is Hector found out about the affair. Followed Jean there. Waited until they were done. Then—'

'Come on,' Chatty scoffed. 'He's lurking in the trees watching some other guy with his wife. Wouldn't happen.'

'I hate to disabuse you,' Flora said, stony-faced. 'But it happens all the time.'

'What if Hector waited until Jean drove off?' Morag posited. 'Confronted Stuart. They fought. Then—'

Heather said, 'You're making the evidence fit your theory. I can think of umpteen reasons Stuart didn't want his car to be spotted.'

'Such as?'

'He could have bunked off early from work. Didn't want to publicise the fact.'

'Suppose.'

'He might have needed to pee.'

'Could have done that at the roadside or in a layby.'

'Say there were cars there already, he had to evacuate his bowels.'

Morag hooted. 'A jobbie? Whatever. According to my source, the police had a look around, found nothing to arouse suspicion.'

Flora said, 'We can spend all day conjuring up fanciful hypotheses. Seems to me this whole P-plate thing has taken our focus off the central issue: how did Stuart Thom die, and was anyone else involved?'

'I don't agree. Chances are – if an assignation did take place – we've identified the exact spot Stuart went in the river.'

'What good is that?' Chatty complained.

'Could narrow our suspects, give us another leg up on the police.'

Taking a genteel sip from her mug, Heather said, 'Still no news from the mortuary on cause of death?'

'Not a peep,' Flora replied. 'I'll chase them up. As to a perpetrator, we've identified Hector Pirie as a person of interest, but we still need to place him at the scene. And we can't rule out the fisher.' She'd briefed them on the car hire feedback. 'Reportedly, Chipper was disaffected. It's just conceivable he laid a false trail and took Stuart by surprise.'

Chatty said, 'So much for being ahead of the police. How on earth can we find out where Chipper was and what he was doing between Thursday evening and Saturday morning?'

Flora rounded on her. 'You tell me.'

'I only asked a simple question.'

'To which there are any number of potential answers: he could have been anywhere, doing any darn thing. And we can hypothesise till kingdom come. Problem is: we're heavy on information, short on facts.'

Clutching a hand to her forehead, 'This whole thing is doing my head in.' Chatty sighed. 'Can we talk about something else for five minutes?'

'What, for example?'

'Has anyone read Harry's book? I'm told the waiting list at the library still runs into the hundreds.'

Flora wrinkled her nose. 'Wouldn't waste my time.'

'Nor money,' Morag added. 'Big sap.'

'I think you're being unfair,' said Heather. 'You don't know the whole story.'

'Nor want to. For all there is to it. At least we've been *spared*—she pulled a comic face—'another raft of so-called revelations in the paperback edition.'

'Not to mention more interviews,' added Flora.

Morag said, 'I hope you're not using it as an excuse to bang on about your flipping book club again?'

With a peeved expression, Heather replied, 'I was only making conversation. We seem to have talked the investigation into a standstill.'

Chatty said, 'It's the King I feel for: losing his mother and then all the unpleasantness. Children can be so cruel.'

'Sounds like you've first-hand experience,' Flora came back. She'd heard tell Sholto MacIntyre was two sandwiches short of a picnic.

Letting this pass, Chatty continued, 'How he looked on the day of the Coronation: the weight of expectation on his shoulders and him in his seventies. Camilla, too. They'd a good enough life without all that. And the King couldn't but think of his mother during the ritual: how young she was, the weight of all that responsibility on her shoulders.'

Heather said, 'When William – 'the young prince' as we called him on Deeside before the accession – kissed his father on the cheek and said those few words, I wonder what was going through Harry's head.'

'Netflix footage, most like,' Morag jibed. 'And everyone forgets about Princess Anne. She was with the Queen at Balmoral when she passed away and by her side on the flight back to London. Plus, she wasn't too high and mighty to get wed in Crathie Kirk, unlike the other one. When you think of the cost to the taxpayer of that Windsor wedding. The Sussexes didn't even last two years before they skipped the country for a cushier life. And now look at the pair of them!'

Flora said, 'Don't get me started on victim culture.'

'Just because Harry and Meghan don't see things the way you do,' Chatty protested. 'There's no need to be so mean.'

'And there's no need to wash your dirty linen in the public eye,' Flora shot back.

'It's our poor dear Queen I'm thinking of,' said Heather. 'What she had to bear, those last years without Philip to support her. "Her strength and stay." Worse, when Philip passed away, the poor woman was left to deal with a bunch of unsubstantiated claims: William flooring Harry, Kate speculating on the colour of Archie's skin. And her at death's door.' Shaking her head mournfully, she added, 'God was merciful, taking her when he did.'

Morag said, 'It's hardly surprising William and Harry are estranged, nor that the royals have kept their distance since. Who'd want to see their private conversation or email end up for public consumption?'

'Queen Elizabeth was nobody's fool,' Flora observed. 'Saw through all the smoke and mirrors. The comment attributed to her that Harry was "a little too in love" says it all. And that press release – "recollections may vary" – was masterful in its understatement.'

'Our truth,' scowled Morag. 'Have you ever heard the like? Truth's truth.'

Flora said, 'I think we can all agree on that. Now, can we please get back to chasing facts.'

Seventy-two

Chatty gunned the Mazda through Dinnet and speeded towards Aboyne. Kincardine O'Neil passed in a blur. Road signs flashed past: Inchmarlo, Banchory, Kirkton of Durris. Foot to the floor, she paid scant heed.

The call had cut the legs from under her.

She'd been in the kitchen, up to her elbows in greasy water, trying to unblock the sink.

It was Etta answered the phone:

'Fella needin' a guest's business details.'

'What fella?'

'Didn't give a name, just askin' after thon fisher.'

'What did you tell him?'

'Said you were busy.'

'Did you take his number?'

'Aye.'

'Let's have it, then.'

'Canna mind what ah did wi' it.'

'Think, woman.'

'Ah'm thinkin'.'

Rummaging in the pedal bin, she'd thrust a scrap of paper into Chatty's dripping hands.

*

By the time Chatty covered the fifty miles to Aberdeen and made her way to the city centre, she was in a lather, armpits damp with perspiration, hair sticking in lank tendrils to her collar.

Once lined with upmarket retail businesses, Union Street, the Granite City's main thoroughfare, is now largely populated by licensed premises and betting shops. Founded in 1873, its flagship department store, Esslemont & Macintosh, closed in 2007 following the collapse of a buyout. Other independent shops followed. More recently, major retailers such as Marks & Spencer have decamped to the nearby Union Square development, resulting in loss of footfall. Add to this, the street is subject to long-term closure to allow for major upgrades.

With the central section controversially closed to traffic other than buses and cycles, Chatty was fit to melt when – finally – she reached her destination. Still, she consoled herself, it would be worth it. She'd been stung by Chipper's brusque rejection. If she could pin something on him …

The guy she'd agreed to meet might be just the conduit.

Her imagination took a leap: a hitman?

Chatty parked the Mazda on a double yellow.

Curiosity was killing her.

If she got a ticket, too bad.

*

The Railway Tavern in Bridge Street was even less salubrious than she expected: doorway strewn with fag ends, sticky lino underfoot. Chatty had done her homework, learned it served as a staging post between the helicopter terminal at Dyce and the nearby railway station.

The place was humming. As she shouldered her way to the old-fashioned gantry, a chorus of heckles bounced off the blackened ceiling.

'Chatty?'

She turned.

He was sitting in a corner, long legs splayed under the table, six-pack straining through a fitted tee.

Chatty's interest quickened. With blond highlights in thick, mid-brown hair, chiselled jaw and the bluest eyes, Dean Foster was a total babe.

Pulling in her stomach muscles, she sashayed towards him.

Rising, he extended a hand. 'Dean Foster.' He flashed a smile. 'What can I get you?'

She clocked the pint glass on the table. *Lemonade? Sparkling water?* 'I'll stick for now.'

Chatty crossed her legs. The drive into the city had put a strain on her bladder. She didn't want to be running to the loo. Guardedly, she continued, 'Your telephone call raised some concerns.'

'Really? Asking for someone's contact details, that a problem?'

'Data Protection. One has a duty of confidentiality to one's guests.'

'I get that. But, as I explained to your receptionist, Chipper and I had arranged to meet. Unfortunately, when we parted company, he left something behind: something I'm anxious to return.'

Chatty's mind flew into overdrive. A gun? No. Flora's mortuary pal hadn't mentioned gunshot wounds. A cosh, maybe. She drew a calming breath. 'Hence my decision to meet in person. In a high-end establishment like mine, one cannot be too careful.'

'You thought the call was dodgy?'

'It did ring alarm bells: why the business rather than the home address? And now you admit to having met the guest, I'm wondering how you found out where he was staying? It appears you don't even have a contact telephone number. Otherwise, you'd have called him instead of me.'

Raising a hand to his forehead, (left hand, Chatty noted, no ring), Dean said, 'Bit of a long story. Sure I can't get you a drink?'

'No, really.' They hadn't even got to the crux of the matter and she was desperate for a wee.

'We were seated next to one another on the flight up from London. Got talking. You know how it is?'

Chatty nodded, though she hadn't been on an aeroplane since she buried Roderick and would happily have taken a flight to anywhere.

'Chipper told me he was on a fishing trip. Back to London that same week. I said I was headed to my base at Dyce, then going offshore. I'm a deep-sea diver,' he explained.

As she pictured Dean encased in rubber, Chatty's heart beat even faster.

'Anyhow, the two of us really hit it off. So when we landed in Aberdeen, I gave him my mobile number, just on the off-chance.'

'He didn't give you his?'

'Bit of a scramble getting off the plane. Didn't think anything of it. To be honest, I didn't expect to see the guy again.'

'But,' Chatty pressed, 'you did?'

'Chipper rang me on the Thursday. Said he got finished early and could we meet up? He had a flight back to London the next day.'

'And?' She was on the edge of her seat, by now.

Dean shook his head. 'I had something on. Couldn't get offshore because of bad weather, so I'd looked up an old mate.'

'Oh,' said Chatty, deflated.

'Nobody was more surprised than me when he offered to change his travel arrangements.'

'Who? Your mate?'

'No. Chipper. Managed to get on a Saturday morning flight. So we arranged to meet at his hotel on the Friday.' He let out a whoosh of breath. 'Some night that was!'

Chatty envisioned Dean and Chipper in the hotel cocktail bar, being eyed up by the local talent. She strained forward. Planting her elbows on the table, chin resting in cupped hands, she squished her breasts together. 'I'm all ears.'

'Guy doesn't look like much, but boy …' Dean rolled his eyes. 'Does he have stamina.'

'A foursome?' The words were out before Chatty could stop herself.

He shot her a pitying look.

'I'm s-sorry,' she stuttered, colour suffusing her cheeks. 'Didn't read him as ...'

'Gay?' His voice softened. 'Sweetheart, Chipper's camp as a row of tents.'

'I know,' Chatty lied. 'Just testing the water.'

Dean chuckled. 'Sorry to have brought you this distance, but I don't swing both ways.'

She made to rise. 'That being the case ...'

He held up a hand. 'Before you go ...'

'Of course.' Mustering what was left of her composure, Chatty said, 'You wanted to return something.'

Dipping into a pocket, Dean extracted a small object. 'Chipper left this on the bedside table.' With a sheepish smile, he added, 'Didn't think it was the best idea to send it to his home address.'

And with that he set on the table between them a gold signet ring.

Seventy-three

'Guess what?' crowed Chatty, swanning into the conservatory.

Morag said, 'Go on, then.'

She flopped onto a chair. 'Found out where Chipper was when Stuart Thom went into the river.'

'Spill.'

She titivated her updo. 'Long story short, he wasn't within fifty miles of Ballochbrae. He'd booked himself into an Aberdeen city centre hotel.'

Flora said, 'You sure?' She'd convened the emergency meeting on the back of Chatty's cryptic message.

'Hundred percent. Got confirmation of his check-in and check-out times from hotel reception.'

'They were okay with giving out that information?'

'Not exactly. Had to shoot them a line: inventive, even by my standards. Wait till I tell you,' Chatty added, eyes like saucers. 'You'll fall about.'

'Don't want to know.'

'Had the receptionist eating out of my hand. She even called up a copy of his bill.'

'What was Chipper doing there? Did you find out?'

'Let's just say it was recreational.'

'Banging, was it?' asked Morag with a sly grin. 'How come you got involved?'

'If you must know,' Chatty replied, crimson-faced, 'I was following up a lead.'

Heather said, 'So if Stuart was still alive on the Friday afternoon—'

'Chipper's in the clear. He was billed for lunch at the hotel, and had an evening engagement. No way could he have driven to Deeside and back.'

'Could have told you,' Morag grumbled. 'Didn't I say all along it's Hector we should be going after. We know Stuart Thom made clandestine visits to his home. We've established Stuart's car was in close proximity to Jean's during the timeframe Stuart went in the river. Hector has to be the person with the strongest motive.'

'But,' argued Flora, 'we haven't placed him at the scene. Even if we did, we'd struggle to prove he caused Stuart physical harm. I put it to you: we've already expended considerable time and effort on this. Do we really have an appetite for more?'

Heather said, 'Having come thus far, I'm of the firm view we should see our investigation through to its conclusion.'

'Given there is one. Very often there isn't a clear-cut resolution.'

'To tie things up, what would we need to do?'

'First, place Hector at – or close to – the riverbank.'

'How can we do that?'

'We can't. Not without an eyewitness. Accept it, we're on a hiding to nothing. We simply don't have the resources. The police are able to draw on CCTV footage, technical support, you name it.'

Chatty said, 'Shame we didn't think to put one of those tracker thingies on his car.'

'I'll pretend I didn't hear that.'

'If we'd had the benefit of a tracker,' Chatty persisted, 'we'd have tied things up in no time.'

'So, short of a witness—'

'We try to establish Hector Pirie's whereabouts that Friday during the timeframe in question. Was he at work? At home? In the pub?'

Flora set down her coffee mug. 'Which begs the question: just suppose we actually get this information, what are we going to do with it?'

'Do with it?' echoed Chatty. 'Act upon it, of course.'

'How, exactly?'

Morag said, 'I propose we pay Hector a visit.'

Flora cast a wary eye, 'All of us?'

'There's safety in numbers.'

'We'll look a bonny sight.'

'Not dressed like this,' Chatty protested. 'We could wear dark clothing.'

'And balaclavas?' sniffed Heather. 'Next thing you'll be suggesting we carry out a dawn raid.'

Flora said, 'Even if we did roll up, Hector's a big chap. He'd see us off.'

'Not if we look like we mean business,' Morag asserted. 'The quiet bairn gets nowt. I've a shotgun licence. I could …'

'Don't even go there.'

'Do you have a better idea?'

Heather said, 'We could produce a report, present it to the police.'

'That big eejit MacDuff?' Morag jeered. 'You have to be joking.'

'Not MacDuff. The Banchory sergeant.'

'And own up to having flouted an explicit warning?' said Flora. 'I doubt Eck was working on his own initiative when he paid me a visit. He'll have been acting on instructions.'

Heather said, 'What about Jean?'

'What about her?'

'You're talking about placing Hector at the scene, but we haven't actually placed Jean there, only her car.'

'Duh!' Flora hit her forehead with the heel of her hand. 'Why didn't we think of that?'

'Because we're a bunch of amateurs,' Chatty replied. 'Why you thought we could beat the police at their own game, I can't fathom. I only went along with this because I thought it would be a lark.'

'Whatever the initial motivation, I think you'll agree we're now heavily invested.' Truth be told, the investigation had furnished a welcome diversion from Flora's own troubles. 'One way or another, we need to wrap things up.'

'And how,' said Heather, with a disparaging look, 'do you suggest we do that?'

'I propose we set ourselves one final challenge: see who can come up with the whereabouts of both Hector and Jean Pirie in, say, the next forty-eight hours. Failing that, we act upon your suggestion and take what we have to the police.'

Draining her mug, 'Fair do's,' Morag conceded.

'If we break our objectives down into manageable tasks. Stay in touch by phone, text, what have you. Keep Heather updated on results, we should get the job done.' Flora looked around. 'Is everyone in agreement?'

Nobody spoke.

'Chatty?'

With a shrug, 'Whatever.'

'Morag?'

'Well …'

Heather said, 'Why don't we have a show of hands?'

Seventy-four

Morag was mucking out the byre when Duncan stuck his head around the door. 'What are you at?'

She looked up. 'What do you think?'

'Fergus not around?'

'He's down the village. Why?'

'Thought he'd be here to give you a hand.'

With a derisive snort, 'Morag said, 'I should be so lucky.'

Duncan moved to her side. 'Here.' He tried to wrestle the fork from her grip. 'You shouldn't be doing that.'

Holding on for dear life, Morag retorted, 'Who will if I won't, tell me that?'

'I could give you a hand.'

'I don't need your help.'

'Didn't say you did,' he countered, fork handle swinging back and forth in a tug of war.

'Let go,' Morag yelled.

With one massive final yank, she pulled the handle clear.

And landed flat on her back.

'Well,' said Duncan, standing over her, a smile playing on his lips. 'Here's a thing.'

Heart thudding, she glowered up at him.

Stooping, he held out a hand.

Story of my life, Morag thought, as she allowed herself to be hauled upright, backside clarted with muck, into his open arms.

Seventy-five

Flora hosts a Zoom call.

Flora opens the call: Where's Morag?

Chatty: Don't ask me.

Flora: Have you heard from her, Heather?

Heather: No. She'll likely have been held up.

Flora: Okay, we'll start with you.

Heather: I've collated everyone's feedback and updated the spreadsheet. Hector Pirie was off work the day before Stuart was found. He wasn't in the pub that Friday evening. None of us have been able to place him at home or anywhere else.

Chatty: It's possible he followed Stuart. Then—

Flora: That's not enough to take to the police.

Chatty: Bottom line – Hector doesn't have an alibi.

Flora: That we know of. He could have been anywhere – shopping at the supermarket, visiting his old Granny at Torphins, driving into Aberdeen.

Heather: We've already ruled out ANPR, so tracking his car isn't an option. What do we do now?

Chatty: Take what we have to the police.

Heather: Forty-eight hours we agreed. There's time yet.

Flora: Not much. And the clock's ticking.

Morag enters the room: Sorry I'm late to the party.

Flora: What have you been up to? You look like you've been dragged through a hedge backwards.

Morag: That's sheep for you.

(Plucks straw from her hair)

Have I missed much?

Chatty: Not a lot. And the sooner we put this to bed and move on to something new, the happier I'll be.

Flora: The nub of it – we've drawn a blank with Hector Pirie. Hope you had better luck with Jean.

Morag: Yes and no. She didn't go to her usual cleaning job that Friday afternoon. Told her employer she had a doctor's appointment, would make up the time on the Saturday.

Heather: Now we're getting somewhere.

Morag: The bad news – I had no joy getting corroboration. Rang the Aboyne Health Centre. Shot the receptionist a line. All I got was Data Protection.

Flora: Woman was only doing her job.

Heather: You're not going to leave it at that. Everything rides on what time that appointment was – if there even was an appointment – and whether Jean Pirie kept it or not.

Flora: I get that. But I don't see—

Heather: What's staring the rest of us in the face. You're the one with the medical background. If your connections are solid enough to obtain confidential details of a post-mortem, getting confirmation of a GP appointment shouldn't be beyond you.

Flora: And you're the one been mugging up on police procedure. We've a thin enough case to take to the police as it is. Plus, we've already been warned off. Why risk a face-off in the Health Centre?

Heather: Given the circumstances—

Chatty: And this whole thing was your idea in the first place, I think you owe us one.

Seventy-six

Midway between Ballater and Banchory, the pretty village of Aboyne – founded in 1671 by Charles Gordon, Earl of Aboyne – spreads out from a large central green fringed by substantial granite villas. With the arrival of the railway in 1853, it developed as a holiday destination, and today still offers a wide range of tourist facilities, including golf, tennis, water-skiing on Aboyne Loch and gliding at the nearby airfield.

Flora was engulfed by a wave of nausea as she turned into Bellwood Road, a manoeuvre she'd performed on autopilot until the day her hitherto well-ordered life blew up in her face. Since she resigned her job, she hadn't gone near Aboyne Health Centre. Nor the Community Hospital. Indeed, she tried to avoid the village altogether, turning down invitations to meet with friends at The Sign of the Black Faced Sheep – a coffee house and gift shop she'd hitherto frequented – or a drink at the historic drovers' watering hole, The Boat Inn.

After the Zoom meeting ended, she'd racked her brains for ways to verify Jean Pirie had kept her – alleged – medical appointment on the Friday in question. Come up with no answers. Pulling into a parking space, Flora sat for a few minutes, trying to compose herself. It wasn't just that Allan's infidelity had injured her pride. There was no arguing the pneumatic Tracey was a younger, more desirable model. It was that he'd chosen to do so at their place of work: somewhere Flora was regarded as being at the top of her game, professionally. Now, with career defunct, finances shredded and self-esteem at rock bottom, if she were to bump into any of her former colleagues …

Get on with it!

Heart pumping, she opened the car door and stepped onto the pavement.

Feet dragging, she crossed the approach road to the hospital and pressed the buzzer to release the automatic doors.

The receptionist looked up from her desk. 'Yes?'

Flora's heartbeat slowed, just a tad. The girl was a complete stranger. Hardly surprising, given the time that had elapsed.

She hazarded a quick glance over her shoulder. On the far side of the waiting area, an elderly man sat hunched on a wipe-clean stacking chair. Alongside, a teenage boy studied his phone. Neither was within earshot.

'Can I help you?

Flora squared her shoulders. She'd spent a sleepless night rehearsing the scene: in and out, speed of the essence. If there were no complications, that was. Were any of the GPs to appear, she'd be scuppered.

She opened her mouth. 'I—' Stopped short, lips parched, tongue sticking to her palate. Her heart thumped painfully in her chest. Flora prayed it wasn't the onset of a panic attack.

She drew a deep breath: in to the count of four, hold for four, out to the count of four, hold, and in again.

The receptionist gave an encouraging smile.

Running her tongue around her lips, 'My sister had an appointment …'

'Today, was it?'

'Yes. No. I mean …'

In a pocket her phone sounded.

'Do you want to take that?'

Flora shook her head.

Her phone stopped.

Started again.

The receptionist eyed her expectantly.

Frantically, Flora scrabbled for her mobile: Morag.

'Sorry.' She gave a muttered apology.

Turning her back, she thumbed the screen. 'What?'

'Glad I caught you,' said Morag. 'I've been back up at the forestry houses asking questions. Turns out Jean Pirie didn't have her car that Friday teatime. She had to beg a lift off her next-door neighbour. To guess where?'

Flora felt her knees buckle.

Leaned against the reception counter for support.

'Aboyne Health Centre. So, you don't have to bother—'

Getting no response, 'Flora?'

And again, 'Flora, you still there?'

Seventy-seven

MacDuff was ensconced in his recliner, shovelling down a forkful of special chow mein from the New Shanghai in Ballater, when his mobile sounded.

He checked the caller display: Flora MacPhee.

Set down the foil container.

Swiped to accept the call.

'Alec?' she began, her voice uncertain.

He stiffened. 'Everything okay?'

'Fine. It's just—'

MacDuff selected a choice morsel.

Savouring the pungent aroma, stuck it in his mouth.

'Do you remember the last time we spoke?'

He swallowed in one gulp. 'Vividly.'

'Well, you know how we've a book club going?'

Guarded voice. 'Aye.'

'And you know how we were wondering about Stuart Thom: how he ended up in the river?'

One eye on his rapidly congealing supper, MacDuff said, 'Get to the point.'

'Well, I know you said not to. Only—'

'And that's for a good reason. As I already warned you in no uncertain terms, there's a live police investigation underway. The last thing it needs is a bunch of bored housewives stirring the pot.'

'We're neither "bored" nor "housewives".'

'I won't argue. Why are you calling?'

When no response was forthcoming, 'Flora MacPhee, what the hell have you been up to?'

'Nothing.' On the line there was silence for a few moments, then, 'Nothing much.'

MacDuff groaned. 'Let's have it.' He dipped a finger in sauce, gave it a sook.

'We think Stuart Thom was having an affair.'

'Tell me something I don't know.'

'Where his car was found,' Flora pressed on. 'There was another car parked close by around teatime that Friday.'

'Doesn't surprise me. There's more than one layby in the vicinity.'

'Wasn't in a layby. It was—' She broke off. 'We think Stuart was meeting his lover there.'

'Why there? Why not in his own car?'

'Only the person who should have been driving the car,' Flora continued, doggedly. 'Not Stuart's car. The other car.'

'What about them?'

'They weren't. Driving the car, I mean. They were—'

MacDuff jerked upright. 'Stop there. Where are you right now?'

'Aboyne.'

He leapt to his feet.

'I'll meet you halfway.'

Seventy-eight

Flora had run back to her car and was about to slip her phone into its dashboard holder when she clocked a missed call.

She scanned the screen: Isla.

Dammit! Kids had an uncanny habit of demanding attention at the worst possible times. And if ever there was an emergency— In her mind's eye, she saw MacDuff scream down the A93 on blues.

Coming after the constable's warning to back off, Flora was nervous enough about what she was going to say. Didn't dare risk jeopardising the entire investigation by turning up late. Plus, it wasn't as if the missed call could have been about anything urgent. She and Isla had spoken only two days before. Besides, if Flora was honest with herself, her daughter's on-off relationship was becoming tiresome. Maybe best stay out of it until this latest stand-off was resolved.

She turned the key in the ignition.

Heard the engine fire.

For some moments Flora sat motionless, fingers glued to the gearstick, head scrambled with conflicting thoughts: a body dragged from the Dee, an embittered fisher, a rapacious poacher, a cuckolded husband, a red Fiesta—

Then, *What's more important: the investigation or your only daughter?*

With a sigh, Flora reached for her phone.

Isla: Mum?

Flora: I'm in the car right now. Can we speak later?

Isla: This will only take a minute.

Flora: Okay. Fire ahead.

Isla: Can I come home?

Flora: Here, you mean?

Isla: Where else have I got to go?

Flora: Of course you can come home. When did you have in mind?

Isla: Soonest I can get on a flight.

Flora: Can you leave it a day or two? Thing is …

Isla: You don't want me to come.

Flora: I do. Been too long. Only—

Isla: I get it. You don't have to make excuses.

Flora: It's the practicalities I'm thinking of. A last-minute flight will cost an arm and a leg.

Isla: I'm not asking you to pay.

Flora: Doesn't matter who pays. If you book ahead, even by a few days, the saving can be put to better use.

Isla: Spare me the lecture. You're not a team leader anymore.

Flora: And, besides, it will give me time to make the house really welcoming. Get some nice food in, and … *see what comes out of my meeting with MacDuff.*

Isla: If that's all I wanted, I'd book a hotel.

Flora: So, what do you want to do?

Isla: I'll get onto the airlines and let you know.

Seventy-nine

It wasn't the first time Flora had sat in the back of a police car. In the course of her career, she'd become embroiled in many a domestic dispute, her own included. But never in a Defender.

The meeting point MacDuff suggested was the car park at Cambus o'May, a hamlet notable for its iconic latticed iron bridge. Constructed in 1905, it replaced a ferry, which transported people across the River Dee to what had once been a station for the Deeside Railway.

Flora got there first. Sat for a few minutes, feeling ready to throw up. What with her visit to the Health Centre, Morag's news and the drive from Aboyne at breakneck speed, her nerves were completely shredded.

It helped none when MacDuff roared up on blues and twos.

Stern-faced, he ordered her into the back seat.

Climbing in beside her, he instructed, 'Run me through that again.'

Clutching her bag in clammy fingers, Flora said, 'First off, we – I mean the book club – couldn't get our heads around how someone with Stuart's knowledge and experience would have gone near the river without the appropriate safeguards.

Then, when it transpired his death wasn't due to drowning, we—'

MacDuff's eyebrows met his hairline. 'Where did you get that from?'

'Can't remember,' Flora lied. 'It was a while ago. But it added to the mystery, so we decided to see what we could find out. Just to satisfy ourselves,' she qualified. 'Not with any ulterior motive.'

'And what did you find?'

'First off, we thought Stuart might have been the victim of an assault.'

'On what evidence?'

'We came up with a few persons of interest.'

'"Persons of interest",' MacDuff parroted. 'Any names you'd care to pull out of the hat?'

'There's no need to be sarcastic.'

He brushed a tired hand across his forehead. 'Go on.'

'We established one of Stuart's fishing party nursed a grievance.'

'How?' Getting no reply, MacDuff said, 'Never mind. We'll come back to that later.'

'There was another chap – traveller possibly – had a spat with him. Then we found out Stuart owed money all over the place.'

'What was the upshot?'

'None of our leads led anywhere.'

He rolled his eyes. 'Join the club.'

'We kept coming back to the affair Stuart was rumoured to be having.'

'And?'

'All the evidence pointed to Jean Pirie.'

MacDuff's mouth twisted. 'What evidence was that?'

'Witnesses placed Stuart at her home when her husband wasn't there. Stuart was observed phoning and texting constantly.'

'Okay.'

'We were able to place Jean's car within walking distance of where Stuart's car was found, and around the time he was last seen …'

His shoulders stiffened. 'That so?'

Flora averted her eyes.

'Do I sense a "but" coming?'

'Jean's car was at the scene,' she mumbled. 'But we don't think she was in it.'

He gave a curt nod. 'Go on.'

'We know the Piries' daughter, Gemma, passed her driving test recently. We think it was Gemma who was driving the car that day. If that's the case …' She looked to MacDuff for a reaction.

None.

'Hector Pirie, don't you see? It's one thing another man having it off with your wife. But your teenage daughter? That really would give someone a motive for murder.'

Eighty

Morag asked, 'Did you get hold of MacDuff?'

'I did,' answered Flora, thankful to be safely back under her own roof.

'Bet he was gobsmacked.'

'Quite the contrary.'

'How come?'

'MacDuff knew Gemma had been seeing Stuart Thom. Knows what all the local kids get up to. He might give the impression he's a village plod, but looks belie. He's been in the job long enough, don't forget.'

Heather said, 'So our investigation—?'

'It's not all bad news,' Flora interrupted, seeing their stricken faces. 'I got the impression the police didn't know about Jean's car being at the riverside.'

'Phew!' said Morag, with a long whoosh of breath. 'I thought for a minute you were going to say we screwed up.'

'Not totally.'

Her brows knitted. 'Go on then.'

'That Friday afternoon – when we placed her and Stuart by the riverside – Gemma was at work in The Fife Arms.'

'Says who?' Chatty demanded.

'She gave a police statement to that effect.'

'But,' Heather puzzled. 'Jean's car—'

'Was by the riverside. Only not when we thought.'

In the conservatory, there was a collective intake of breath. Then Chatty said, 'You're telling us we've run ourselves ragged for nothing?'

'That's what it amounts to. Police were in possession of the intel, right down to Jean Pirie's GP appointment.'

Morag said, 'Which I flagged up.'

'And MacDuff was able to confirm she kept.'

'What did he have to say about the persons of interest we identified?'

'Police interviewed them all: fishers, travellers, folk Stuart owed money to. Eliminated every last one.'

'But ...' wailed Heather, 'my spreadsheet.'

'That's what's been bugging me. Everything hangs on the timeline.' Sighing, Flora continued, 'The more I've thought about it, there are two imponderables: the sighting of Stuart in the minimart, and of Jean Pirie's car by the river.'

Heather said, 'Jessie might have told me wrong, is that what you're saying?'

'Either that, or the band member Morag chatted up at Bayne's garage mistook the time he saw the car.'

'Bummer!' said Morag. 'And we thought we'd got one up on Big Eck.'

Flora grimaced. 'Not to mention Banchory.'

For long moments, they sat in grim silence.

Then, 'One thing we haven't considered,' mused Chatty. 'Hector could have been driving Jean's car.'

'Smashed it!' Morag yelled. 'I fingered him from the get-go. He had the strongest motive. He had the means. He had the opportunity. He'd knocked off work, remember.'

'Maybe his forestry vehicle was too recognisable,' Chatty chipped in. 'So he took the Fiesta instead.'

'We need to nail the guy.'

Heather said, 'Best leave strong-arm tactics to the police.'

'But,' Morag protested. 'Forty-eight hours we agreed. And time's running out. Between the four of us, we—'

Flora said, 'I started this. I'll finish it. Leave Hector to me.'

Eighty-one

Flora's heart beat a tattoo as she approached the forestry cottages. She'd dressed for the occasion: dark hoodie and jogging pants. Tucked her hair under a black woollen beanie Isla had left behind on her last visit. Hidden the Peugeot in a thicket of trees.

Despite her earlier bravado, she recoiled from confronting Hector Pirie. Judging by the intel, she was no match for the man. Besides, who knew what he was capable of? Her best course of action, Flora concluded, was to beard his wife. Where the book club was concerned, Jean was in the clear for involvement in Stuart Thom's death. She might, however, be able to provide her husband with an alibi. If not, Flora could seek out further intel from neighbours, workmates, whoever.

Having first established Hector's hours of work, and confirmed Gemma was due on shift at The Fife, Flora identified a window of opportunity. Jean Pirie would almost certainly be at home in the late afternoon when her son was due back from school. Even if Lewis was involved in an after-school club, his mum would likely be in the process of preparing the evening meal.

Flora's spirits plummeted as she neared the Pirie home. There were no cars in view, no lights visible in the front rooms.

Stealthily, she tiptoed up the drive.

Bingo! Although it was not yet dusk, light blazed from what looked like a kitchen window.

Flora dropped to a crouch.

Crept up close.

Cupped a hand over her eyes.

Her nose was pressed to the glass, when a heavy hand gripped her shoulder.

A male voice. 'Looking for someone?'

Flora near fainted from fright.

'N-n-no,' she stuttered, fearful to turn her head, for the kitchen showed no sign of life.

'You're up to no good,' the deep voice growled. 'That's for sure.'

'No,' Flora squeaked.

'Dressed like that? Come off it. You're here to check no one's around …' His grip tightened. 'Then you'll call your mates. Drain my tank.'

'No,' she said, again.

'Three times this year I've lost a tank of oil, and no one held accountable.'

She fought for breath. 'You've got it all wrong.'

'I'll tell you this: it's going to stop. Right now.'

Squirming from his grasp, she turned.

It was only then Flora saw the axe in Hector Pirie's left hand.

Eighty-two

Flora said, 'Transpires the last known time Stuart Thom was seen alive, Hector Pirie was out on the hill with no phone signal.' She'd briefed the book club on her brush with The Axeman, as she'd henceforth think of Hector.

Snorting in disbelief, Morag said, 'And you'd buy that?'

'No need.' She took a reviving swig of red wine. 'I was able to confirm Hector was on a training exercise with Mountain Rescue.'

'Did you speak to them direct?'

'What do you take me for? I had a fruitful conversation with their Operations Manager. Team members can also testify. There's absolutely no doubt.'

Morag threw up her hands. 'I don't believe it. So you put yourself in harm's way for sod all.'

'My choice. I'm a grown woman.'

'Of a certain age,' Chatty smirked. 'As you keep reminding us.'

'Let's call it an exercise in teamwork,' said Flora, diplomatically.

'Stand us in good stead,' added Heather. 'When it comes to—'

'Don't even go there,' Morag snarled.

Chatty said, 'Before you start a cat fight, I want to hear how you got on at Birkhall with the conservation group.'

'If you think you can fob me off by changing the subject,' Morag retorted, 'you think wrong.' Reaching for her near-empty glass, 'What I want to know …'

Chatty said, 'We'll get the details in due course. But right now, to help get over our disappointment, tell us: how did the visit go?'

This was met with a murderous look.

'Come on,' she wheedled. 'Don't be such a killjoy.'

'Along with all major salmon rivers,' Morag trotted out, 'the Dee has seen a significant fall in catches, with high levels of mortality at sea. The subject of major conservation efforts, projects include—'

'It's not the salmon I'm interested in,' Chatty interrupted.

Heather said, 'Perhaps it hasn't occurred you don't speak for all of us.' Giving Morag the nod, 'Carry on.'

'Projects include river restoration schemes, which have provided immediate benefits. Longer-term projects include planting a million native trees in the upper catchment, providing shade and mitigating rising water temperatures, which can be lethal to juvenile fish. A comprehensive tracking project has also been initiated to monitor the success of the young salmon, and—'

Chatty heaved a theatrical sigh. 'Tell us about the house.'

'Dates from 1715 and was left to the then Prince of Wales by the Queen Mother.'

Chatty stifled a yawn. 'I already knew that.'

Flora said, 'What you might not know: the estate was once owned by the Farquharson clan, who originally owned Balmoral.'

She perked up. 'Now you're talking.'

'The then Duke and Duchess of York spent time there until the Duke's accession as George VI, when the King and Queen stayed at Balmoral and Philip and Elizabeth and their children spent summers at Birkhall. After the King's death, the Queen Mother used the house more frequently until her own passing.'

'Thanks for that,' said Chatty, looking bored witless. 'Anything left in that bottle?'

Whilst Flora was topping up their glasses, Heather said, 'The gardens are wonderful: a stumpery planted with hostas, gunneras and ferns. Woven wire arches fastened with antlers. Clipped yews to give structure. And there's the produce: fruit from espaliered trees, vegetables and herbs.'

'Too much information.'

'It was you broached the subject in the first place,' Morag groused.

'It's the house I want to know about,' Chatty sulked. 'Not the pesky garden. I've seen plenty of photos in magazines. I want to know what it's like for real.'

'Big.'

'Can you be more specific?'

'Sort of L-shaped.'

She strained forward. 'Give me more.'

Morag raised her eyes to the ceiling. 'It's a feckin' house.'

'An early Georgian stucco-fronted house. I don't suppose you registered the colour it's painted?'

'Double cream is the nearest I'd get. With a porch on the front supported by tree trunks. And before you ask, they were painted a funny shade of blue.'

Frowning, Chatty deliberated for a few moments. Then, 'Farrow & Ball De Nimes, at a guess. Either that or Etruria from Little Greene.'

Flora made a comic face.

Chatty either didn't see or didn't care. 'What's it like inside?'

'Pretty much as you'd expect. Crammed. Stuff everywhere.'

'Specifically?'

'Antique furniture. Paintings. Books. I was with a bunch of other people,' Morag protested. 'And we were only in one room.'

'Which was?'

'The drawing room. One of the reception rooms, anyhow. And we were only there for an hour.'

'Long enough to have scoped the ground floor,' said Chatty, voice dripping with envy. 'If I'd the chance to see inside the King's home, my eyes would have been all over the place.'

Flora said, 'Morag's a farmer, not an interior decorator.'

'I get that,' Chatty said with a petted lip. 'Only I thought she'd have made more of the opportunity.'

'I was there to do a job,' Morag asserted. 'Not case the joint. Anyhow, I was busy taking notes.'

'So busy she doesn't remember a darned thing.'

'There were loads of table lamps. They were blue and all.'

'Chinese,' said Chatty, with authority.

'Photos in silver frames. Tons of those.'

She pounced. 'Any of Harry and Meghan?'

'Not that I noticed.'

Her mouth turned down. 'What else?'

'Grandfather clocks. I counted nine.'

'In one room?'

'God's honest truth. And not one of them chiming at the same time. "One of my grandmother's little eccentricities", the King remarked.'

'You're making this up.'

Hauling herself out of the chair, Morag made a beeline for the sofa. Stooped so her face was only inches from Chatty. 'You calling me a liar?'

Flora pushed between them. 'No need to get worked up.'

Eyes like slits, Morag said, 'She wants to watch her mouth.'

'I won't argue. We've bust a gut on this investigation, and tempers are running high.' When Morag had sat down, 'There's no denying Hector's alibi has come as a disappointment. What we have to do now is regroup.'

Chatty said, 'Then what?'

'Revisit Heather's timeline. And fast.'

Eighty-three

'Good of you to see me.'

'Nae bother.'

'All the same ...' Flora clocked the rash of stubble on MacDuff's chin, the carpet slippers on his feet. 'It's late, and you're off-duty.'

'Never off-duty in this job. It's a twenty-four-hour commitment.'

Bit like a district nurse, thought Flora, with a pang of longing.

Once they were seated in the police house living room, 'What can I do you for?' he teased. 'Solved any more crimes since I saw you last?'

'That's just it. There's a couple of things been bothering me.'

He raised an eyebrow. 'Only a couple?'

'Seriously. What you told me at Cambus o'May, I was disappointed, to say the least. But then, when I went back to our timeline—'

'Timeline, is it, now?'

Flora didn't rise to the bait. 'Jessie in the Post Office told Morag that Stuart Thom came in for cigarettes around two o'clock the day before his body was recovered. I verified the intel at the time, and again at a later date. Can you confirm: is that what Jessie told the police?'

'No comment.'

'Come on, Alec, it's not a state secret.'

'Okay. From memory, I'd say yes.'

'You're not sure?'

'We'll have it on record.'

'Thing is, I nipped in past the minimart on the way here.' Colour flooding her cheeks, 'Made a nuisance of myself, to be honest.'

The corners of his mouth twitched. 'Never!'

Ignoring the veiled sarcasm, she continued. 'Jessie told me Stuart was in a tearing hurry that Friday afternoon. Said he needed to make Perth before his kids' teatime, otherwise Sheena would kick up.'

'Aye.' MacDuff rubbed his temple. 'That would be about right.'

'Except,' Flora persisted. 'Today, when I pressed her, Jessie put the time nearer three. She'd heard the church clock strike, she recalled. Had to get ahead of a Post Office collection.'

He shrugged. 'Doesn't make a whole load of difference.'

'I disagree.'

MacDuff eyed her with asperity. 'You do, do you?'

'I think you should have another look at your timeline.'

'To what end? The police have finite resources. There's more urgent matters than—'

'Finding the truth?'

'Well, I—'

Flora leaned in. 'Please?'

He made to rise. 'I'll give it some thought.'

'Thought?' she repeated. 'Is that all you've got to offer? A man is dead before his time.'

MacDuff said, 'You're treading a dangerous path, Flora MacPhee.'

And with that he showed her the door.

Eighty-four

Heather said, 'Did you get hold of MacDuff?'

'I did,' Flora replied. 'Said he'd "give it some thought."'

'That all?'

'Yup. But that's not why I've dragged you back here today: my contact at Aberdeen City Mortuary rang late last night. I'll keep it short: the final post-mortem report states Stuart Thom died from a spontaneous subarachnoid haemorrhage.'

Morag said, 'What's that in layman's terms?'

'Bleeding in the space between your brain and the membrane that covers it. SAH results from rupture of an aneurysm, a little balloon of inner parts of the wall which occurs due to a weakness in the wall.'

'Wow! Sex must have been banging, right enough. Assuming,' she added, 'I've been right all along: there actually was an assignation.'

Curled in one of the conservatory's cane chairs, shoes on the floor, 'Seriously?' asked Chatty, goggle-eyed. 'Can sex bring that on?'

Flora said, 'It's possible, if Stuart was susceptible.'

Heather said, 'How so?'

'The rupture often occurs when there is transient elevation in blood pressure, such as during vigorous exercise.'

'How can they tell?'

'When the pathologist opens the head, they'll rapidly appreciate the presence of SAH and seek a source to establish it is a "spontaneous" rather than "traumatic" SAH due to injury.'

'How do they decide between the two?'

'By seeking a source: in this case a leaking aneurysm.'

Morag said, 'Nightmare! If Stuart died of an aneurysm, it lets our so-called suspects off the hook.'

'Not necessarily,' Flora countered. 'The haemorrhage could equally have been brought on by other stress factors: an altercation, for example.'

'Didn't you say the pathologist's report ruled out injury?'

'I did. Traumatic SAH would result from a blow to the side of the neck or sometimes a punch to the chin or face.'

'My point, exactly.'

'What I'm suggesting is the spike in Stuart's blood pressure could have been triggered by a heated argument.'

Morag said, 'Who with? Not Hector Pirie. You said yourself he has a solid alibi. Not Jean. She was at the Health Centre. Not Chipper what's-his-name. He was occupied with the beefcake. Which only leaves …'

Flora nodded. 'Precisely.'

Eighty-five

MacDuff said, 'Talk me through that Friday.'

Gemma gave him the side-eye. 'All of it?'

'From when you left the house.'

They were in the Pirie living room. Hector was at work, his wife at home. But Gemma had refused to have her mother present while the constable had what he described as 'a quiet chat'. Through flimsy walls, MacDuff could hear Jean Pirie in the kitchen going about her chores. Suited him fine. Time enough to dot the i's and cross the t's.

'I've already done that,' Gemma argued.

'Do it again.'

'Missed my bus,' she muttered. 'I was like, out the night before. Slept in.'

'Out where?'

'Ballater.'

'Who with?'

'Old mates from school. There's five of us, and—'

'We'll come back to that,' MacDuff interrupted. 'So, you missed the bus. What did you do then?'

'I was like, in a state. Had to get to work.'

'At The Fife Arms, that right?'

She nodded.

'Enjoy the job?'

'No way. Housekeeping's harder than I thought: stripping beds, cleaning bathrooms and stuff. Plus, you've to work to a timetable. The housekeeper's never off my back.' She pulled a tragic face. 'It's just like being at school.'

'You must have days off.'

'Don't come around fast enough.' She gave him the side-eye again. 'I've taken more than a few days off, claiming sickness.'

'Bet that didn't go down well.'

'Too right. I'm on my final warning.'

'So …' MacDuff prompted. 'That Friday?'

'My dad had gone to work. Mum was in the kitchen. And I'm like, "Mum, can I borrow your car?" And she's like, "No." And I'm like, "Please?" And she's like, "It's your own fault you missed the bus. If you hadn't stayed out until …" Gemma broke off. 'Yak. Yak. Yak.'

'What was the upshot?'

'I'm like, "If I don't turn up, I'll lose my job." She's like, "Get the next bus. Make some excuse." And I'm like, "What, for example?" And she's like, "I don't know. You haven't been short of excuses the days you skived off."'

'Did you catch a later bus?'

'You kidding? The way the service operates, I'd have been an hour late. At least. So, I'm like, "Just this once?" And she's like, "I already told you: I'm sick and tired of the way you treat this house like a hotel, it and everyone in it. You're not having free rein of my car." And I'm like, "It's not free rein, just to Braemar and back." And she's like, "Doesn't matter." And I'm like, "I'll be super-careful. Put petrol in." And she's like, "Whatever. I'm needing it myself." And I'm like. "What for?" And she's like. "I've a doctor's appointment."'

Feeling as if he'd gone five rounds in the ring with Tyson Fury, MacDuff asked, 'Did you get the car?'

'On one condition: after work, I had to bring it straight back.'

'So, to recap: you drove your mum's car to Braemar.'

'That's right.'

'Where did you park?'

'In the public car park at the top of the road.'

MacDuff nodded in acknowledgement. 'And after your shift ended did you drive it straight back?'

Not meeting his eyes, she ducked behind her hair.

'Gemma?'

Her chin came up. 'No.'

'Why not?'

'I was meeting someone. It wasn't planned,' she added quickly. 'It was a last-minute thing.'

'And that someone was?'

Eyes downcast, she wound a lock of hair around one finger. Unwound it.

Repeated the action.

'Gemma?'

'If I tell you, will you get me in trouble?'

MacDuff said, 'I can't answer that. Depends.'

'What on?'

'A lot of things: who it was, what you were doing.' He fixed her with a steady gaze.

For long moments there was silence. Then, 'It was Stuart.'

'That would be Stuart Thom, would it?'

Her face flushed.

'I'll take that as a yes.'

'He texted me at work. Said he was heading to Perth, could we like, meet up? I said okay and I had Mum's car. He said in that case he'd wait for me by the riverside.'

'Where was this?'

'Between Invercauld and the suspension bridge. There's like, a wee secret place you can pull off the road. We've been there before.'

'Can you be more specific as to the location?'

'Not really. There's nothing there: no buildings, just trees and a bonny view of the river.'

MacDuff said, 'If Stuart usually drove you there in his car, how did you know where to pull in? Are there any road signs or markings?'

'No. There's a funny-shaped tree, is all. You have to be quick or you'll miss it.'

'Go on.'

'I didn't see Stuart at first. Thought he'd maybe not have waited. But he was there, right enough. Said two cars would draw attention and, besides, there wasn't space, so he'd left his up the road.' She sat back in her seat and folded her hands in her lap.

'Umm,' mused MacDuff, chewing his pinkie nail. 'I've a wee problem with that.'

She sat up. 'How come?'

'In your statement – made to my fellow officer – you said you left the hotel just after 15.30.'

'Correct.'

'Is that the truth, Gemma?'

'That's when my shift ends. Anyone will tell you.'

'According to my information, Stuart left Ballochbrae the back of three.'

'So?'

'He was due in Perth by five.'

She frowned. 'I'm not with you.'

'Journey takes coming on two hours, longer allowing for Friday night traffic. Even if you'd left The Fife at 15.30 on the dot, there's no way the numbers add up.'

'That's your problem.'

MacDuff leaned forward. 'I'll ask you, again: did you tell the officer the truth?'

No response.

For some minutes the two sat in silence. Then, MacDuff said in a soft voice, 'Gemma?'

Her eyes welled. 'I bunked off early. You happy, now?'

'How early?' he pressed.

'Not long: an hour, something like that.'

'And you went to meet Stuart Thom.'

'I just told you.'

'Lying to the police is a very serious matter, Gemma. Do you understand?'

'What did you expect?' she burst out. 'I'd have lost my job. Got in trouble at home. Not been able to drive Mum's car. And then how would I have seen Stuart?' She dissolved into noisy tears.

*

When Gemma had composed herself, MacDuff said. 'So, you're in the car and Stuart's outside. Then what?'

'He like, gets in. We talk.'

'Talk? Is that all?'

'We like, smooched for a bit. Then he got out while I climbed into the passenger seat and …' She shrugged. 'You know.'

Running a finger around his shirt collar, MacDuff said, 'And afterwards?'

'Stuart said he had to get down the road. Sheena would give him a bad time if he was late.'

'How did that make you feel?'

Her chin quivered. 'How do you think?'

'The relationship was how old?'

'Six weeks. But it wasn't what you …' She broke off, eyes bright. 'Stuart said him and Sheena were going for a divorce.'

'Did the two of you exchange words?'

Gemma's pupils dilated. 'If you're asking did we have a fight, no, we didn't.' Her eyes slid away. 'Not what I'd call a fight.'

'I'll rephrase that,' said MacDuff doggedly. 'Did you two speak after that?'

'Not really.'

'What was Stuart's frame of mind, can you recall?'

'Huh?'

'Was he in a bad mood, would you say?'

Gemma shook her head. 'He just got out the car. To sort himself. You know?'

MacDuff gave a brief answering nod.

'What did you do?'

'Got out the passenger seat. Walked around to the driver's side. Got in.'

'Who left the scene first, you or Stuart?'

'I did.'

'And you didn't say goodbye?'

Her lower lip jutted. 'Nobody asked me that.'

'I'm asking you, now.'

'I said something, like, "Gotta run. Mum will go nuts if she's late for her appointment."'

'What did he say?'

Turning her head away, Gemma muttered, 'Can't remember.'

'Think,' urged MacDuff. 'This is important.'

Getting no response, 'Gemma?'

Slowly, she turned back.

Choking back tears, 'Stuart said, "Forget your mum. If your dad gets wind of us …"'

'Go on.'

'"I'm a dead man."'

Eighty-six

In the snug at Albert Villa, Flora sank thankfully into her dad's big chair. The events of the past twenty-four hours had completely drained her.

As she raised a much-needed mug of tea to her lips, her mobile rang: Isla.

Flora: Hello, pet.

Isla: About the other day—

Flora: Sorry I was so distracted. I've had a lot on.

Isla: It's not Gran, is it?

Flora: She's fine. I'm going to see her later.

Isla: Give her a hug from me.

Flora: I'll do that. Have you booked a flight?

Isla: That's why I'm calling.

Flora: Bet you had difficulty getting a seat at a decent time. Those morning flights are usually chock-full.

Isla: I'm not coming.

Flora: Not at all?

Isla: Another time, maybe.

Flora: Any particular reason?

Isla: Change of plan.

Flora: It's not something I said?

Isla: Always. Just joking.

Flora: I know I'm straight from the shoulder, but I do make an effort, you know.

Isla: Wouldn't have you any other way. Sorry, got to go.

Flora: Take care.

Isla: You, too.

Isla ends the call.

*

Flora wasn't off the phone five minutes when the doorbell rang. Setting her tea aside for a second time, she levered leaden limbs out of the chair and hurried out of the room and down the hall.

Her heart sank when she saw Chatty silhouetted in the half-glazed inner door. Opening it, 'Didn't expect to see you back here so soon.'

Chatty looked down at her feet, shod in a pair of Louboutin knock-offs. Looked up. 'Wanted a quiet word.'

'What about?'

'I'll explain. Can I come in?'

'Of course.' Inwardly bemoaning her lack of grace, Flora stood back and beckoned Chatty into the hallway. Hesitated for a beat. Feeling as deflated as she did, if she didn't make her guest too comfortable, maybe she wouldn't stay long. 'In here.' She opened the sitting-room door. Was gratified to find the temperature on the chilly side. 'Take a seat.'

Chatty perched on the edge of a sofa, knees together, hands clasped.

Flora sat down opposite. 'There's something you wanted to say?'

Nervously, Chatty cleared her throat. 'It's obvious you don't like me.'

'It's not a question of "like". It's …' Struggling to complete the sentence, she ended lamely, 'I'm sure you'll agree we don't have a lot in common.'

Eyes flicking from Flora's FootGlove loafers to her own scarlet-soled heels, Chatty forced a smile. 'Diplomatic to the death.'

'If you weren't such a snob.'

'And you weren't such a … '

'Control freak?'

'You said it.'

Flora shrugged. 'We're polar opposites, that's the truth of it.'

'Just so happens we find ourselves in the same boat.'

'How so?'

'A house this size is a money pit. Same goes for Castle View. Thing is, I've got myself in a bit of a pickle. And—'

'Stop right there,' Flora interrupted. If Chatty was looking for financial assistance, she'd come to the wrong place.

'It's not what you think.'

'Isn't it?' Flora had heard the stories: Chatty taking advantage right, left and centre.

With a shrug, Chatty said, 'Won't pretend I'm not stretched financially. But money isn't what I've come here to talk about. Fact is, I've worked my socks off to talk up Castle View and now, what with the Queen's passing and Harry and Meghan's Netflix series and Harry's book and the coronation, I've been swamped by a deluge of advance bookings.'

'Isn't that a good thing?'

'Would be, if I had a hope in hell of honouring those bookings. I was so keen to build up the business, I said yes to everyone, and now my reservations calendar is one giant mess. If I don't get it sorted tout de suite I can wave goodbye to my VisitScotland ranking.'

'I'm sorry to hear that,' said Flora, completely flummoxed. 'But what has it got to do with me?'

'There's no way I can ring all those people and say, "I've messed up, would you like to come another time?" Now, do you understand?'

'Not really.'

Chatty puffed her cheeks, let her breath out in a slow stream. 'If I can't do that, they'll have to be accommodated somewhere else.'

Flora said, 'I don't see what the problem is. There are loads of B&Bs in Ballater. There's bound to be someone would—'

'Be happy to take business off me. I'd never get it back, that's the thing. Meantime, here are you sitting in this big, empty house. What I came to ask: would you be willing to take my overspill?'

'Oh,' said Flora, wide-eyed. 'No. That wouldn't do at all.'

'Why not?'

'This is my family home.'

'You've no family within spitting distance,' Chatty countered. 'Even if they were to visit, you'd have bedrooms to spare. And it's not as if you have a job.'

'That's not the point,' snapped Flora, stung. 'It's different for you: a business enterprise.'

'Which I've knocked my pan out to get off the ground. After all I've been through, I'm not going to watch it go up in flames.'

'Wouldn't happen. Not overnight.'

'I disagree. Word gets around, and—'

Flora cut her short. 'Another thing: you're a social animal. You can smooch to your heart's content. Not me. I'm more …'

'Straight from the shoulder?'

'Whatever. Can't help.'

'Shame. I was counting on you.'

'I'm sure you'll come up with another solution.'

Chatty made to rise. 'I'm sorry you feel that way.'

'Hang on.' Flora held up a hand. 'It's as well you called. There's something you ought to know.'

'Can't wait.' Chatty sat down again.

'Your fling with Mark Outhwaite is the talk of the village.'

Her jaw dropped. 'But we've been so careful.'

'Not careful enough. What you have to understand: Ballochbrae is a tight-knit community. Never mind Ballochbrae, the whole of Deeside. If you don't know someone in person, you'll know someone who does. There's nothing stays secret around here for long.'

Fists balled, Chatty hissed, 'Must be down to Etta. If I could find anyone else to do the job, I'd show her the door.'

Flora said, 'Etta's the least of your problems. When we embarked upon our investigation and I started asking questions, I turned up all sorts of surprising facts.'

Clasping a stricken hand to her forehead, Chatty said, 'Tell me the worst.'

'Turns out your late husband – the Commodore as you would have him – wasn't a commodore at all.'

Her hand dropped into her lap. 'Is that it?'

'Isn't it enough?'

'Roderick was a naval commander. That's two ranks below commodore, if you don't know. With correspondingly lower pension benefits.' She uttered a bitter laugh. 'And you wonder I choose to embroider?'

Flora said, 'I get where you're coming from.'

'No, you do not.' Her voice rose. 'You've no idea what it's like being a service wife: the pecking order, the niceties that accrue to rank.'

'That's not the exclusive preserve of the Royal Navy.'

'Maybe not. But—'

'That's not all, though, is it?' Flora pressed.

Chatty couldn't meet her eyes.

'I ran an internet search.'

Her face drained of colour.

'It informed me Roderick was killed in a freak accident.'

'"Freak"?' Chatty shrilled. 'There was nothing freak about it.'

'He went under a bus on the way to a disciplinary hearing, am I right?'

She nodded.

Flora said, 'I'm very sorry.'

'I'm not.'

'Do you want to talk about it?'

Chatty shook her head. 'Would take all day. Suffice to say there is absolutely no doubt in my mind Roderick stepped off that pavement in order to avoid responsibility for his actions.' Her mouth twisted in an ugly grimace. 'A path he followed his entire life.'

Flora said, 'The disciplinary hearing, I read something about Malta.'

'I might as well fill you in. You'll find out soon enough: Roderick was caught in flagrante at an official function in the British High Commission.'

'That's tough.'

'What's worse: it happened on the Queen's birthday.'

'Yikes!' Flora exclaimed. 'That's quite something, especially for a serving naval officer.'

'And there's more: the act took place on a first-floor balcony in full view of pedestrians in the street below.'

Fanning her face with one hand, Flora said, 'Blimey! And I thought I had problems.'

'Did I mention Roderick's coupling was with one of the waiting staff?'

'You did not.'

'A male waiter.'

'*No!*'

'Maltese citizen, need I add. You can imagine the diplomatic fallout.'

'I don't know what to say.'

Chatty shrugged. 'I'm unclear how much of this is already in the public domain, but, given I'm trying to run a business, I'd prefer you didn't broadcast it.' Getting no response, 'Look, I know we don't see eye to eye, but we're two single women trying to keep our heads above water.'

Flora said, 'I'm not disagreeing with you. It's a lot to take in, is all. I always suspected there was something, but a Maltese waiter—' She put a hand to her mouth to stifle a fit of the giggles.

'Tell me about it. If it wasn't so sordid it would be hilarious.'

Assuming a straight face, Flora said, 'I shouldn't laugh. You didn't come here to air your dirty laundry.'

'No, but it helps to get it off my chest. As to my business proposition, will you think about it?'

'Well, I really don't—'

'Please?'

For an instant, Chatty's composure slipped. And Flora saw her for what she was: a lonely, middle-aged, disappointed single woman.

Not unlike herself.

Voice softening, she said, 'Maybe. As to the other thing …' She tapped the side of her nose. 'Mum's the word.'

Eighty-seven

'What are you doing here?' Kate asked, when Flora came through the door. 'It's past your usual time. Is something wrong?'

Flora dropped a kiss on her forehead. 'Nothing's wrong. Just fancied some company.'

'You should be keeping company with folk your own age.'

'My age? You talk like I'm still a teenager.'

'You'll always be young in my eyes,' Kate said wistfully. 'I wish we were back at that stage: Jock, me, your brother—' She broke off. 'What's his name?'

'James.'

'That's it. James and you.'

'Happy days.' Seeing Kate – now – Flora couldn't help but think of the randomness of it all.

'How are things at home?'

'Fine. Funny thing happened, though. Chatty MacIntyre—'

'Who?'

'Lives at Dalnacreich.'

'No, that's Xanthe you're thinking of.'

'Xanthe's dead, Mum. Chatty's her daughter-in-law.'

Kate shook her head. 'News to me.'

'Anyhow, Dalnacreich's a guest house now. And, would you believe, Chatty asked me to take her overspill.'

'At Albert Villa?'

'That's right.'

'What did you say?'

'Told her it was a ludicrous idea.'

Frowning, Kate asked, 'Was that wise?'

'Think about it,' said Flora. 'What would Dad have to say about giving houseroom to total strangers?'

'He'd say cut your coat according to your cloth.' When Flora didn't respond, 'Do you imagine I don't know how much it's costing to keep me here?'

'That's not the point.'

'It's a factor, surely.' Kate reached out, took hold of Flora's hand. 'They think old folk are feeble. Even the ones without dementia.' She gave a little laugh. 'They're wrong. We're tough. That's why we're still alive.'

'I suppose.'

'You've done your best for me, Flora. Like you give everything your best shot. But you have to learn to accept help. Maybe this Catty person's offer has come at the right time.'

'Chatty,' Flora corrected.

'Whatever you say, pet. You know I'm not good at names.'

'It wouldn't bother you: me taking in boarders?'

'What bothers me is you having to worry yourself sick. If you had a bit extra coming in—'

'It's not a question of money so much as trust. Chatty MacIntyre and I are like night and day. She's everything I'm not: shallow, a total snob, a chancer is what it boils down to.' Flora looked to Kate in exasperation. 'How could the pair of us possibly go into business together?'

'Same way you've managed to rub along with folk throughout your career: compromise.'

Flora's mind flooded with images of her ex-husband: Allan's rugged good looks, his sharp intelligence, his dry sense of humour, the give and take, the deep-rooted affection that had sustained their marriage for so many years. She'd thrown that all away. And for what? A bleak, cash-strapped old age?

She wondered how Allan was coping. He never was a great organiser. Whether he was living with a new partner …

'And …' Her mother's voice broke Flora's train of thought. 'That Catty wouldn't be the first woman had to live by her wits,' Kate added, with another rare flash of insight. 'You might have more in common than you think.'

'Doubt it.'

'Promise me you'll give it serious thought.'

'I will. But right now,' said Flora, 'how about we cosy up and watch *Coronation Street*?'

Eighty-eight

'Woohoo!' Morag whooped. 'We got a result!'

Flora said, 'Not the one we were looking for.'

'Still, we brought our investigation to a satisfactory conclusion.'

'Satisfactory for whom?' asked Heather, dispensing tea into her best bone china cups. 'Not Stuart Thom, God rest him.'

They hadn't been back in Thistle Cottage since Morag unearthed the raunchy book. Heather was still out of sorts. What with that and the stushie at The Old Royal Station, she'd girded herself to extend an invitation to afternoon tea.

Chatty said, 'Not Sheena.'

'Poor woman. Those children—'

'Not Gemma,' Morag added. Turning to Flora, 'Heard any more from MacDuff?'

'Thought you'd never ask. He dropped past not long since to bring me up to speed. Decent of him, I think, in the circumstances.'

'Go on, then.' She set down her cup. 'Let's have it.'

Flora put a finger to her lips. 'Strictly within these four walls, Banchory police have interviewed Gemma Pirie under caution.'

Chatty sat forward. 'And?'

'Her story differs in salient respects from what she told them first time around.'

'Such as?'

'Turns out she knocked off her shift early that Friday.'

Heather said, 'Didn't anyone notice? I'd have thought – if Gemma was on her final warning – her supervisor would have been on her back.'

'The hotel was gearing up for a function that evening, apparently. Everyone running around like mad.'

Chatty brightened. 'Anything I should know about?'

Morag threw her a disparaging look.

'Next up: Gemma confessed to leaving her jacket in the staff cloakroom, to make it look like she was still there. If anyone asked, she planned to say she felt sick and shut herself in the toilet. Same for the assignation with Stuart. If her mum's car was spotted, Gemma would say she'd been nauseous and pulled off the road in case she threw up.'

Morag said, 'If she was prepared to lie to the police about that, makes you wonder what else she was hiding.'

'And there's more: Gemma now admits she and Stuart had a set-to, which she earlier denied.'

'Doesn't surprise me.'

Heather asked, 'How so?'

'Think about it: Gemma risks dismissal to sneak off early from work. When she makes it to the assignation, Stuart announces he can't stay long. Why? Because he's rushing to see the wife and kids.' Morag sat back in her seat.

'Don't know about you, but I'd be raging. For all we know, she pushed him in.'

Flora said, 'Why would she? According to MacDuff, she was besotted with the guy.'

'The size of her,' Heather added. 'I doubt she'd have the strength.'

'You'd be surprised,' Morag argued. 'Imagine: the pair of them get out the car. There's barbs flying back and forth. Bit of pushing and shoving. Then he loses his balance. And bingo!'

'More likely,' Chatty came back, 'Stuart's at the water's edge, relieving himself. Gemma sneaks up behind him, and—'

Flora cut her short. 'It's these kind of wild hypotheses led our investigation in the wrong direction. We can speculate till the cows come home. Doesn't make any difference to the outcome.'

'What will happen to Gemma?'

'Apart from losing her job?'

Morag said, 'Can't the police charge her with anything?'

'Not according to MacDuff.'

'But you've just told us Gemma confessed to fighting with Stuart. So—'

'If you're still thinking murder, forget it. Police would have to prove intent. They've reached the conclusion – backed up by the PM report – Stuart Thom did, indeed, succumb to a spontaneous subarachnoid haemorrhage.'

Morag snorted. 'Accident waiting to happen.'

'On that score,' Flora conceded, 'you're spot on. The aneurysm may have been present for several years and the SAH occurred when it ruptured.'

With a serene smile, Heather said, 'God works in mysterious ways.'

'Poor Stuart.'

'You reckon?' quipped Chatty. 'What a way to go!'

Handing around finger sandwiches, Heather shuddered. 'We get the picture. But think of his poor wife. When is the funeral? Anybody heard?'

'Could be a while, yet,' Flora replied. 'Meantime, the Clach has set up a JustGiving page.'

Morag said, 'One thing's for sure: I wouldn't like to be living in the Pirie household right now.'

'If you're casting blame, that rests squarely on Stuart's shoulders. He is – was – old enough to be that wee girl's father. Plus, for all her outward sophistication, I think it unlikely Gemma was the manipulator in the relationship.'

'Couldn't agree more. Stuart's track record with women speaks for itself.'

Flora caught Morag's eye. 'Not that we're biased.'

Chatty said, 'Don't get me started on men.'

'It's the boy I feel sorry for.'

'I wouldn't worry about Lewis,' Heather responded. 'That age, their minds are on other things.' (As, indeed, was that of Ruaridh Shirras, who had fallen out with Lachlan Burnett and formed another alliance, assuaging his parents' concerns.) Offering sultana scones, 'What did MacDuff have to say about us? After he warned us off, we didn't exactly play ball.'

'You can say that again! We've been investigating the length and breadth of Deeside. But to answer your question, '"Considering their position", is how he put it.'

'Pompous fart,' muttered Morag. 'As for that jumped-up sergeant in Banchory …'

'All the same,' Flora argued, 'best keep our heads down.'

'Speaking of which,' said Heather, resuming her seat. 'How does everyone feel about—?'

'If it's books you have in mind,' Morag interrupted, 'I'd have thought you're the last person to be voicing an opinion.'

'I'm not going to argue.' Crestfallen, Heather offered the Victoria sponge.

Morag helped herself to a large slice. 'So what are you on about?'

'As Flora said, some while back, investigations don't always find a resolution. We may not have come up with all the answers, but I think you'll concede we've learned a great deal.'

'And got one over on the cops,' Flora added. 'I'd give anything to have seen MacDuff's face when he realised that wee girl had led them up the garden path.'

'Was it him took Gemma's original statement?'

'No. Some rookie from Banchory.'

'Bet he got torn off a strip.'

'Just goes to show: one slip can throw an entire investigation.'

Chatty said, 'Investigation aside, I've enjoyed meeting up. But – no offence – the books were a screaming bore.'

'Precisely why I broached the subject,' Heather retorted. 'When I was in the library the other day, I hit upon the complete answer.' From behind a cushion, she brandished a volume with a striking black cover bisected by yellow police tape.

'*Forensics,*' Flora read. '*The Anatomy of Crime.*' And roared with laughter.

'I don't see what's so funny.'

Chatty said, 'I do.'

'Me and all,' said Morag.

Turning to Flora, Heather asked, 'What's the verdict?'

With a glint in her eye, Flora said, 'Dare I suggest a show of hands?

Glossary

bairn	child
bam	trickster, criminal
bidey-in	mistress
breeks	trousers
clart	mud
doin' awa	okay/fine, thanks
fit like	how are you/how's things?
ghillie	helper on fishing/shooting expedition
loon	boy, lad
neeps	turnips
quine	girl
shufti	quick look
thrawn	awkward

A Letter from the Author

Thank you for reading the first instalment in the Ballochbrae Book Club series. I hope you enjoyed shadowing Flora, Chatty, Heather and Morag on their adventures as amateur sleuths.

If you enjoyed the book, please spare a few moments to leave a short review. It would be greatly appreciated, and help introduce new readers to the village of Ballochbrae and its cast of quirky characters.

I am fortunate to have lived and worked in the Scottish Highlands, hunting for antiques at village auctions and farm sales. Family holidays are spent on Deeside, where the majestic Cairngorm mountains form a backdrop, and locals rub shoulders with the Royal Family when they visit Balmoral Castle and Birkhall.

You can get further insights into Ballochbrae and its surroundings by becoming an Honorary Member of the Ballochbrae Book Club at **visitballochbrae.org.uk**

Don't miss out! If you want to hear about the next book in the series, sign up for my newsletter at **mcmackay.com**

Acknowledgements

For editing, Craig Hillsley, and proofreading, Heather Belleguelle.

For specialist input, Dr James H.K. Grieve, Emeritus Professor of Forensic Pathology at the University of Aberdeen, Archie Hay, fishing ghillie for the Crathie beat of Invercauld Estate, Police Scotland former Constable Donald Macleod and William Meston of Coilacreich Inn.

Invaluable feedback was provided by early readers Pauline McBain and Sheila Reid.

To my family, for their love and forbearance, heartfelt thanks.

And not least, to the good folk of Deeside, my apologies. I have manipulated your geography and diluted the Doric language in pursuit of a good story.

Inaccuracies in the narrative are wholly mine.

The Ballochbrae Book Club's next case ...

Flora MacPhee speed-walked into the village, chin tucked, elbows churning like pistons. The hills were darkly forested with Sitka spruce and Scots pine, the sky over Lochnagar streaked with grey, a spit of rain in the air. Alongside the stony footpath, trembling bracken fronds fronted a carpet of heather. Tugging at the collar of her Lovat quilted jacket, she powered onwards,

Rounding a bend, the village came in view. Gaining the imposing three-storey Ballochbrae Arms Hotel, a flash of red caught her eye. Panting, she pulled up short. The stout storm doors were defaced by graffiti.

Shaking her head in disbelief, Flora was about to walk on when a warning sparked in her subconscious. With a covert look over her shoulder, she crept up close. Spatter pattern indicated spray paint. With the tip of one forefinger, she gave it a rub. Bone dry.

She was ready to turn away when she spied a run. Delving into her shoulder bag, she extracted a clean tissue and blotted a fat drip. Then, folding the tissue, stowed it in the inside pocket of her jacket.

Tutting, Flora turned on her heel and made for Ballochbrae's one remaining provisions outlet. Above twin display windows crammed with a jumble of tinned goods and souvenirs, a fascia board proclaimed McTavish Grocer.

An old-fashioned iron doorbell jangled as Flora pushed through the entrance. The minimart – that was what everyone called it – was laid out like any small supermarket: aisles bisected by tiered gondolas, bank of freezers, wines & spirits nearest the checkout. A Post Office counter occupied one front corner.

'Have you seen the hotel?' she called.

Behind a glass screen, Jessie McTavish raised a face blank as Buddha. 'Aye.'

'When did that happen?'

'Who knows.'

'Any idea who's behind it?'

Jessie quirked an eyebrow. 'Now you're asking.'

'So the story in the *Deeside Piper* is right enough?'

'You might say.'

'Have the new tenants been in?'

She nodded.

'What are they like?'

'Gay couple.' Publican's wife, Janet Kinnear, joined the conversation. 'Well enough turned out, but not a sock between them.'

'You've made their acquaintance?'

'Wouldn't go that far. When I passed yesterday, they were standing outside with the contractors. We exchanged a few words.'

'When are they moving in, did they say?'

'From what I gather, they've already taken occupation.'

'Haven't wasted much time.'

'Won't want to miss out on more of the season than is necessary, I expect. Plus, if they want to bring the place up to a decent standard, they've got their work cut out.'

'Starting with the graffiti. I take it you've seen it.'

'Couldn't have missed it.'

Turning to Jessie, Flora asked, 'Has Constable MacDuff been in this morning?'

Shuffling forms on the counter, 'Bit early for Big Eck,' she replied.

'Don't suppose any of your customers have bought spray paint lately?'

Jessie's head jerked up. Fixing Flora with a challenging look, 'You're the one plays private detective. You tell me.'